I0556698

Ravishing Our Queen

Copyright

Second Edition, February 2023
Copyright © 2023 by Melony Ann

Copyright notice: All rights reserved under the International and Pan-American Copyright Conventions. No part of this book may be reproduced or transmitted in any form or by any means, electronic or mechanical, including photocopying, recording, or by any information storage and retrieval system, without permission in writing from the author or the publisher.

This book is a work of fiction. Names, places, characters, and incidents either are product of the author's imagination or are used fictitiously. Any resemblance to actual persons, living or dead, organizations, events, or locales is entirely coincidental.

Warning: The unauthorized reproduction of distribution of this copyrighted work is illegal. Criminal copyright infringement, including infringement without monetary gain, is investigated by the Federal Bureau of Investigations (FBI) and is punishable by up to five years in prison and a fine of up to $250,000.

Paperback ISBN: 978-1-961966-16-1

Published by: Carxander Publishing
Minnesota

Disclaimer

The books in this series are based completely on dreams that I've had or that one of the other people in my relationship has had. They all have a little bit of real life thrown in so that you, the reader, can get to know us a little bit better.

These books can and should be read as standalone books. There isn't an order to them. All of the characters in the books are the same, as they are all based on characters from real life.

As you read these books, please keep in mind that other than the characters and the city they are based in, these books are not connected to other books in the series. They aren't a continuation of other books. They are all novellas based on dreams that revolve around the same characters.

As you keep that in mind, please enjoy reading this book. I do hope you will also read the others in this series and love them as much as I loved writing them!

Opening Quote

I wish someone would have told me that this darkness comes and goes. People will pretend, but, baby girl, nobody knows. And even I can't teach you how to fly. But I can show you how to live like your life is on the line. You throw your head back, and you spit in the wind. Let the walls crack, 'cause it lets the light in. Let 'em drag you through hell. They can't tell you to change who you are. That's all I know so far. And when the storm's out, you run in the rain. Put your sword down. Dive right into the pain. Stay unfiltered and loud. You'll be proud of that skin full of scars. That's all I know so far.

All I Know So Far by Pink

Chapter One

⭐ Matt ⭐

I scrub my hands down my face after getting into my truck with a groan. I love my truck. Jet black. Leather seats. It's a Ford F-150. Brand new. After getting all the bells and whistles, it cost me just about eighty-grand, but I couldn't care less. Stock dividends are good for something other than retirement funds.

DJ climbs into the passenger seat and reaches over, resting his hand on my thigh. Captain DJ Rens has been my best friend ever since I started with the Gainesville Police Department fifteen years ago. He was not only my training officer, but also my partner. And he became more than just a partner on the streets. A couple of years after we met, he became my partner in life, too.

DJ was the one who encouraged me to become a Sergeant, and then a Lieutenant, as I am now. He's constantly encouraging me to be the best cop, and man, I can be. I do the same for him. I suppose that's the kind of thing people do when they're in love.

"Matt, you need to let it go. It wasn't your fault. There was nothing you could have done differently." DJ lightly rubs my thigh.

I sigh and drop my head on my arms on my steering wheel. "I know."

Just after I got to work this morning, there was a report of a young kid threatening suicide. His parents called and were beyond worried. Rightfully. Officers were dispatched out. When they couldn't quickly resolve the situation, SWAT was brought in. Not because there were hostages or anything. It's because our SWAT is a highly trained machine.

Our SWAT officers are all tactically trained. We're like a small military. But that's not all we do. We have officers trained in negotiation and others trained in mental health crises. As one of the commanders of our team, I'm fully trained and certified to train my officers. DJ, being our other commander, is trained the same as I am.

When we got to the scene, I knew I had my work cut out for me. The kid was sitting on the roof of his parent's house. And when I say kid, I mean that. He was only fourteen. He talked enough to me for me to learn that he was being bullied at school. Terrible shit. He'd get locked in his locker during gym class. They wouldn't find him until after the class was over, and only because he screamed for help.

And that wasn't even the beginning of it. The horrors the kid dealt with are fucking unimaginable to me. He'd been beat up. Pushed. Trapped in lockers for hours until cops were called by the parents to get him out when he didn't return home. His clothes were hung from the flagpole while he was in the shower after gym. He had to run to his locker in the school's corridor in just a towel to get his phone to call his parents to get him from the school. I can't figure out what the fuck the school has done about the bullying. I say bullying, but fuck if it shouldn't be called abuse. It infuriates me because it seems like they've done nothing. This kid was suffering, and no one helped him.

I close my eyes as I drop my head against the headrest. "It reminds me of Beckett," I say in reference to my nephew. "Same fucking age. I know he doesn't get bullied, but fuck. My sister treats him like shit. He's getting bullied at home. Maybe that's worse. I don't know."

"I know, Matt. But there was nothing you could do for this kid. You can't beat yourself up. You did all you could. We all did."

I open my eyes because if I keep them closed I'm going to envision the same fucking sight I have been for the entire afternoon.

Instead of that kid laying on the sidewalk with his head busted open; his eyes wide and staring at me, it's my nephew.

Beckett.

"If I'd just been a little quicker, DJ, I could have caught him."

"Matt. Stop it. There was nothing you could have done. You didn't expect him to jump right then. None of us did. He was talking. He seemed to be coming out of it. He was listening to you. He believed you when you said you could help him, and that you'd fight the school with him. He was all in when you said you'd stand right there by his side and fight the bullies. That you'd bring charges against everyone, including the school. When he stood up, Matt, I thought he was coming down. I didn't expect him to take a running leap off the fucking roof. No one did." DJ leans over and kisses me. "Get out of your head." He leans back in his seat. "Let's head home."

I look at my watch. "I don't want to go home. It's been a fuck of a day. It's late. I need a drink. Blow off some steam."

He chuckles. "Well, we can go for a run and grab a beer after. Order in. Or we can head over to Sapphire's. I think steak is on their menu tonight. We could pair it with that house wine you like."

I shoot him a weak smile as I take my gun out of its holster. He does the same. I hand him mine so he can put them in the gun safe I have installed in my glove compartment. "Now you're talking. I just can't get too wasted tonight. In case Beckett calls. I don't doubt this will affect him. It happened to a kid who goes to his school. Same age. He probably knew him."

We both remove our holsters. DJ's is a shoulder holster. He prefers those damn things. I hate them. Mine is attached to my belt, just like it's supposed to be. DJ puts them both in the gym bag behind my seat as I put my belt back on. I start the truck.

"You have too much self-control to get wasted. I don't think I've ever seen you drunk off your ass."

I can't help but chuckle. "You just might see it tonight if you don't stop me."

"You never have to worry about me letting you do something stupid. I love you too much. Now, let's go. I'm fucking starving. And before you say what you're about to, you need to eat something. You need to compartmentalize this. You need to let yourself let this go and fight this

7

shit the way only we as cops can. We're going to gather the evidence. We're going to bring charges against the bullies and the school. And we're sure as fuck not letting anyone get away with what happened today."

I start driving towards Sapphire's. "I'm taking every single one of these fuckers down."

"And I'll be right there with you the whole fucking way. What happened today was senseless as hell. But in order for us to get justice for that kid, we need to focus. Cry it out when we get home if you want to. I'll sit there and rub your back the whole damn time. But right now, we need to keep our strength up. Work through the restlessness and the anger."

"I don't think I'm in the right frame of mind to go home with a woman tonight." That's usually what we do when we go to Sapphire's.

DJ chuckles. "On the contrary. I think taking back control is exactly what you need."

I focus on the road as I drive. Sapphire's is an underground BDSM club. It's exclusive. Not everyone is allowed in it. In order to be a part of it, a person has to pay a membership fee yearly that isn't at all cheap, or they need to be sponsored by someone who is a member.

Anyone who frequents the club is required to be tested for any sexually transmitted diseases weekly and must have those results emailed to the owner. Any person who comes up with a not clean test is immediately removed. To avoid any kind of tampering, the owner requires the medical facility who did the test to email the results to them. Which means any member is required to authorize the owner to receive the test results.

The cost to be a member is worth it to those of us who choose to keep our sexuality and sexual preference a secret. Many people DJ and I work with speculate that we're both gay and together, but no one dares to approach us about it. They know we won't hesitate to put them in their place. And that place is that it isn't any of their fucking business who we're in a relationship with.

The truth is, we're pansexual. While we're in a relationship with each other, we both quite often share a woman. We never go out and fuck around with anyone on our own. That isn't how we operate. It would feel like we're cheating. But we share. We love to share, and the women we choose to be with love to be shared just as much as we love to do it.

But the biggest thing about us that we choose to keep away from anyone we aren't close to is that we're both dominant men. Our relationship works because I'm slightly less dominant than him. I don't often back down to him, but I know when I need to. DJ allows me to have control over him and in life when he knows I need it.

Regardless, we've both talked at length about where we see our relationship in the future. While we love each other with all we are, we want a woman in our life to share who would join our relationship and be with both of us for the rest of our days. It's an unrealized dream. We've been looking for her for thirteen years and still haven't found that special woman. We haven't given up looking, though.

Which brings me to Sapphire's. DJ and I both need a submissive woman. Not that we want a weak woman, which is how most people view submissives. We want a woman who can not only appeal to our dominant sides, but someone who can also compliment it. We're cops. It takes a special kind of woman to be with a cop. We need a woman who is also strong and confident in her ability to take us down a notch when we need to be.

Most submissives we've found, though, are either one or the other. They aren't that perfect balance of both. They either submit to us fully and can't stand on their own two feet, or they're the definition of brat and don't appeal to us in any other way than us wanting to spank them and send them back to mommy.

Not to say we aren't holding out hope. They say there's someone out there for everyone. Lightning struck once when it came to me and DJ. We both believe it can happen again. Everyone deserves the perfect relationship. While ours is perfect, we've always felt like something is missing. We both feel like we'd be okay without the addition of that perfect woman, but she's the missing link. We know she's out there. We'll find her. One day.

I pull into the parking lot of Sapphire's. No one who comes to this five-star restaurant for dinner would have a clue what goes on above them. Most think it's a bakery, but above the bakery is a club. There are no windows. The music, while club music, isn't overpowering. A person can have a conversation without having to scream over the noise. They can enjoy drinks and dinner without being bothered. And they can watch the show without being stared at.

It's the show I'm looking forward to tonight. It's not strippers or dancers. It's dominants and masters with their submissives. There are no sexual acts. Nothing more than a lot of play that is a huge turn on to both doms and subs. When they leave the club, they go home and do whatever they do. DJ and I both love watching some of it, but we like making fun of the crazier shit even more.

It's also a place where doms like us can find subs who are looking for doms. Many of them like the play. They aren't looking for relationships. Some, though, are. This is a place where they can do that relatively safely. Most crazy people don't frequent a club they have to drop ten grand every single year to be a member of. It's not a surefire method. There are all kinds of people that frequent this place, but it goes a long way in keeping those who aren't serious about this world out of it.

DJ takes my hand when we get out of my truck. He leads me into Sapphire's. We didn't bother going home. It's long past dinner. DJ is wearing black dress pants and a dark green dress shirt without a tie. I'm wearing jeans and a dark blue dress shirt without a tie. I hate dress pants. They feel restricting and don't feel strong enough to hold my gun to my hip. It's the reason DJ usually wears a shoulder holster.

It's one of the few things we differ quite a lot on. I'll take my gun belt any day of the week. DJ prefers the shoulder holster because it allows him to wear the dress pants he loves so much without feeling weighed down by his gun. I like the weight of my gun at my hip.

The hostess looks us up and down with a slight frown. Sapphire's has a pretty strict dress code. Neither of us meet it. "Name?"

"Chance," I say to her. "You won't find us on your reservation list, though."

She looks up at me with a bored look. "Then, you won't be able to get in, sir. We're booked solid for an entire year."

I chuckle. "We'll be on the red list," I say quietly so no one but her hears me.

Her eyes widen as she looks around at the few people standing around waiting for a table for the reservation they do have. "Oh! Um... y-yes, sir. Follow me."

DJ leans into me. "She must be new."

I nod. "Probably."

She leads us to the back of a lobby and uses a keycard to open a door. She blushes as she pushes it for us and lets us in. She says nothing as she closes the door behind us. DJ finally starts laughing as he turns towards the elevator.

I laugh with him. "She must have just started her shift. I doubt we're the first ones here. It's almost nine o'clock," I say.

"First shift. First day." DJ shrugs. "I don't know. She'll get used to it real quick or quit."

I smile as the elevator doors open. The calming ambiance of the club makes everything just slightly better. At the very least, I can think past the kid's age and stop my mind's eye from thinking about my nephew. I need to talk to him. I need to clear my mind before that conversation, but I know I need to talk to him.

"Hey, there, Mr. Rens and Mr. Chance," a perky, young blond girl dressed in red lingerie says. She's been working here for a few years. She's not a submissive or dominant, but she doesn't have a problem with the world. She's just working her way through college.

"Hey, Lauren," I say with a grin. "Usual table, please. Usual meal. Usual drinks."

She smiles. "Bad day?"

"Very," DJ responds for me as she leads us to our table in the back. We can see everything and not be bothered.

Lauren is one of very few people in this entire establishment who knows what we do for a living. She needed help once and is good at keeping secrets. One of the other people is the owner, and that's only because part of our membership approval involved an interview and background check. The attention to detail is what makes this establishment one of the safest and best in the city. The owner truly wants everyone to have fun while protecting them the best he can.

The lights dim a little more than they already are just as DJ and I are getting our food. We both look up as the curtains rise at the far end of the club revealing seven different rooms with seven different couples all engaged in seven different types of play. One couple is using a feather. I've done that and fucking love when DJ gets off on it. Another is using a whip.

I chuckle and shake my head. "I'll never understand whip play."

DJ grins and shakes his head, too. "Me either. Maybe we're on the vanilla side of all of this because I don't understand half the shit going on in here. I mean, breath play?" He gestures to another room with his fork. "Who the fuck gets off having their air supply cut off?"

"I guess, if done right, it's supposed to be all sexy and shit."

"No. I'd never do that. Give me blindfolds and cuffs any day of the week. I'd never use a whip or suspend anyone in the air. It doesn't seem like fun to me. It seems like far too much control over someone."

I chuckle because it's a conversation we've had a lot. It's the reason we're looking for a specific type of woman. One who will allow us to have the control we want and will submit fully to us, trusting us to bring her the pleasure she desires and needs while still being an actual individual. We want balance in our relationship. We want what DJ and I have with each other. Finding a woman like that, though, has proven quite a difficult task.

As we're finishing our meal and just about to give up on finding someone for the night, the elevator doors open, and out steps the most beautiful woman I have ever seen. I glance at DJ when I hear him gasp.

"Jesus," he whispers.

The woman is petite. Her thick, beautiful, auburn hair falls in waves just past her shoulders. Her slim black jeans hug her curves in all the right places. Her purple V-neck t-shirt dips just enough to make me wish I could see more while putting several inappropriate thoughts in my head. Like what my dick would look like between those ample tits. Her eyes are submissively downcast. Her hands are clasped in front of her, respectfully.

The immediate reaction I have to her forces me to adjust myself before I rip a hole in my jeans. My dick is hard as steel. It's a reaction no one but DJ has ever gotten out of me. Even though we've both been with women, I've never been solid as a rock within seconds of looking at one.

The woman walks past us with a blond girl I hope like hell is just a friend. She looks up at us both through her lashes and blushes a beautiful shade of pink before looking away. DJ groans and reaches down to adjust himself.

"What the fuck just happened?" I ask, blinking like I'm coming out of a daze.

"We aren't leaving without that girl," DJ mumbles. "She's the one."

My eyes snap to him. "What did you just say?"

His eyes never leave her. "She's the one, Matt. The one we've been waiting so long for. You can't tell me you didn't feel that. It was like…" He pauses as he watches her. I let my eyes fall back on her. She's just about to take a seat when a male who looks like he fell out of the corporate world sidles up to her.

"A kick to the chest," I finish for him. "Which is how I'm feeling right now seeing that guy with his hand on her arm."

"Like he's touching what's ours."

I look up as Lauren stops at our table to gather our plates. "Lauren? Who's that girl? The one standing near the table closest to the breath play show? Purple t-shirt."

Lauren glances where DJ and I are looking. "Oh. Her name is Lyric Sharpe. She's been coming here for years. Her friend pays her membership. Josh, I think his name is. He doesn't live locally, I don't think, but visits when he can. He has a membership here, too, but he bought hers a few years back. The woman sitting down at the table with her is her friend, Alice." I raise an eyebrow when she makes a face as the word 'friend' leaves her lips. I file it away for later.

"Why haven't we ever seen her before?" DJ asks.

Lauren tilts her head. "Um… honestly, she doesn't come here a lot. She's probably either gone by the time you get here or just didn't come here that night. On a few occasions, she'll be in the back in Cooper's office waiting to be picked up by her brother. Sometimes, if she wants a quiet night to just relax, she sits at the back of the room observing everything. I know she's been there a few times when you've come in." She watches her for a couple of moments before looking back at us. "If you'd like some inside information, though, I think she'd be perfect for you two. She's asked me about you before." She flicks her eyes towards the guy Lyric is with as she takes a deep breath. "And I'd be quick about picking her up because that guy is a true charmer and real asshole. Lyric deserves better than the likes of him. She's so, so sweet."

The words are all we need to move. DJ drops a hundred dollar bill on the table. I drop a fifty. We both get up and kiss Lauren on top of the head as she stares at the money on the table in confusion.

"Rest is for you, sweetheart," I say as DJ and I both make our way towards the woman who stepped out of our fucking dreams.

"Thank you guys," Lauren says. "I'll be able to pay rent this month."

We both stop and turn to her. I raise an eyebrow. "What?" I ask.

She sighs. "It's been tough. My shifts are getting cut. The new manager here doesn't like me much. He's kind of a dick."

DJ looks at me then back at Lauren. "You have our numbers. If you ever need anything, you know you can call."

She nods. "I know. He hasn't tried anything. He's just an asshole." She looks past DJ. "Hurry. He's about to steal her away."

I take out my wallet and press a few hundred dollar bills into Lauren's hand. "Don't argue. I don't need this. You do."

Lauren's eyes widen and shine with sudden tears yet to escape. "He takes half our tips," she whispers, frantically looking around.

I assume the guy near the kitchen is the manager, so I pull her close to me, like I'm kissing her. I tuck the money in her bra and push her back, making sure it's not seen. "Then, don't tell him."

She sniffles and nods. I make a mental note to have a conversation with Cooper, the owner. No fucking way I'm letting this new manager take half the tips these girls make. There's nothing about it that is right in my book

DJ and I turn towards Lyric just as the charming asshole takes her hand. He starts walking towards the elevator. She follows submissively behind him, but her body language is all wrong. Her friend is too busy flirting with another guy to notice her discomfort, or the fact that she's trying to make eye contact with her, but I do. I see her shoulders are hunched over. I see she's looking down at the ground. And I see she's chewing furiously on the inside of her lip.

"She's uncomfortable," DJ says, quickening his strides.

"Let's find out why." My cop instincts kick in. I know something isn't right. But it's the dominant instincts that overrule everything else. A submissive should never be nervous. Never afraid. Lyric is all of that and more.

I notice the bartender, Kieran, moving to intercept, but pauses when he catches sight of DJ and I approaching her. I nod to him, telling him we have her, as we reach her side. He nods in return and mouths, 'Take care of her' before turning to serve the new customer in front of him. I smile a little because that's exactly what we plan to do.

"Hey, Lyric," DJ says, using our advantage right out of the gate. She has no idea who we are, but we know who she is. "Sorry we're late, honey. Got tied up on a call." He looks at the guy with her with a glare. "Who's this?"

Lyric looks between us both through wide, beautiful hazel eyes. "U-um… I…," she stutters. It's obvious she doesn't know what to say, but what's even more obvious is the tremble she tries to hide and the bleeding lip she has from biting it so hard. "T-tried to t-tell him I…" She sniffles. "I d-didn't w-want to go…" Her eyes fill with tears.

"Doesn't matter," I cut in, tearing my eyes from hers and glaring at the guy. "She's taken."

He looks at us as if we've grown a second head. "Excuse me? We're leaving. Now." He pulls her with him as he steps around us. She stumbles, but I catch her, pulling her into me.

"I said she's taken." I gently push her so she's behind me because I know guys like this. He'll start a fight. I don't want her involved in it.

I watch DJ flick his eyes towards the security guard standing near the elevator. If a person wasn't looking for him, they'd never know he's there. But our job is to be observant. We're good about knowing where everyone is. Especially if they can be of assistance to us. Even more so if they can harm us.

The security guard immediately walks towards us. "Problem here?" he asks, putting a large hand on the charming asshole's shoulder.

"Yeah," the guy says. "These two seem to think they can have anyone in the club. Including what I've claimed as mine," he growls. His eyes fall to Lyric. They're cold. Calculating. I can feel her shiver behind me, and I don't even need to see or touch her. This guy isn't getting his hands on our girl.

Not tonight.

Not ever.

"She doesn't want to go with him," DJ says calmly. "Do you, honey?"

I look over my shoulder and give Lyric a wink of encouragement and slight nod. "It's okay. You can be honest," I say, my voice low enough for only her to hear.

Lyric shakes her head. "No, s-sir," she whispers. "I r-really don't." She sniffles. "I've been trying to tell h-him no since he approached me at the t-table." She grips the back of my shirt with a terrified whimper that stabs me in the chest. "He is into S-sadism. Please don't let him h-hurt me," she whispers.

"That's not what you said before these Neanderthals showed up!" the guy yells, getting more and more agitated.

Lyric bites her lip again, hard enough to split her lip open in a second place. Luckily, she doesn't. But it does start bleeding again. I wince at the sight of it. Not because blood makes me queasy, but because she's hurting herself. She's so scared that she's *hurting herself.*

"Time to go for the night, Mr. Tanison." The security guard escorts the man out as DJ and I watch.

"Why would you go off with a guy like that, honey?" DJ asks, turning his attention to Lyric and holding out a hand for her to take.

"I tried n-not to… He said submissives aren't a-allowed to say n-no," she says quietly, not looking at either of us as she takes his hand.

"That's not true, sweet girl. Submissives are always allowed to say no. Anyone who tells you otherwise is lying to you, baby." DJ leads her to our table and lets her scoot into the circular booth first.

I slide in next to her, leaving a little distance between us. DJ does the same. It's a little trick to make her feel like she's in charge of what happens next. And she is. It's her choice to choose us, and we'd never want her to feel uncomfortable or forced into her decision.

Not to say that we don't want her to choose us both tonight. I've never wanted to take a woman home with us. Home to me and DJ is like a sanctuary. But ever since my eyes landed on her, sharing our sanctuary is all I can think about.

Talking to her.

Touching her.

Loving her.

I want it all, and I know DJ does, too. He's right. She's the one we've been waiting for.

And I'll be damned if I let her walk out of here with anyone but us.

Chapter Two

☆ DJ ☆

I don't know why, but I didn't think it would be so easy to get Lyric to sit down with us, let alone talk to us. But seeing her smile and her eyes light up is something I didn't know I needed in my life. I've always been content with Matt. I love him more than breathing. I like the relationship we have. I enjoy going out with him. I love sharing a woman here or there with him.

Matt and I have felt for a long time that something was missing for us, though. While we've looked for the woman that could complete us, we've never found her. No one really fit. They were fun for a quick night, but they didn't make us whole.

Not until her.

Lyric Sharpe.

This girl has no idea what we want from her, but the more she talks, the more I'm hoping she'll say yes because I feel like she's the one we've spent years looking for. She's gorgeous. The only other person I've felt like this about is the man sitting on Lyric's other side.

Lyric has her hands folded politely in her lap. She keeps her eyes down. When she looks up at us, she does it through her lashes. It's both adorable and sexy as fuck. Every time her eyes meet mine, my stomach does a somersault. Her soft and subtle scent floods my senses. It's clean and simply her. Vanilla bean. It's beautiful.

I watch as Matt brushes his hand against her face while he tucks a strand of hair behind her ear. She blushes, just like she always does when one of us finds a way to touch her, and leans into his hand like it's instinctive. She's done the same thing to me when I've brushed my hand against her cheek. She doesn't have any idea what she's doing to us. With most other girls, I wouldn't believe for a second that they didn't have a clue, but not her. Lyric is oblivious to her beauty. It's one more thing that makes her the one.

"So, what are you doing in a club like this?" I ask her, my voice a little raspy. I clear my throat.

She looks up at me through those damn long lashes again. I swallow. Hard. She licks her lip. "U-um. Looking for a relationship with someone who…" She shrugs and looks down again.

I reach up and gently grip her chin with my thumb and forefinger, tilting her head up so she's looking at me. "Don't be shy. Someone who what?"

She swallows. "Gets me…" She clears her throat and takes a breath. "Someone who understands me. Someone I can be myself with. Someone I can trust with all I am and let go with. Someone who will be my guide and partner. I… I'm not… good at decisions. Sometimes, I need someone to pull me back when I get a little…" She tilts her head so adorably, it makes me groan. "Out of control. Like when I bite my lip. I make it bleed, but I can't stop. I need someone to help me be accountable for things like that. I… want… someone who won't hold me back. Someone who will push me when I need it. Someone who will support my dreams and help me realize them when I feel like they're just unattainable goals I won't be able to reach." She looks down once more. I let her this time. I watch as she takes a deep breath. "Someone who will love me as much as I love them."

"Someone who will hold you up when you feel weak," Matt adds. He's tangled his fingers in her hair.

She nods slowly, keeping her eyes on her hands. "The only time I ever go home with anyone is when I desperately need to get back into control." She furrows her brows and shakes her head. "That didn't come out right."

I chuckle and put my hand over hers. They're tiny compared to mine. "I think it came out exactly the way you wanted it to. When you feel like your life is out of control, you feel like you need help getting it back. But can I ask you something?"

She nods as I link my fingers with hers. "Okay," she whispers.

"When it's all over, do you feel in control? Or do you feel like you fucked up and feel more out of control then before?"

When her eyes jerk up to mine, and she bites her lip, I have my answer. Matt tugs her hair slightly and runs his thumb across her lower lip until she releases it. I hate that she hurts herself by biting it.

She licks her lip and trembles slightly. Though, I'm not sure if it's at our touch, or if it's because the answer scares her. "I feel worse," she says softly. "No one has ever really interested me like that. It makes me feel like a bad person, a slut, even though I don't sleep with them. When I ask someone to help me feel back in control, that's all. Nothing more. It's like I'm leading them on."

Matt's eyes flick to mine. I know he's thinking exactly what I am. He clears his throat. "What about us?" He takes her other hand in his so she's holding both of our hands. He kisses her knuckles. Her eyes flutter closed. Ours never leave her. "Do we interest you?"

She nods slowly and takes another breath. Her hand shakes in mine. "More than anything," she whispers as she opens her eyes.

I rub my thumb soothingly over the back of her hand. "Both of us?" I desperately need to hear a yes to those words.

She opens her eyes but doesn't look up as she nods. "Yes."

"Then, would you allow us to show you what it could be like with us?" I ask, my eyes flicking to Matt's. Neither of us liked her calling herself a slut.

She watches us both silently as a torrent of emotions plays out behind her beautiful eyes. Like she's waging a war with herself as she thinks about what being with us would mean. I can't help but be even more impressed by her as she works it all out.

Finally, she nods. "Okay….," she says softly. She nods once more, as if giving herself strength. "Yes, sir."

Matt and I both get up. I hold out a hand for her. She takes it, tilting her head slightly. I can see she's confused, but she's about to find out that we aren't going to tolerate her talking down about herself. We just aren't going to show her here. I help her out of the booth.

"Will you allow us to take you home?" Matt asks as he takes her other hand when she stands. "You can say no."

Her eyes widen. "It's been a while since anyone has actually asked me or given me the option… They've just assumed I wanted to go. Or, like the guy tonight, didn't give me the choice and just told me that good submissives don't say no." She adds even softer. "I've always had a difficult time telling people no anyway. I hate conflict. I hate letting people down."

I smile, even though I feel like my heart has been ripped out of my chest. What kind of man doesn't give an option to say no to something like this? "It's your call. You can come with us. Or you don't have to. You can leave anytime if you choose to. Just know that we've never taken a woman home with us. You'd be the first. We've always gone to her place. Not ours. Our place is our sanctuary."

"We've never wanted to share it with anyone," Matt adds. "Not until you."

She looks up at us both in shock and a little bit of wonder. "You want to share it with me? Why? I'm nothing special."

I narrow my eyes and lower my voice to a far more dominant level. "We haven't discussed rules yet, little girl, but I'll tell you this. Rule one. You will not hurt yourself. It's a form of self-harm that we will not tolerate. That includes biting your lip. You've already made it bleed today. Rule two. You will not talk down about yourself. Ever."

Her eyes snap to mine. She nods. "Yes, sir. I'm sorry."

"You've done it twice within three minutes of each other. Don't let it happen again. I won't let the next one slide," I tell her with authority and the dominance I sense she needs.

Matt kisses her knuckles once more before we both lead her to the elevator. I can feel a few glares on our backs as we leave with her, but refuse to acknowledge them. Lyric watches both of us curiously, but makes no move to try and walk away, though I can feel she knows we'd let her. She knows leaving with us is her choice.

As we stop by Matt's truck, he turns to her. "Did you drive here?"

She shakes her head. "No, sir."

"Are you sure this is what you want? Coming home with us?" Matt's intense brown eyes darken just a little, but his voice is soft. Soothing. Exactly what Lyric needs.

She nods slowly. "I'm a little scared."

"Why are you scared, sweetheart?" I ask.

She nibbles her lip again but immediately stops when a low growl escapes my throat. "What about your girlfriend?" she asks quietly, not meeting our eyes. She wraps her arms around herself. "I won't be your bit on the side. That's not who I am."

I smile. She has no idea that what she just said reassures me that she really is the one we've been waiting for. "What girlfriend?" I ask.

She furrows her brows and looks up to the building. "The pretty server. Lauren. I saw you both really close with her. I even saw Matt touching her. It looked like they kissed." She looks up at Matt.

Matt smiles. "Honey, she's a friend. I'll be having a conversation with the owner because the new manager of the club has been cutting her hours and stealing half of hers and the girls' tips. I gave her five hundred dollars so she could eat this month and pay her bills. All of her money she's made is going to rent. I slid it in her bra because I didn't want the manager to see what I was doing. He was standing by the kitchen behind you. I wanted it to look like I was flirting with her and not draw attention to the fact I was giving her money."

She smiles softly. She relaxes as she releases her grip on her sides and links her fingers together. "You gave her money for food and her bills?"

"And a hundred dollar tip that gave her the rent she needed for the month," I tell her. "I guess she'll only get fifty of that, but it's okay because she has the extra money Matt hid in her bra. There isn't another woman. There's only me and Matt. We're a couple. And being totally honest with you, we've been looking for a woman for years that we can share. But not just in the bedroom. We're looking for a relationship. We've never found a woman we've felt a connection with. Just like you've never felt a connection with the guys you've gone home with. We've never stopped looking for her."

"We're pretty sure we've found the woman we've been looking for since we decided this is what we wanted."

Lyric shivers as she nods slowly. "And you… think that's me…?"

"How about we get in the truck and talk about it? You're cold," I say.

As if on cue, she shivers again. Matt unlocks the truck and opens the door. I help her in and climb up next to her. I shut the door as Matt climbs in the driver's side. She folds her hands in her lap again and looks down. I grab the jacket I keep in the back of his truck and wrap it around her shoulders.

"What questions do you have for us, Lyric?" Matt asks. "Because we want you to be comfortable."

She's quiet for a long time, subtly inhaling my scent. Finally, she looks up at both of us. "It's not that I'm not comfortable. We talked for quite a while upstairs. It's… just that for the first time in so long… I feel something. Like a connection. But it's not just to one of you. It's to both. Which makes me feel like a slut because I want two men."

"Lyric," Matt says. His voice has taken on his own dominant tone. It sends shivers down my spine and makes Lyric jump slightly as she looks at him. "What's rule number two that we shared with you upstairs?"

Her eyes widen in realization. She looks down submissively. "Not to talk down about myself."

"I'm going to ask you again, and I want you to understand that if you don't want to come home with us, if you don't want us, it's okay," I tell her as I take her hand. "Look at me." I wait for her to look up at me. "Do you want this? Do you want us?"

"Yes, sir," she says, her eyes not leaving mine.

My heart soars as I smile. "You don't know how happy that makes me." I nod towards Matt. "Us."

She blushes and ducks her head. "I'm not sure if it's right. But I do want you both. It's a little scary. I don't know how to describe it, but the more we talk, the more I feel like I've known you my whole life."

"Good girl," Matt says as he starts the truck.

The ride home is silent. All of us are lost in our own thoughts. Talking to Lyric and learning about her while telling her about us was the easiest conversation we've ever had with anyone. Lyric fits. I know it. Matt is on the same page with me. I'm hoping after tonight, Lyric won't want to run away. I want her to stay.

But I also feel like she needs this. She's admitted it herself. She only goes to the club when she feels out of control.

Matt pulls into the garage of our home. We both get out of the truck. I grip Lyric's hips, helping her down. I have to fight the groan from escaping my lips at the feel of her perfect curves beneath my fingertips. Curves I want to explore with my tongue. Especially when the sexy little moan I'm sure she didn't intend to let out hits my ears.

I close the door to the truck and lead her into the house. It's time to show this girl that we're everything she wants and doesn't know she needs. That she's the piece we've been looking for to complete us. That we're all she's been missing.

I sit down on the arm of the couch, keeping her hand in mine as I look deep into those beautiful eyes. "Do you remember what I said in the club before we left after you called yourself a slut?" I run my thumb over her knuckles. Matt leans on the back of the couch.

Lyric looks down at our hands. "That you wouldn't let the next time slide," she whispers.

"Good girl," I say. I bring her hand to my lips and kiss it. "I had other plans tonight when Matt and I saw you. But plans change. I was serious about that rule, Lyric. You are the furthest thing I can think of from a slut. I have every intention of exploring why the hell you feel that way, but right now, you're facing a punishment for breaking rule number two."

She blinks a few times before nodding slowly. I know she has no idea what's coming, but the way she's just withdrawn into herself sets me on edge. I look up at Matt questioningly. I'm curious if he's thinking what I am. Judging from the way his face mirror's mine, I'd say yes.

"Lyric," he begins. "Sweetheart, have doms you've been with subjected you to punishments before?"

She doesn't look up at us, but nods. "Twice. Only one was really bad," she whispers. "It was when I still lived in the United Kingdom." The tears in her voice break me. "It was my first and last time at a club there. We moved here a week later."

I pull her closer, so she's standing between my legs. I reach up and run my fingers through her hair. "Tell me."

She sniffles. "He tied me..." She pauses and takes a breath. Matt wipes the tear that's begun falling down her cheek. "He tied me to his bed. And left me there all night. I couldn't... go to... the bathroom... I wet myself…," she whispers in embarrassment and shame. "He untied me in the morning and sent me home. He said I wasn't a good sub and not what he wanted. I barely made it down the street before I had to call my brother to come and get me. I could barely walk, my legs were so shaky. I was weak from not being able to move for so long. He wouldn't even… let me… clean up…" She sniffles. "He… made me… clean his sheets and bed and blankets…"

"Jesus, baby," Matt says. He slips his arms around her as he walks behind her. "That's not a punishment. That's abuse and not what we're about or what you deserve." He kisses her neck and sways with her. She begins to relax.

I kiss her hand again. "Five spankings. With my hand. We aren't into whips and chains and all that shit."

She relaxes more and nods. "Yes, sir."

"While we finger fuck you," I continue.

She gasps slightly. "W-what?"

I grin. "Not allowing you to come," I finish.

Her eyes grow hooded when it dawns on her what the punishment is. She lets out a low whine that sounds like she's both turned on and sad she's about to get punished. Adorable as fuck. Though, I'm positive she has no idea.

She nods and looks at me through those long lashes. "Yes, sir," she whispers.

Matt kisses her neck and up to her ear. "Think you can handle that?"

She nods and melts against his lips. "Mmm… Yes, sir…" She closes her eyes, leaning into Matt.

"My God, you're fucking perfect," I whisper. She blushes and slowly opens her eyes as I start undoing the button on her jeans. I slowly push them down her hips to her knees, keeping my eyes on hers the entire time.

When I have her jeans at her knees, I slowly stand. I move to her side as Matt gently lowers her down so she's bending over the arm of the couch. He slides his foot between hers and gently nudges her legs apart. The sexy whimper she lets out goes directly to my cock.

Matt groans. "Fuck…" He runs his hand down the globe of her ass. She whimpers. "I've been waiting for you my whole life, beautiful." He kneels and kisses her ass. She lets out a surprised squeak right before my hand comes down on her perfect bottom.

"Oh!" she shouts with a whimper.

"Count," I say, giving my voice that dominant edge.

"O-one, sir."

"Good girl." I watch Matt slide one finger into her pussy and wish like hell I was that finger. Soon. Very soon. Matt starts thrusting slowly and deeply.

"Oh…," Lyric moans. She grips the couch and lets her head fall forward.

I smile. "So fucking beautiful." I force myself to continue and slap her ass again.

She jerks forward. "T-two, sir."

Matt looks up at me as he keeps thrusting, adding a little twist. Lyric moans again. I can see how wet she is. How reactive she is to us. I kneel down slowly and let my hand trail down her leg. Soft. Silky smooth. Everything like I envisioned it would feel under my fingertips.

I trail my hand back up her leg. "Tell me why you're getting punished," I say. I lean in and press my lips against her ass because I can't fucking resist. She's intoxicating.

"Mmm…," she moans again, pressing back into my lips and twisting her hips slightly around Matt's finger. "Because I talked down about myself."

"Good girl," I say, sliding one finger alongside Matt's and thrusting at his pace.

"Oh, yes…" She clenches tight around us both and starts riding our fingers. We stop. I slap her ass again. She jumps. Her pussy clamps down around us. "Ah! T-three… Three, sir."

"Tell me I'm never going to hear you call yourself a slut again. That I'm never going to hear you say you feel like one again." I start thrusting once more with Matt. We both twist our fingers inside her.

"Oh! N-never again." She shakes her head with a moan and pants, moving with our fingers.

"No. Say I will never call myself a slut or say I feel like one again, sir," Matt says.

"I w-will never call myself a slut or say I feel l-like one a-again, sir." Her thighs start to tremble. We stop once more. She whimpers and tries to catch her breath.

"Good girl," I say as I slap her ass again.

"Ah! F-four, sir…" She sniffles. Tears. I don't do well with tears.

"You okay, baby?" I ask, dropping my timbre to a more soothing than dominant level. Matt and I keep our fingers still inside her. It's hard as hell not to make her come. She's wet, and so fucking tight. Trembling. She's ready.

She nods and lets out a shuddering breath. "Yes, sir."

I kiss her ass where I've spanked. "Can you handle one more? This isn't meant to hurt you, baby. It's meant to give you that sense of accountability you're looking for. I want you to tell me if it's enough."

"I understand," she murmurs. "I can handle it."

"That's our girl," Matt says as I give her a last slap to her perfectly round ass.

"Ah! F-five, sir." She lets out another shuddering breath and clenches once more around our fingers as she grips the cushions and sniffles.

Matt and I slowly pull our fingers out and suck her sweet taste off them. "Fuck, pretty girl. You taste like sin," Matt says with a grin.

We both stand and help her up. I pull her pretty, purple, satin panties up her thighs, followed by her jeans. I take a seat on the brown leather couch again and take her hand. I tug her into my lap as Matt heads for the kitchen.

"You okay?" I ask.

She nods. "I feel… centered. I don't know why, or if it makes sense, but I feel less…" She trails off and furrows her brows adorably as she searches for the right words.

"Out of control?" I offer after a few moments.

She nods and looks at me with a soft smile. "Thank you. It might seem a little…" She tilts her head. "Different? But I really do feel better. More centered than I have in a long time."

"It's not different. It's you. It's what you need. A lot of submissives are just like you, honey. You just haven't found the right dominant to make you feel whole and give you the things you need."

"Until now, I hope," Matt says with a smile. He hands her a bottle of cold water as he sits next to us. He kisses her cheek and takes her hand. "There is something important that we need to discuss. Something that may affect you wanting to be with us." He tucks a strand of hair behind her ear.

"What is it?" She tilts her head adorably. I chuckle and kiss her neck. I shift her until she's sitting sideways in my lap with her legs over Matt's.

"Matt and I have both had vasectomies. Matt had his done about fifteen years ago. I had mine around thirteen years ago. Not long before we got together. We had never really wanted kids. We felt that even when we found the woman that would complete us, we wouldn't want children. Are kids something you would want? Do you see them in your future? With us?"

I watch her for her reaction. I'm not sure what I was expecting, but it wasn't the tears glistening in her beautiful eyes. I hug her close, rubbing her back, glancing at Matt. He's watching her, concerned. He rubs her thigh soothingly as she takes a deep breath.

"I can't have children…," she whispers softly. "Well, I could. But not without extreme health issues." She takes a deep breath and sniffles. "A few years ago, I got pregnant by my then boyfriend, Josh. About two months after we found out, I had a miscarriage. It almost killed me. I was weak for months after. Depressed. Broken. I barely ate. Josh rarely left my side. My brother, too, when he could finally get time off work. They were so worried about me. They got someone for me to talk to. It took a long time for me to recover." She pauses and wipes her eyes.

"Oh baby…," Matt murmurs softly. He runs his fingers through her hair as we sway with her.

"It might seem silly to most people…," She sniffles. She takes a breath to steady herself before looking back up at us. "Josh and I had a memorial plaque created. We named him Jaxon. Jaxon Austin Lucinio. Josh always joked we could give him the nickname Jail if I had let him add Isaac as a second middle name." She chuckles a little sadly. I smile softly and chuckle with her. "We had it placed in his mom's beautiful garden that his friend had done for her. A place we could go to remember. Josh flies me to Chicago every year on the anniversary."

My heart is breaking for the pain she must have gone through. I'm just grateful that she had the support and help she needed. I hug her closer and tighter. I feel Matt wrap his arms around us both, rubbing her back.

"At my last checkup, they warned me that there was a high chance that if I was to get pregnant again, not only was it unlikely that I would carry to term, but that it was highly likely that I wouldn't survive it." She takes a shaky breath to compose herself before continuing. "I made the decision that I didn't want to have children after that. Even before, whenever I imagined my future, I never pictured myself pregnant. It might sound selfish, but it just wasn't something I wanted." She wipes her eyes and looks up at us again. "So, you both having vasectomies actually sets me at ease. There's very little risk of me getting pregnant. I'm not on the pill. It affected me badly, so I haven't actually taken it since I was sixteen."

"I'm so sorry that you went through that, baby girl," Matt says softly. He kisses her softly and hugs her just as tightly as I am. "I'm glad you had people there to help and support you. And I don't think the plaque is silly at all. Everyone grieves differently." He kisses her again and takes her hands.

"Not silly at all, little one." I murmur into her ear as I kiss her head.

"The hard talk is done now. Our relationship, if that's still what you want, will be much easier being on the same page about everything." He taps her nose lightly with a teasing smile. "I have to admit, I'm becoming a fan of your brother. He seems really -" He cuts off when his phone rings. Lyric takes a drink from the water bottle while he takes his phone out of his pocket. She leans into us both as she relaxes. "Shit. I have to take this." He kisses her softly as he stands. He moves away slightly as he brings his phone to his ear. "Beckett? What's up, buddy?"

I glance at my watch. My heart quickens. "Fuck. It's two in the morning. What the hell is he calling for at this hour?" I mumble. I'm trying not to show it, but I'm worried. He would never call this late unless something was wrong.

Lyric tilts her head. "Is everything okay?" She tenses in my arms.

I look at her. "Uh…" I don't want to be dishonest with her. "I don't know, baby."

I watch Matt pace and rub his temple. "Fuck, Beckett. Where the hell are you?" He stops pacing and looks at me. "Beckett, listen to me.

Turn around and walk back to Sapphire's. Go to the back door in the alley. It's next to the big garbage bin. It's a red door. Ring the bell and tell them I sent you. Don't move until I get there, Beckett. I'm not even close to kidding."

"Who's Beckett?" Lyric asks me.

"Matt's nephew. Ours. He's fourteen. I don't know why the fuck he's out at this hour, but my guess is his mom did something. She's never been violent towards him, but she has never been really kind to him either. A lot of her aggression has been taken out on him. She yells at him a lot. Punishes him by grounding him to his room, or not letting him hang out with his friends, or his boyfriend." I rub my forehead. "Matt has been trying to convince his sister, Liz, to give up custody to him for a couple of years now. This just might push him over the edge."

Lyric reaches up to rub her chest, just over her heart. She turns to watch Matt closely. "Poor kid," she whispers.

"Beckett, I'm still right here. Where are you?" He pauses a few moments before looking over at me and gesturing with his head towards the garage. "I'm coming now, buddy. Just tell them I sent you when they answer." He strides towards the garage, not hanging up.

Lyric starts to stand to follow, but I hold her in my lap and shake my head. "No, honey. We have some things to do here. Namely, getting his room ready for him. I washed his bedding last night and haven't had time to put it back on."

"I'll help," she says, looking after Matt worriedly. She sniffles and looks back at me. "Just tell me what you need me to do. And what Beckett needs."

I lean in and kiss her with a small smile as I run my fingers through her hair. My heart skips a beat because despite how this night just took a drastic turn, I'm more certain by the second that she really is the one we've been looking for. She doesn't have to care about a kid she's never met, but she does.

Selflessly.

Chapter Three

✫ Lyric ✫

"Lyric." DJ's timbre hits my ears. My head snaps up like a wolf who just heard her prey.

DJ.

All man.

All muscle.

All dominant.

The guy makes me weak in the knees. He doesn't even have to say anything. So, when I meet his pretty green eyes, I'm almost instantly calm.

"You've been pacing so much, you might actually wear out my hardwood floor."

I sigh and droop slightly as I look back out the window. "I just can't sit still. I mean, that poor kid is out there all alone." I sniffle a little thinking of all the things that could happen to him before Matt gets there.

I hear DJ stand from the chair he was sitting in. I don't know how he can be so relaxed at a time like this, but I'll be honest when I say I need him to be because I am freaking out. So many scenarios are running through my mind. None of them are good. Beckett could be hurt. He could have been taken. He could be getting thrown into a river after having unimaginable things happen to him.

I go back to pacing, but run directly into DJ. All solid titanium of his over six foot frame. "Ow. What were you in a past life? A linebacker?"

He grins as he steadies me. "Close. A wide-receiver."

I just blink at him. "Seriously? Can you be any more perfect? A dominant cop who played football. Tall. Gorgeous." I wave a hand up and down his body. "You smell incredible. You're like walking sex. Where's the flaw?"

He laughs. "Your British accent is adorable, little one. So is that bewildered expression on your face that's trying to hide the look in your eyes that's asking me how the fuck you got so lucky."

"Valid question."

He grins as he tucks my hair behind my ears and takes my face gently in his hands. He brushes his lips over mine, but doesn't actually kiss me. "You aren't the lucky one in this equation. You deserve it all." His lips ghost across mine once more. I close my eyes just as he presses down and kisses me. My entire body erupts in flames.

I look up at him after he pulls back. "How do you know that? I could be a crazy psycho or something."

He throws his head back and laughs. "But you aren't."

"Well, no... But I could be. You know nothing about me."

"I know all I need to. You're very kind. You put others before yourself. Probably to a fault. You refuse to go home until you see that a kid you don't even know is okay. You're submissive. A natural submissive. You're okay with being with two men. I know you're beautiful and smart. And just by the interaction with the fucker at the club, I know you've never been treated like a woman should be, except by the one you told us about. Josh. You have a very low sense of worth, which I have every intention of building up. Though, I suspect the Josh person might have had a hand in getting you this far." He kisses my nose. "I've got your number, honey. But if that scares you, if this is moving too fast for you, I'll back off."

My eyes widen, and my heart races. "No!" I shake my head. The idea of the two of them backing off in any way freaks me out.

"Hey. Shh…" He hugs me hard and close and sways with me. "I didn't say forget all of this, Lyric," he says softly after a few moments.

I take a deep breath. "I'm sorry."

He rests his chin on my head. "You have nothing to apologize for."

"I just feel this connection to you and Matt already. I've never felt it before. I mean, I have. Sort of. Just… not this intensely. It scares me, but the thought of you not being around scares me more."

I close my eyes and let myself breathe in his fresh, earthy scent. It calms my racing heart so much. Matt's is spicy. Not spicy in the sense that it makes me sneeze and burns my sinuses. But a comforting kind of spice. Opposite of DJ, but between the two of them, I've never been able to calm so easily. It usually escalates into an anxiety attack that I can never seem to come down from on my own. I might be submissive, but I always feel like I need to be doing something. If I'm not, I feel out of control.

Even around my brother and friend, who are amazing at bringing me back to the ground when I'm in space, have never had this effect on me. I don't feel like I'm crazy when I'm near them. Everything feels right. Well, at least with Luca. Sometimes, my friend makes me feel a little crazy. But I'm sure she doesn't mean to.

I jump when I hear a door close and dart towards the garage. "Matt?" I ask softly, opening the door from the house to the garage.

Matt smiles. "I thought DJ would have taken you home by now."

I shake my head. "I couldn't leave. I needed to make sure B- Beckett was okay." I wipe my eyes when tears sting them.

"He's good. He's pretty pissed off, but he's okay." Matt kisses me softly when he reaches me, then turns. Behind him is a boy with light-brown hair that looks more bleached from the sun than actually light-brown. He has pretty blue eyes and is fairly tall for his age. At least in my opinion. I guess I don't really know. "Lyric, this is Beckett. My nephew. Beckett. Meet Lyric."

He watches me a few moments before nodding and extending his hand. "I'm Beckett. The annoying kid always hanging around your boyfriends."

"Oh! We -" I start, but I don't have a clue what I'm going to try and say.

"Beckett," Matt interrupts as I shake Beckett's hand. "Why don't you grab something to eat. I smell soup, so I'm pretty sure DJ and Lyric warmed some up."

Beckett raises an eyebrow and looks up at Matt as he drops my hand. He doesn't have far to look though. He's easily six feet. He shrugs. "Okay."

I just blink after him. "I…" I shake my head, convinced he knows what's going on here before actually asking. Did Matt say something already? Am I bad because I want him to?

DJ chuckles. "He's very observant. He knows Matt and I are pansexual. We're together. He knows that. But he also knows we want more. You, specifically."

I blush and quickly change the subject to the one on my mind. "So, his mother." I look up at Matt.

Matt lets out a breath and shakes his head. "Long story. To make it short, though, she sees her late husband in Beckett. She can't let him go. It hurts that he's gone. The older Beckett gets, the more he gains his own personality and is less like his dad. So, she pushes Beckett away. Especially when she drinks, like she is tonight. Beckett is gay. He's been with a kid who lives around here for quite a while. They've been friends for years, but started dating this year. His mom absolutely hates it because it's one more thing that makes him different from his dad."

I hug myself and look after Beckett as he makes his way to the couch. "So, what made him run?" I ask softly.

"She slapped him," Matt says. "She's spanked him before. That's nothing. But she slapped him."

"I noticed the cut on his lip. And his cheek is red," DJ says.

Matt crosses his arms over his chest and glares. "Yeah."

DJ leans against the wall and looks at Matt as he takes a breath. "We can't let him go back this time."

My eyes widen. I look up at Matt. "Is that an option? Tell me that can't happen."

"Not if I can help it," Matt says. "I need to open a case." He rubs his head before tangling his fingers in my hair. I lean into his hand. "Which means DJ will have to drive you home. I have to deal with this. It's not that I don't want you here, but I think you need to have some time to think about things. I don't want to sway your decision on being with two men, and now a teenager, even though we both feel like you're the one for us."

"You… think I won't want to be with you both if Beckett is in the picture because I said I didn't want kids... That this will change… everything… for me. You think that I will walk away," I say softly.

I nod, leaning up on my tiptoes to kiss his cheek.

I step back and turn away from him to DJ. I don't want to, but he's probably right sending me home. Beckett needs to be his priority right now. He is what is important. Not me. He needs family. I'm not.

I'm not a violent person, but if I ever meet Matt's sister, I would love to slap her for laying a hand on him. Beckett seems like such an amazing kid for his age.

"Can you take me home, please?" I ask DJ quietly. "I think it's time for me to go."

"That's not -"

DJ cuts Matt off by shaking his head at him. "Matt, I think we need to focus on one thing at a time. Go get a report started with this Beckett incident. We can't allow her to have him back after this. I'll take care of our girl."

Matt looks at me hesitantly but nods anyway. He tugs my hair and leans down. He kisses me when I tilt my head back, and it makes me weak. "I'll call you," he whispers when he pulls back.

I know some guys use that line as a line, but for some reason, even as a whisper, I can feel the weight in his words. The promise.

I bite my lip and nod. I glance at Beckett, sitting on the couch. "Make sure he comes home."

Matt smiles and kisses my forehead as he walks the rest of the way into the house. DJ takes my hand and walks me to his convertible, a black Ford Mustang. He opens the door, and I slide into the soft, black leather seats.

"Wow," I whisper when he closes my door.

He slips into the driver's side and turns the engine over. It purrs to life, and he smiles. "I love this car. Matt loves his truck, but this. This is where it's at."

I smile softly. "It's a really nice car."

"Thank you." He pulls out of the garage. I can't help but notice he backed into it so he doesn't have to back out of it. It's not often I see many do that. It makes me wonder if it's a cop thing. "So, what questions do you have?" DJ asks after I tell him where I live.

I look down at my hands. "I'm not sure."

"How about we start with your reaction when Matt suggested I take you home?"

I play with my fingers. "Okay," I whisper.

"Why did you shut down so quickly? It was like you just closed yourself off."

"In a way, I did." I shrug slightly. "I wanted to make Beckett his priority. You both have only just met me. I would never expect to come before him. Nor would I want to. I just…"

"You got scared, and a little insecure?"

I nod. "I worried that he would think that I couldn't handle it," I whisper. I pause to collect myself. "The responsibility that comes with a partner who has a kid. I'm not saying that I would automatically become a parent to him. I only just met him. But I wouldn't shoot down the idea. That was the way it felt. It was how Matt sounded to me when he said I needed to think about things. I agree that I do need to think things through. Being with one man is hard enough, but two? I can see why he would want me to think it over. Now, when you add Beckett to the equation, I can see why he would want me to be one-hundred percent sure in my decision. It's not just adults in this relationship, but there is also a teenager to think about now, too. But do you want me to be honest?"

"You know I want you to be honest, baby."

"It might sound crazy…" I look at him hesitantly.

"Doubtful."

"I don't have a single doubt that I want to be with you and Matt. Even knowing that Beckett comes as part of the package now doesn't cause even an inkling of doubt in my mind. It has taken me a few minutes to understand that Matt wasn't pushing me away. That he just wants to take care of both me and Beckett. I don't need to, but I will take the time to think about it like Matt asked, even just to ease his mind. If I am completely honest with myself, I have wondered what it would be like to be with you. I've seen you both at the club a few times, though I kept myself to the back tables of the club where I wouldn't be noticed. I felt… drawn to you both. Every time you both walked in, it would be like my eyes would automatically lock onto you, even if there was a guy trying to take me home with him. The number of men I have actually been with would probably shock you." I look down at my hands as I twist my fingers.

DJ swallows. Out of the corner of my eye, I can see his grip tighten on the wheel. "How many?" he asks quietly. But there's an edge to his voice.

A little dangerous.

A lot possessive.

I shiver because his tone warms my entire soul. "One," I say softly.

"One?"

I nod. "Kieran, one of the bartenders, keeps an eye on me while I'm there. He does it as a favor for my brother and my friend. Kieran is my brother's best friend. He can tell by my body language if I'm even the slightest bit uncomfortable. Kieran, or a security guard he has sent after us, interferes if someone does try to take me home. I go to the office or a breakroom to wait for Kieran to finish his shift."

DJ lets out a relieved breath. "You have no idea how much that eases my mind. Knowing you've had someone watching out for you."

I hesitate to continue but know instinctively that I need to be honest with him. "There's something else you should know."

He reaches over and takes my hand as he stops at a light. The move instantly calms me. "You can tell me."

"Those I did leave with…," I trail off in a whisper, looking down at my hand linked with his as my courage leaves me. I take a deep breath and look up at him when I feel him squeeze my hand and rub his thumb over the top of my hand. "They only helped center me by giving me commands. Nothing… nothing sexual, just… a kind of order to the chaos in my mind. Kieran would speak with them himself before we left. He would make sure that they knew from the start that I wouldn't be sleeping with them. Unless I wanted to. I never wanted to."

He doesn't say anything as he glances at me when I pause. He kisses my hand and starts driving again when the light turns green.

I take a deep breath and continue softly. "When we left, they would take me to my apartment. They would give me the dominance I needed by creating a list of things I had to complete. They would stay and watch as I got them done. Then kissed my forehead and left." I take a deep breath when I finish talking.

DJ opens his mouth but closes it. His thumb keeps moving in a circle over the top of my hand. Finally, he looks at me as he pulls into a parking space in front of my apartment. "Why did he let us leave with you? He never talked to us."

I smile softly and blush. "I've talked to him about you both. When he saw me with you, he winked, then smiled and mouthed 'have fun' on our way out." I blush and look down at my lap. "I may not be a virgin. You know I've only ever been with one person. And that was after we moved here. We were together for a long time. In the end, we realized we're much better best friends than lovers."

DJ smiles and shakes his head. He leans over and cups my cheek with his hand, keeping my hand securely in his other. "Where have you been hiding? We've been looking for you for so long, Lyric."

His lips are just a breath from mine. "Admiring from afar. Certain you wouldn't be interested in a woman like me."

"Very, very incorrect," he whispers just before his lips meet mine in a soft kiss that ends far too soon. He pulls away slowly. "You'd better let me walk you to your door. Otherwise, I'm turning this car around and never letting you out of my sight."

My heart flutters. "Would that be so bad?"

He lets out a low rumble that I'd think was a chuckle if I didn't see the heat in his eyes.

But it's not only that.

It's the promise behind the words, and the fact that I want it all.

I don't want him to let me go.

I yawn and stretch, blinking sleepily and reaching for my phone vibrating somewhere. "Okay, okay. I'm up…," I mumble. I finally find my phone and sit up in bed. After my vision clears a little, I feel the smile turn up my lips. Text messages. I smile even wider when I see that it's a group text between me, DJ, and Matt.

DJ: Good morning. How's our girl?

Matt: I had a fun dream. Was yours just as pleasant?

I bite my lip and tilt my head as I think of what to say. The truth is, my dream was incredible. I didn't want to wake up. With a smile I snuggle into my pillows.

Lyric: It involved me straddling DJ with you both buried inside me... I would say I had a fantastic dream.

DJ: Ha! Matt just spit out his protein shake!

I snuggle under my purple fleece blanket and giggle. Before I lose my courage, I take a quick selfie with me under the blanket. I quickly peek at it then send it with my eyes closed and a squeak. I throw my phone.

"Holy shit, why did I do that?" I hiss and cover my mouth. "What if they hate it? Oh, God!" I flail around on the bed until I'm hidden underneath my fleece. "I'm never coming out."

My phone vibrates, though. I peek out at it like it's a bomb about to go off. When it goes off again, I squeak and hide. I clutch my chest and take deep breath after deep breath. Maybe there's a way to unsend it. Can a person do that with texts? I've never tried.

Fuck.

Oh fuck.

I take another deep breath when my phone vibrates a third time. "I can do this. I can do this. No big deal. Just a picture." I snatch my phone and quickly look at the replies with wide eyes.

DJ: Fuck, baby girl. You trying to kill us?

Matt: I'm going to have to go to work with a hard dick. You're paying for that.

DJ: Nice little tease, brat. I'll get you back.

I cover my mouth and blush furiously when I see what they saw. "My nipple is showing!" I whisper as I type a furious reply.

Lyric: Oh my God! I didn't mean for the nipple to show! I meant a cute picture! I'm sorry!

Great! Now they're going to think I'm some kind of tease or something! I silently berate myself as I furiously and nervously chew my lip while I wait for their reply.

Matt: Don't be sorry, pretty girl. Gives me an assist later.

"Oh my God," I whisper, catching his meaning.

DJ: We'll both be jacking off in our offices by lunch. Have a good day, baby.

Matt: Dinner later. I'll swing by and pick you up after I'm off.

I blink.

Lyric: That's... not the reaction I thought I was going to get...

Matt: Get used to it, gorgeous!

DJ: See you later, beautiful.

I can feel the blush spread over my entire body. I giggle like a schoolgirl with a crush as I get out of bed to clean up, but voices catch my attention. I furrow my brows and stop next to my bedroom door. I open it just a small crack so I can hear better. It's not that I intend to eavesdrop. It's that the two voices are speaking rather hushed. That's unusual.

"I just don't know what to do, Luca. This is going to destroy her... We might not have thought much of that stupid bitch, but Lyric did. She was her friend."

"What?" I whisper to myself. I peek out the door. Mariah Carter, my twin brother, Luca's girlfriend is curled into his lap on the couch. He's rubbing her back soothingly.

I furrow my brows when I also see Uncle King, the Chief of Police of Gainesville Police Department. He's a really good friend of my dad's and has been for years. I'm not sure how exactly they met, but they're like brothers. He's mine and Luca's godfather, but we both call him Uncle King.

"We'll do this together, baby. And if it's as bad as you're thinking, we'll call your ex in. You said he can help. But at least this is one death notification you don't need to do on your own."

I gasp and step away from the door, covering my mouth. "Death?"

"You have us both, Mariah," Uncle King says. "It'll be okay."

When I hear movement, I quickly and quietly hurry back to my bed, and sit down covering my lap with the fleece so it looks like I have just woken up.

Moments later, Luca gently opens my door. I look up at him. Luca is over six feet. He's well-built and has light-brown hair and golden skin that women fall over. Add in his British accent, and he could have any girl he wants. Or guy.

But he only has eyes for Mariah Carter. Which is great. I love her. She's become such a good friend over the past couple of years since they've been together. She has such pretty and long hair. It's dark and silky. Compared to Luca, she's tiny. She honestly looks like she's half his size. They make the perfect couple. They fit together so well. I've always wanted what they have. They're who I've based my idea of the perfect relationship off of.

They actually helped me talk through things last night. Or this morning, I guess. We talked until almost five in the morning. They listened without judgment and gave their own advice while letting me come to my own decisions. It really helped me become even more certain in myself and my decision to take a chance with Matt and DJ. I never would have been able to make that type of decision a few years ago. I'm truly proud of my growth.

Uncle King is a tall man. African American. He's the first African American Chief for Gainesville Police Department. He's very good at his job. He's so kind and caring. I'm sure people think he's intimidating, just based on his size, but he's never been that way to me. Protective, maybe. Never scary.

"Lyric?" Luca calls softly. When he sees me in bed, he furrows his brows. "Did you hear us?"

I look down and play with my fleece before slowly nodding. "Not everything…"

Mariah sighs and slowly walks into the room. She sits on the bed next to me and takes one of my hands in hers. "So, you heard what I said about Alice…"

"She's…" I sniffle. "I just saw her last night… She was still at the club when I left…" I wipe my eyes when the tears start to fall.

"Do you remember who she was with?" Mariah asks softly while she rubs my hand. Luca sits behind her and gently rubs my leg over the blanket. Uncle King crawls into the bed and wraps me in his strong arms.

I burrow into him and shake my head. "I've never seen him there before." I wipe my eyes again. "She was smitten with him, though," I say quietly. "What happened to her?"

Mariah bites her lip and looks at Luca. Luca kisses her shoulder and hugs her close with one arm, keeping his other hand on my leg.

"She was killed, sweetie," Unkle King says quietly.

I can't hold back anymore. I burst into tears. Mariah and Luca both wrap around me and hug me as close as Uncle King is. I cry harder because while I was having a good night, Alice was going through the worst struggle of her life and lost the battle.

"We're doing an investigation," Uncle King whispers in my ear. "Mariah is on a taskforce I set up."

Mariah, a police officer with Gainesville PD, hugs me a little tighter. "I know this might not be much comfort, but there has been a few other murders in the area linked to the club. I just found that out this morning when I was put on the case."

"We don't want you going to Sapphire's anymore, sweetie. At least not right now," Luca says as he hugs both of us harder.

I hear his words and just nod. "I wouldn't be anyway... I told you about Matt and DJ. I'd only go with them."

"I know, sweetie," Mariah says.

Uncle King kisses my head. "I'll need a full statement from you, but not right now. We'll have someone else do it anyway. Someone other than me or Mariah. Just to be ethical..."

I nod again. A statement is the furthest thing from my mind, though. I know they know that. One thing I do know for sure is that I can't let Alice's death be in vain. They said there's an investigation happening. That there had been previous victims. I want to do something. I don't know what, but I know I can help. I've been going to Sapphire's for a long time. I could know things I don't think I do that could help them.

As I lean into their embrace, I become steadily more determined. Alice was my friend. She might not have been the best one in the world, but she was still mine. She had her flaws, many of them, but she didn't deserve this. I'll do whatever it takes to bring her killer to justice.

Maybe, when I'm feeling stronger and not reeling from this information, I can find out whoever is heading the investigation through Mariah or Uncle King. I can tell them all I know. Everything I've observed. Maybe I can discuss who seems shady.

I can't sit here and do nothing. I just can't. They probably don't think that I can do much to really help the investigation, other than the statement from last night, but I know I can. I have an advantage they don't.

I'm an insider.

Even better, I am a submissive. Dominants in the club can't resist me. I get hit on all the time.

This asshole, whoever he is, isn't going to know what hit him. I'm going to help put him away forever.

As soon as I figure out a plan...

Chapter Four

☆ Matt ☆

(Two Weeks Later)

Spending two weeks getting to know Lyric has been one of the most fun things I think I've ever done. The girl is vivacious. She's got a wicked sense of humor. She's fun to be around and brings a dynamic to mine and DJ's life that we've longed for.

Not that she opened up right away. We've spent almost every single night with her, but the first few nights, as expected, Lyric was very quiet. Like she was observing us and how we not only react to each other, but her.

We've also had Beckett with us. I'm ecstatic that Beckett and Lyric seemed to have hit it off. I've walked into a room or out by the pool several times and seen them deep in conversation or goofing off. It warms my heart to see her fitting in so well with my little family.

DJ couldn't agree more. Just like me, he loves walking into a room or outside and seeing Lyric completely free and open. It's a beautiful sight. Neither of us could be more pleased with her decision to give us both a chance. Everything has clicked so perfectly with all of us.

Which is why I'm sitting in my office right now slightly confused. Maybe things were going too perfectly or something because things feel very off right now. Something is just not right. DJ and I text Lyric every single morning. Fuck. Even Becket texts her. Not in our group chat. That's gotten pretty sexy and nothing I want my nephew a part of. Lyric always responds almost right away.

Last night, though, she didn't text either of us back or Beckett for almost two hours. When she finally did, she was very vague about what took her so long. It's something that is incredibly unusual for someone who is as honest as she is. The girl can't lie to save her life. When she didn't text us this morning at all, though, is when I knew for sure that something is going on.

I growl low as I press a button to answer my office phone. "What?" I snap.

"Lieutenant Chance?" a soft, meek voice says. Fake as fuck. I know what she's like face to face.

I just glare at the receiver. "Yes?"

"Chief King would like to meet with you, sir." She clears her throat. "Now."

I glance at the bright purple folder on my desk. It's been sitting there since I got here four hours ago. It's already noon. I haven't even opened it. I have enough work to do. Several priority cases that need my attention. I can't deny the purple folder among the numerous plain tan ones piqued my interest, but I refuse to look at it.

"Does this have something to do with the purple folder on my desk?"

"Um -"

"I'll be there." I hang up before Chief King's secretary can say another word.

Her voice gets on my nerves, but it's the way she traipses around this department with her short skirts and non-existant tits hanging out that really bothers me. When she bends over, and she does it a lot, everyone around her can see what color panties she's chosen to wear that day. Most of the time, it's the flesh colored kind, meaning she doesn't wear any.

She really loves her pink, remote controlled bullet. It's constantly buried in her pussy. Panties or not. She's so desperate that I bet it's her that controls the thing. I have never met a man who can stand to be in her proximity for more than a few minutes at a time. No way anyone here is on the other side of that remote. At least not any respectable cop.

How the hell she's still working here with the amount of complaints against her is something I couldn't understand for the longest time. Until I found out that she's the daughter of our district's State Representative. It all made sense then. She fears me and DJ, though. Neither of us give a shit about her political connections, and we've both turned her down flat on many occasions. Not that she doesn't keep trying.

I grab the folder and flip it open as I leave my office and walk towards the Chief's. I read over the case notes, barely glancing up when DJ joins me as I make my way past his office. I shake my head a few times and grumble.

"Does he not realize he's given me seven priority cases in the past two days?" I complain, finally looking up at DJ.

"I don't think he gives a shit," DJ responds with a grin before he sobers immediately. "Did you hear from Lyric?"

My bad mood grows exponentially. "I have not. I'm both worried as fuck and pissed the hell off. Something is going on with our girl. And whatever it is, she's not comfortable telling us about it."

"Have you done more than glance at the file in your hand?"

"Nope." I close it. I know I'm being stubborn, but I don't really care right now. "There's only been one thing on my mind since this morning. Family will always supersede work in my life, and Lyric is our family."

"While I agree with you, you need to look at that file."

I sigh and open it again. I scan it a little more before nearly choking. "The fuck?"

"Yep. Remember when Lyric told us about her friend, Alice?"

I raise an eyebrow as I read the file. "Yeah. She's still extremely upset about it. Despite how incredibly well she's doing." I can't blame her, but it's because of that I'm having such a hard time with her not answering texts. Or calls. Because I've tried that, too.

"Well, there's a taskforce that has been set up. They haven't gotten anywhere. Chief has you and I leading it now at Mariah's request. From what I know, she's pissed the taskforce hasn't gotten anywhere. There've been nine murders linked to Sapphire's."

I sigh and rub my head. "I thought my days of leading taskforces were over."

"Chief is pulling us in on this one special. Like I said. Mariah requested it. And Mariah is being a very secretive little brat."

I laugh. Mariah Carter is one of our closest friends. She also just made the investigation squad, which is something she's been working towards ever since she started with Gainesville PD. She's the only woman we know who is so close to us that she's like family.

"Of course she is." I shake my head. "You think she knows something more than just the taskforce isn't up to par in her mind?"

"Oh, fuck yes." DJ chuckles as we reach Chief King's office. The chuckle dies on his lips as soon as he sees the Chief's secretary. "Chief King is looking for us," he growls. Neither of us bother using her name. She's not important enough for it.

She smiles wolfishly. Her eyes light up as she looks us both up and down. "Of course!" She stands and makes a show of adjusting her skirt.

I roll my eyes. "Thanks, but we'll manage." I walk past her with DJ on my heels. She pouts and bites her lip but sits her ass back down.

DJ shakes his head as he knocks on the door. "Every time I see her, I want to fucking puke."

"You're not kidding."

"Come in!" Chief King commands.

DJ opens the door. I follow, but he stops so quickly, I plow right into him. "The fuck?" I say as I catch him before he crashes to the ground.

"Please, for the love of God, tell me that the thoughts running through my head aren't even remotely close to what's going on here," DJ growls after he composes himself.

After I help steady him and close the door, I turn and see what he did. "Oh shit," I whisper. My heart jumps into my throat. "This is not happening."

"Take a seat," Chief King says.

I do, but only because if I don't, I'm going to fall to the ground and start begging the woman in front of me to tell me that she's not doing what I think she is. DJ sits next to me. The Chief squeezes her shoulder before he sits behind his desk. DJ is growling low enough that only I hear. I glance at him because I'm a little unsure how he's not having a panic attack right now, but I am.

Mariah puts a hand on DJ's arm. Sitting on the other side of me is Lyric. Her hands are folded in her lap, and she's looking down at her feet. To anyone who didn't know her, it would look like she's just waiting for the conversation to continue.

But I do know her.

I know that she's terrified of what's coming. I know that she can see DJ gripping the chair as hard as he can. She can see the vein in his neck ticking. And I can see the trembles that she's trying to hide.

I reach over and rest my hand on her thigh with my palm up. Lyric takes a shaky breath and glances at me before she hesitantly, and very shakily takes it. I squeeze her hand as hard as I dare without breaking it just so she knows it's okay. While I'm doing that, I tap DJ's thigh to get his attention. As soon as he sees her, the anger I feel radiating off him and slamming into me dissipates.

"Fuck," he whispers.

I stand, keeping Lyric's hand in mine, and pull her up with me. She looks at me a little confused as she bites her lip. I switch places with her so she can sit between me and DJ. I switch the hand I'm holding. She leans towards me and grasps my hand with both of her small ones. She keeps her head down, refusing to meet DJ's eyes.

I lean over and kiss her head. "It's okay, baby," I whisper. I squeeze her hand.

DJ lets out a low sound of regret and puts his hand on her thigh with his palm up, just as I had. One very important thing we've learned about Lyric is that she hates when people are angry. She feels it so much more than most other people that I've met.

She also hates feeling like she's done something wrong or disappointed someone, especially those close to her. She instantly shuts down. Much like she is right now. DJ and I knew she was and is a very natural submissive when we started this. We know she needs the domination and control to her life that she feels like she lacks. We know when she needs to feel centered. We know how to get her there.

Lyric does better with routine. She needs it. She needs guidance. A lot of people only need that in one or two aspects of their life. Lyric isn't like that. In order for her to thrive, she needs a schedule. She needs lists. Without that type of routine, Lyric feels like her whole entire world is tilted on its axis.

"I called you here because -"

DJ holds up a hand, effectively cutting Chief King off. "Just give us a minute, Chief." He leans into Lyric as he cups her cheek with the hand he doesn't have on her lap.

She tilts her head as he whispers in her ear low enough that only she can hear him. After a few moments she grips his hand like she's hanging onto a life raft. I smile because I know it means she's okay again after DJ reassured her.

Keeping her hand in mine, I turn to Chief King. "Okay, Chief. Lay it on us."

He chuckles. "Did you do your homework like good boys and read those files?"

DJ sighs. "Yeah. But when you said CI, I expected the confidential informant to be someone within Sapphire's. Not our girlfriend."

Chief King nods. "I can see where the worry comes from. I wouldn't want to put my daughter in there. Or my wife. Hell. I don't want to put my goddaughter in. I don't want her anywhere near this. But Lyric came to us. Mariah already put up a huge fight. So did Luca. Nothing either of you say to me is going to change my mind. Unless you want her going in and trying to investigate on her own, because believe me, she already threatened me with that. Lyric is our only option."

I look down at her in horror. My pulse has reached an unnatural level. "Tell me you wouldn't dare do something like that." I sigh when she bites her lip and looks down. "Fuck," I whisper with a shake of my head.

"I can't stand by and do nothing." There's a tremble in her voice that I don't like. I don't say anything. Instead, I just rub my thumb over the back of her hand.

DJ glares at Mariah. "Why would you not say anything to me about this?"

Mariah returns his glare. "Because I know you, DJ. It's far better for her and all of us if she has backup when she goes in because she's going to do it with or without us. I don't know about you, but I'd prefer she goes in with us. And if you'd shut up and listen for five seconds, you'd realize that she has a really good plan. One she had already come up with before she approached the Chief. Luca and I only found out about this today. So, if *we* can sit and listen to her, the woman you claim to be falling for, then so, damn well, can *you*."

I fight back the smile and chuckle. "I think we need to just hear what this idea is. There's nothing saying we can't talk about it afterwards."

Chief King sits back in his chair. "Whether the two of you like it or not, Lyric knows the club. She's been going there for years."

I raise an eyebrow. "I could argue that so have we."

"Lyric informed me, and I agree, but you're not submissive women. You both are big guys. You're not the type that is being gone after. The description of the women differ in physical appearance except -"

"Except for one thing," DJ says, glancing at Lyric with a sigh. I'm not sure what I'm missing, but it pisses me off that I didn't take the time to look at that damn folder. DJ rubs his head. "They're all small women. Easy to overpower."

"Exactly," Mariah says. She smiles at Lyric softly. "Sending in Lyric is a good idea for us. I'm small, but we've already ruled me out. I'm not submissive enough. Someone looks at me the wrong way, and I'm punching them. I have too much training to come off submissive in any manner. But Lyric? She's shy. She's naturally submissive. She responds to dominant men. I do, to an extent, but not enough to pass myself off as the type of woman who frequents Sapphire's."

Lyric lets out a breath. "Not only that, but people know me there. They've seen the reaction men have to me. And a lot of them..." She shrugs a little. "They don't give up. And they get upset if they are turned down. If they start to see me actually leaving with men, they'll pay even more attention to me."

"She has a really good plan," Mariah says soothingly. "Tell them, honey. I really think they'll go for it if you tell them all the ways you've come up with to protect yourself."

"Well..." She looks at us both hesitantly. "I'm not sure if you know, but each of those killed were girls I knew. Well, sort of. I mean, I knew they were popular among the dominants, but they didn't stay with any of them. It was like they were with them for a night, then they went back to the club for more."

"It was a link we hadn't seen, and never would have, if not for her observation," Chief King says.

His praise bolsters her confidence. She nods and smiles a little. "I thought me going in there and appearing to go home with a lot of men would pique the interest of the person doing this. But the men I go home with would be undercover officers. A different one each night."

I furrow my brows. "So, how would getting you in the sight of our killer help us? I see that as doing absolutely nothing but putting you in harm's way."

She smiles even wider. "Well, that's where you come in. And other members of a… what do you call it, uncle?" She glances at Chief King. "Oh! A taskforce. You would be doing surveillance. So, you'd be there making sure I'm safe, and everyone else is, too."

"Wait a second. Uncle?" DJ asks, bringing my own confused thoughts to fruition.

Lyric's eyes widen. "Oh! Um… Yeah. He and my dad have been friends forever. He's mine and my brother's godfather, but we call him Uncle King."

I raise an eyebrow. "A discussion on how that relationship happened a little bit later. Back to all of this." I wave my hand in front of me. "How are we keeping you safe?"

Chief King chuckles as he leans forward and shuffles through his papers. "All of the bodies are found in the alley behind Blue Stone. One block away from Sapphire's. The bodies were not moved. The medical examiner believes they were killed right there. I know that behind the buildings in that area is basically one long alley that zig-zags over the span of the block, weaving behind a building, then stopping near Sapphire's. There is only one entrance and exit, and that's near Sapphire's. There wasn't a struggle. They believe the person is known to them. They were all strangled by someone taller than them, judging by the way the ligature marks on their necks are. Medical examiner believes the weapon of choice is some kind of durable wire. Not a fishing line, but something similar to that. She hasn't been able to narrow it further than that because whatever it is doesn't seem to leave behind any trace evidence other than the mark. Which is something very unique. Make sure you look at the images. It's a zig-zag pattern."

"A male who is taller than Lyric." DJ chuckles and squeezes her hand as he winks at her teasingly. "That's a lot of suspects."

She smiles as she opens her mouth like she's going to say something. She closes it again, though, like she's unsure whatever she wants to say has a place in this room. Instead, she crosses her feet and nods her head.

"Honey, what were you going to say?" I ask her quietly.

She looks up at me hesitantly. "Well…" She trails off and tilts her head.

"It's okay, Lyric. Tell us," DJ says just as quietly. "You know we want to hear what you think."

"How are you keeping the taskforce confidential?" she asks quietly.

"Is there a reason we should?" I ask, concerned at how much she is.

She takes a deep breath before letting it out. She looks up at me. "It's just that you and DJ aren't the only cops who go there. And you're right. It could be anyone. It could be a short man who wears heels, or has platforms in his shoes. Hell, it could even be a tall woman, or a woman in heels." She slumps slightly but tries to stay strong.

"She's right," DJ says. "Not all cops are good cops. If we have cops who frequent the club, we need this entire operation to be discreet."

"That's the other reason I pulled you both. You have experience leading taskforces. You know who can keep their mouths shut. As the Chief, I'd vouch for everyone in this department because that's my job."

Lyric let's out a noise that sounds a little like a snort. "Really?" she mutters under her breath.

"But the truth is," the Chief continues with an amused expression. "All I have to go off of is paperwork. I'm not sure I can trust that. Two of my best officers have complaints against them in their jackets. I've fired a few whose jackets are squeaky clean."

Lyric chuckles, but still continues to speak quietly. "I've been here many times since we moved here. I could point out eight people I wouldn't trust further than I could spit."

Mariah stares at her a moment as DJ and I watch her in shock. Chief is chuckling as he leans back in his chair. Mariah clears her throat. "You can't spit."

Lyric looks at Mariah with a deadpan expression. "My point."

"A conversation I'd love to have with you," Chief King says.

I smile when Lyric relaxes more and more the longer this discussion goes on regarding her plan. To say that I'm not intrigued at her initiative would be a lie. It could work. It will.

But I don't fucking like that Lyric is involved with it in any way.

Or that I agree she's the best choice for the job.

Chapter Five

☆ DJ ☆

This meeting has gone on for far too long. Every reason for Lyric to not do this that I've come up with have all been countered, very smartly, by our girl. It impresses me and makes me want to fly to the United Kingdom to kick every single ass of the people in her life who told her she wasn't smart enough to do whatever the fuck she wanted to in life. It also makes me want to lock her up in our bedroom so she can never get hurt.

"I think I've had about enough of this meeting, Chief," I say with a sigh. "I'm obviously not winning this, even though I don't want Lyric anywhere near this shit, so I need to get a team together." I look down at Mariah as I stand. "Don't think you'll be spending much time with your boyfriend over the next few days." I nod to Lyric but don't take my eyes off Mariah's. "You kept this whole fucking thing from me as much as she did. You're on the taskforce."

Mariah opens her mouth to say something but quickly closes while I pull Lyric to her feet. It's a wise move. I love her to death, but I'm pissed off that someone I consider family didn't bother to tell me about this. She knows how much I hate when things are kept from me. If she were mine, I'd be punishing her.

She may not be, but Lyric is. I pull her gently to her feet. She looks up at me. I know she knows what's coming, but I also know she trusts me and Matt. It hasn't been that long, but Lyric has grown to love us more and more. Seeing that love and trust grow within her is something I never knew I needed in my life. Her trust is a huge turn on, and something I'll never break.

"I want the taskforce finalized by the end of day," Chief King drawls. He looks down at his case notes. "We start tonight. And Lyric?"

"Yes, Uncle King?" she says quietly. She looks up at him through her lashes but keeps her head lowered.

"You can get me a list of all of the officers you recognize that you said you wouldn't trust. Give it to Captain Rens. He can give it to me with his taskforce choices. I'm not sure if I'll see you before he does, so it saves you a trip."

"Yes, sir," she whispers with a shy smile. He chuckles and waves us out.

I squeeze her hand as I lead her out of the office. Matt follows. We both shoot the Chief's secretary a glare when she starts to stand. She furrows her brows when she sees Lyric. I'm sure she thinks I miss the hatred that crosses her eyes. I don't. She thinks she owns all of the men in this department. I don't doubt a few of them have taken her up on her advances. No cop that I know would, but I know not everyone in this department is respectable.

I pull Lyric into my office and set her in a chair as Matt closes the door behind us. I lean on my desk and fold my arms over my chest as I look down at her. She's so beautiful, it's hard to believe she chose us. She could have anyone. That thought sends me to a very dark place. Her not being ours is something I don't think I can handle.

Matt leans on my desk in front of her and next to me. He crosses his arms over his chest just as I am and looks down at her. Lyric looks at her feet. She doesn't like the feeling she gets when she thinks people are angry at her, but it's the disappointment she feels that really gets to her. I know all of that, yet I still stand in front of her like this.

Finally, though, I let my hands fall to my sides. "Lyric, honey, I don't know how to feel right now. I don't know whether to spank you for lying to us -"

She looks up with wide eyes. "I didn't lie!"

"You didn't tell us what's going on!" I retort. "That's lying by omission, baby." I kneel in front of her and take her hands when she sniffles and looks down with a blush and sad whine. "Lyric. Baby, look at me."

"I'm sorry," she whispers and shakes her head. One of the tears falling hits my hand and breaks me.

I wrap my arms around her. "Baby, you have to understand where I'm coming from." I hug her tighter and relax slightly when I feel her melt against me. Her arms wrap around me, and I sigh in relief. "I don't want you in harm's way. I don't. This is a very, very dangerous job. I don't want you anywhere near it. You've literally put yourself right in the center of a game of cat and mouse with a psychopath." I tangle my fingers in her hair as I pull back. "Do you understand what you've done?"

"I just want to help, DJ. Alice was…" She wipes her eyes. "The police haven't gotten anywhere, and I have so many suspicions about why."

"Let's talk about those suspicions," Matt says as he sits down next to her. He takes her hand and kisses it. "You said there are cops out there you recognize and don't trust. Why?"

She sucks her lip into her mouth, but I run my thumb across it. She releases and takes a breath. "They go to the club. I thought you knew."

"A few of us go there," I agree. "I know some, but we tend to go on days that others don't. That's intentional. But why does that make them untrustworthy?"

"Well…" She closes her mouth and chews on the inside of her cheek hesitantly.

"Honey," Matt says as he tucks her hair behind her ear. "You have no reason to be hesitant with us. We trust you. You know that." He kisses her check. "What's going on? What do you know?"

I slowly let go of her hands and slide mine up her thighs to her hips as I lean forward. It's been far too long since I've had my lips on her. Eventually, that need wins out over everything else. I kiss her throat with a low rumble before pulling back slowly. She relaxes even more, certain now that I'm not pissed with her.

"One of them? He's a Sadist. Like that guy who was leading me away when you both saw me. He whipped a girl unconscious once.

Security removed him. He's never been back. The girl had to go to the hospital."

Matt raises an eyebrow. "How the fuck did I not hear about that? I don't remember anyone getting an assault charge on their ass. That would have gotten him fired."

"He was never charged," Lyric says with a shrug. "The girl said she asked for it. It was consensual. The club never brought up charges because she wouldn't testify. No victim. No crime. The club just banned him for life. It was before the new owner took over."

I share a look with Matt before shaking my head. "We'll circle back to that. What else?"

"Another one refuses to take no for an answer. He took Alice home a few times. I don't know all the details, but she always made it home afterwards. He tried taking me once, but security faked a phone call from Luca and said it was an emergency. I've seen him a few times, but every time I have, I've ducked into the back and either left the club right away or stayed in the office until Kieran finished his shift."

"Details? What did she tell you? Even if it was small." Matt kisses her forehead. I don't even need to look at him to know how protective he's getting.

"Well, like, even if she said no to going with him, he didn't like that. He always leaned into her and whispered something that made her back down instantly. She never told me anything more than he just likes control and knows where to hit people to get them to cooperate. At his house, she said that he liked disobedience, but wouldn't elaborate. I always thought he was a Sadist, too, but she never told me the things he did to make her obey."

"Fuck me," I say with a shake of my head.

"The thing is, I think I know a couple of the people she might be talking about," Matt says. "Sick sons-of-bitches, but don't have a single complaint against them. Glowing jackets. Do a lot of shit with the public." Matt pinches the bridge of his nose.

Lyric takes a breath. I rub my thumbs over her hips. "They aren't even the worst," she whispers. "Some are just assholes, but there's one that terrifies a lot of the girls. He usually shows up later at night before closing. He picks his girl quickly and leaves, but a few of them have told me he has a…" She shudders and hugs herself. She leans closer to Matt and shifts so her legs are touching as much of me as possible. "A rape fantasy." She shivers.

I furrow my eyebrows, but my heart feels like it might explode out of my chest because it's beating so fast. I tamp down my anger for her, but I'm beyond livid that one of the cops who works here has a fetish like that. I can handle a foot fetish. Fuck. I can even deal with the gross shit, like the golden shower fetish. I don't get it and won't take part in it, but to each their own. But rape? Come on.

"A rape fantasy." I shake my head as Matt and I both lean forward and hug her. "You're safe, baby. No one is getting close enough to you to play that shit out."

"I know. I was lucky to have back up in the form of Kieran at the club. He always stepped in or had a Security Guard step in if he even tried to approach me. Mostly, though, I just stayed away." She shivers again. "Some of the things they said, though. He'd make them pretend like they were being forced. He'd tie them up. Sometimes, he'd even beat them. By the end of it, even if they said they didn't want to roleplay anymore, he made them keep going. But again, they never reported it. He made it very clear no one would believe them."

I sigh and pull away slowly. I kiss her throat before reluctantly standing. I walk around my desk and find my legal pad and a pen. "Do you know their names? Or do you want to go through pictures and identify them? I need to know who they are. Firstly, so they don't come anywhere near this case, but also so we know who to watch for when we're watching you."

She smiles softly and starts writing down names. "A few of them I don't know the names of, but I can point them out at the club. One of them has a desk right across from your office. The first desk in that cubicle area."

I look up at Matt. "Will?"

"Wouldn't surprise me. Something always threw me about him. During his hiring process, I was one of the interviewers on his interview board. We gave him a scenario. You're called to the University. A cheerleader for the football team asks for an escort to her car because she saw her stalker around. You arrive. Cheerleader runs to you. She's terrified. You can see she's been crying. Her top looks tattered. What do you do? His response? Call Campus Security."

I shake my head. "What?"

"Yeah. I said she tells you she's called them. They didn't come. She's scared. Hysterical. Clinging to you. Looking for you to help her. You're gaining a crowd. People are looking. Some are taking out phones. He said he'd give her the comfort she needs while hiding her from the onlookers. He'd take her somewhere private to talk and figure out what's going on. He'd keep her close."

Lyric furrows her brows. "Wouldn't… that kind of be a lawsuit waiting to happen…? She could say he did something to her."

Matt nods. "Yep. There's a lot of things wrong with that answer, but one of the things that struck me was his body language. Like being her hero was a huge turn on. One of the other interviewers asked him to walk them through everything step by step. We even gave him a body camera and a simulated duty belt with fake equipment. Like the recruits get in the academy. He put it all on. We had him start from the beginning. We had Mariah come in and play the victim. She does scenarios all the time for the academy classes. She was good. She acted it all out. We had a couple of other cops come in with camera phones to simulate the onlookers. We blocked off an area of the room to simulate his private room. Then we watched."

"And he failed?" Lyric asks.

"Epically." Matt chuckles and crosses his arms over his chest as he leans back in the chair. "He started out okay because he knew calling Campus Security wasn't the right answer. We made him start all the way from stepping out of the squad. First thing I noticed is he didn't turn on the camera. Mariah clung to him like her life depended on it. She didn't let go for anything. Babbled incoherently while she cried. Real fucking tears. Hysterical. He took her to the private room. Still didn't turn on the camera. Kept her close. Asked her shit about what happened. Called her pretty girl. Beautiful. Touched her leg. Arm. I stopped it when Mariah shot me a what the fuck look."

"How the hell did he get hired?" I shake my head. "And how the fuck did I not know this shit?"

Matt laughs. "He was hired because guess who his daddy is?"

I sit down in my chair. "The mayor? Senator? The President?"

Matt shakes his head. "State rep."

I raise an eyebrow. "Are you saying what I think you are?"

"Chief's secretary is Will's sister."

Lyric wrinkles her nose and hands me the list. "She's on that list, too. She's at the club almost every night, according to Kieran. I've seen her. She's all over everyone. She watches everyone. And I've seen her getting off to some. But no one there has ever taken her home. Not that I've seen. Not that Kieran has seen. And she's caused several scenes with others out of jealousy. She'll slide right into the booth with a guy who is talking to a girl and trying to get to know her. She'll flirt with anyone and make sure that everyone knows how available and easy she is. I don't think she's ever seen me. I tend to stay to myself. But she has approached Alice and one of the people she was with one night. The manager kicked her out. Or so everyone thought. Kieran and I left shortly after and saw him behind a dumpster in the alley with her."

I gag. "Fuck, that's gross." I look at Matt. "We need to get our taskforce together. But let's talk to our confidential informants. Keep the department out of it. Chief can have it out with me, but that's my decision. I want unrecognized people in there that we can trust."

Lyric let's out a breath and closes her eyes. "Uncle King might be upset, but I don't know why that makes me feel better," she whispers.

"You're priority, baby," Matt says. He drops a hand on her thigh. "He's right. Even if we throw cops in there that we know and trust, they'll be recognized by the ones you have listed as well as the ones you'll point out when they show up." He rubs her thigh lightly to soothe her.

It stirs something in me, though. When she subtly squeezes her thighs together, I about lose it. I groan low. I know it's only audible to my ears. We haven't done anything more with Lyric than what she's been ready for. Which is pretty much everything before full intercourse. We'll wait for her forever. We'd never pressure her, but the waiting is killing me. I've wanted her since the second I laid eyes on her. Just tasting her has only whetted my appetite for her.

"Keep squeezing your thighs together like that, you're going to end up with my tongue inside you," I say as my eyes zero in on the part of her I crave but really shouldn't do anything about right now. I stand anyway and walk around my desk.

She blushes and ducks her head as she watches me lock my office door. "I can't help it," she says shyly. "I always want you both." She looks down. "Especially since I know neither of you hate me."

"What the hell reason would we possibly have to hate you?" I hold out a hand to her.

She takes it and looks up at me. "Because I didn't tell you what was happening. I thought... maybe... you wouldn't want me anymore." Her voice is barely audible. I pull her up.

Matt chuckles as he stands. He kisses her cheek and taps her ass. She jerks into me. "We know the shit you've been through, but that's never happening," Matt says.

I throw him a wink and tilt my head towards my desk. Taking my hint, Matt moves behind it. I turn Lyric so her ass is against it and grip her thighs. I lift her onto my desk as I lean down. I take her mouth with mine, growling low and possessively. One of my favorite things in the world is when Lyric submits instantly to me and melts against my body.

Like right now.

I kiss down her jaw to her neck. Matt leans over my desk as he unzips his jeans. He pulls his dick out and strokes it slowly as we both kiss her neck. She moans softly and trails her fingertips up my arms. Her soft touch makes me shiver.

I slowly unbutton her shorts and tug them down her hips while we both kiss her. Matt, still stroking his dick and managing to make me even harder while I watch, turns Lyric's face towards his. He kisses her deeply, plunging his tongue into her mouth. I strain against my slacks so hard that I have no choice but to unzip them. I pull out my dick and moan at the instant relief.

My intention was to lavish Lyric with the attention and reassurance she needs to feel that we're okay, but watching Matt stroke himself changed my plan drastically. Now, all I can think of is chasing my release while I give her hers and she gives Matt his as I watch.

So, I lean her back into Matt as he kisses her. I kneel between her legs and grip her hips. As soon as Matt pulls away, I pull her a little roughly towards my mouth. She lets out a quiet squeak. I grin and squeeze my dick while I start stroking it slowly.

"My God, you're beautiful," I rumble against her pussy. "You're just glistening for us." I take a long, slow lick from her pussy to her clit, but it doesn't come close to satisfying my craving for her. She jerks into me and lets out a noise from her throat that makes me look up. My eyes widen. "Fuck."

Matt lets his head fall back when Lyric nips his tip as she takes his dick in her mouth. "Christ, Lyric." He slides his hands down to her tits and gently squeezes them while she sucks him off. She arches into his hands and moans again.

I slide my tongue into her sweet center and pump my dick faster. I thrust fast, hard, and as deep into her as I can while swirling my tongue and moaning low. I know it sends vibrations through her pussy because she jerks and arches into me.

Matt fucks her mouth with slow thrusts. She grips his ass with one hand and spears my hair with the other. She tugs my hair as she grinds into my tongue and meets my thrusts. I watch her scrape her teeth down Matt's length when he pulls out of her. Her tongue darts around his dick, nipping under his tip, making him groan before he pushes himself back into her mouth. I watch her throat work as she sucks harder and faster around him. I squeeze my cock a little harder and twist my wrist while I lick and suck her.

"Mmm!" Her thighs start to tremble. Her fingers tighten in my hair, and she tugs a little harder. I lick and suck and nip harder and faster, growling low and sending vibrations shooting through her again. Her pussy pulses around my tongue. She moans and whimpers around his dick as she bobs her head faster, sucking him. I watch as Matt's cock thickens. He groans as she swallows around his tip as he hits her throat. When his eyes roll back in his head, I know he's about to come.

"Oh… fuck…," Matt groans as he does just what I thought he would. He comes hard down Lyric's throat. I watch as she swallows it all with soft moans.

She bucks into me as my tongue darts in and out of her pussy. She gets tighter and tighter; wetter and wetter. The taste of her is driving me insane. I glance at Matt. He's slowly pulling out of her mouth and packing all ten inches of his thick dick away. Lyric is bucking and arching uncontrollably.

"Please… please, sir," she whispers.

"You know what you have to do, little one. What do you want, sexy girl?" I thrust my tongue into her pussy again, shaking my head relentlessly as I rumble, sending vibrations through her. She jerks and arches as her pussy gets impossibly wetter.

"Please, sir! Please let me come for you!" She quietly whimpers and she whisper screams as she bucks into my tongue.

"Good girl," I rumble as I meet her pleading eyes and nip her pussy. "Come, baby. Let me see this beautiful pussy come."

She slaps her hands over her mouth as she arches with a scream. She comes hard. Her hips jerk into me as I thrust my tongue into her. Her pussy clenches and pulses as she rides her release. I moan low as I lick and suck everything she gives me. I'm addicted to her taste. So fucking sweet. My cock is more than ready for release. I feel that familiar shock that shoots down my spine straight to my cock. My stomach tightens in anticipation, but I stave it off.

Matt kneels next to me. I grin when he leans over. We both take turns licking Lyric's pussy as she pants while she comes down. Still holding my dick and giving myself gentle squeezes and strokes, I stand. I help Lyric sit up.

Matt guides her down to his side and gives her a wicked smirk. "I think he's waited long enough to come. Don't you?" He tilts his head towards me.

Lyric nods slowly as she watches me. No one would miss the hunger in her eyes, and damn if that in itself doesn't nearly make me come. Matt grabs my wrist as Lyric takes me in her mouth. I let go of my cock while they both take turns licking and sucking it.

"Oh, fuck…" I whisper. I close my eyes and let my head fall back. I tangle my fingers in their hair and tug lightly.

Their lips meet as they kiss around my tip; their tongues flicking in just the right spot to make my dick jerk. I groan. Both of their mouths and tongues are all over me. My shaft. My tip. My balls. I feel her teeth lightly scrape along the vein running along my length. I can't stop the moan that comes from deep within my chest. I'm already so fucking close that I grip Lyric's hair as I look down at her. She takes me in her mouth and looks up submissively through her lashes. I haven't even hit the back of her throat before I'm coming.

Wave after wave of pleasure courses through me as my dick throbs in her mouth. She swallows around me as Matt strokes me. In one smooth motion, Lyric pulls back when I'm only halfway through and Matt's mouth replaces hers without spilling a single damn drop. I finish shooting my load down his throat as he looks up at me. He moans low as I come, swallowing the rest of what I give him. Lyric licks her lips and wipes her mouth watching with beautiful, wide eyes as Matt sucks me dry.

I reach down and help Matt slowly stand after I've come down. He takes Lyric's hand and pulls her up with him. I push my cock back into my pants as I watch them both with a grin. Matt kisses me first. His tongue slides over mine, and I taste a mix of myself and Lyric. His hand finds its way to my dick. He pushes all nine inches of it down as he slowly zips my slacks.

He pulls away slowly. "I love how thick you are, and the way you taste, but I think I might like the way she tastes on your tongue more." He winks.

I laugh, but Lyric cuts it off when she stands on her tip toes and kisses me just as deeply as Matt had. When she pulls away, she sucks on my tongue and nips my lip. "I really love the way you both taste," she whispers with a blush.

I kiss her again because I can't resist. When I pull away, I let my hand fall to her ass. "Can Luca come get you and take you home? And by home, I mean our home, where you belong." I feel like I have to specify because, though I know she feels like our house is her home now, she still hesitates to call it that because she thinks we think it's too fast. Which couldn't be further from the truth. If we could, we'd move her in today.

She blushes. "Yes, sir." She nods submissively.

I tap her ass. "Good girl. Matt and I are going to text a few people. We'll meet with you at home and discuss who we're using for the taskforce. We'll probably meet somewhere so you can meet them all."

"Yes, sir." She nods as she sits down and texts Luca.

Matt sits next to her and starts texting a few of the contacts he's made over the years. I sit in my chair behind my desk and text a few of my own. It's unconventional to be texting people I've busted for shit throughout my career, but this entire fucking thing is unconventional.

These people have proven over and over to be both trustworthy and reliable. Telling Lyric that the people I'm trusting with her safety are gangbangers, drug dealers, and a couple of people from a local motorcycle crew isn't a conversation I'm looking forward to having, though.

It's necessary. If it means Lyric's safety, I'll do anything I have to. Including getting her things packed and moved into our home where she will be safe.

But mostly? Dangerous case aside, I want to show our girl just how much we need and love her. Beckett adores her, and he doesn't like anyone.

She belongs with us.

Forever.

Chapter Six

✯ Lyric ✯

(A Week Later)

It's been about a week since the meeting with Uncle King. Matt and DJ have been really busy trying to get everything in place to make sure I'm safe. Ever since they told me they would be reaching out to their confidential informants, I've been on edge. I trust them, but I don't know how to feel about it. If I'm honest, I don't think I'll feel comfortable about using them. Or safe. These are drug dealers and thugs. I can't tell them that, though. They are putting in so much effort to keep me safe.

The house is quiet as I make my way from the kitchen to the den. Beckett is at his boyfriend's place. He stayed over there last night. Matt and DJ had to go to work this morning. They left me a note on the pillow for when I woke up, so I wouldn't worry. They should be home soon.

I pace anxiously around the room as I clean up from our movie night last night. I stretch and tug on the hem of my favorite hoodie of Matt's when I finish. I'm only wearing panties underneath. It's my go-to outfit for when I'm relaxing. I've lived in Florida for years now, and I don't think I will ever get used to how hot it can get. Matt keeps his house cool, so I've started wearing hoodies instead of t-shirts or tank tops.

I smile softly as I finish putting the couch back up, it folds down into a bed, and look around to make sure everything is done. I glance at the clock and make my way to the kitchen. I want to have a meal ready for when my men get home. They have been working so hard. This is something that I can do to make their day a little easier.

I pull the ham, egg and cheese croissants I made this morning out of the fridge and slide them into the oven. They both love when I make them. I thought we'd have breakfast for dinner tonight. I also want something quick since they said we'll be going to meet the people who will be making up the taskforce.

I dance a little as I clean up and sing along to *Show Yourself* when it starts to play over my phone's Bluetooth speaker. I finish the dishes and bend to pull out the croissants, swaying my butt to the music. I place them on top of the stove to cool a little bit and turn the oven off. I'm so into the song that I don't see the men I have fallen in love with leaning against the wall watching me. I jump and spin around with a squeak when I hear them chuckle.

Matt grins as they both converge on me. I watch them with wide eyes. DJ quickly wraps the croissants with aluminum foil as Matt grips my ass and lifts me onto the counter. I squeak again and watch them both curiously, and a little cautiously.

"I appreciate the dinner," Matt says, stepping between my legs. He grips the waistband of my panties as he leans in. His lips just brush mine. I shiver. "But I'll take my dessert first." He kisses me with a low growl, stealing my breath with the heat of it. He tugs my panties down as he fucks my mouth with his tongue.

"Holy God," I pant when he pulls away. He winks and puts my panties in his pocket. My mouth drops. "Hey! Those are mine!"

"Not anymore," DJ growls against my neck as he leans in. He nips it and sucks lightly. I won't tell them because it would stroke their already rather impressive egos, but I love when I wear their marks.

"Mmm…," I moan. My head starts to spin with desire. My pussy is instantly soaked for them.

DJ pulls away slowly and kisses the mark he left behind. Matt tugs me to the edge of the counter and leans into my neck. While DJ is driving me insane with his lips and tongue as he kisses up my leg to my thigh, Matt is sucking on the other side of my neck, leaving his own mark.

Matt pulls away slowly and kisses his mark before dropping to his knees next to DJ. I watch them both as they spread my legs wide. They each kiss up my inner thigh as my head falls back on a soft moan. My core is already throbbing for them. I lean back on my elbows relishing in their mouths and tongues. The way their teeth lightly scrape my skin as they make their way up.

I jerk my head back up as my body jolts into DJ's tongue when he dives into my pussy. I moan, trying to say his name, but I can't. All I can do is whimper, making incoherent sounds while his tongue twists, turns, flicks, and crooks inside me.

Matt's thumb finds my sensitive nub. He begins rubbing as he kisses my thigh while he watches DJ take me. I buck and arch into them both, writhing under them and digging my nails into the cold marble underneath me.

"Oh... fuck...," I finally manage to say as DJ expertly takes me higher and higher. But then he slowly stops licking me and pulls away with a grin as his eyes meet mine. I whimper and pant, reaching for him and silently begging for more.

Matt doesn't make me wait long, though. Taking DJ's place, he slams his tongue into my pussy and licks relentlessly. He growls low. I jolt again and buck into his tongue. He knows exactly what that does to me.

"Holy fuck!" I fall back against the marble counter. My pussy tightens almost instantly around him and pulses erratically as I get closer and closer to my breaking point.

Not to be outdone, DJ begins rubbing my clit, forcing me to arch into them both as I become a quivering, arching, writhing mess beneath them. Matt thrusts his tongue fast and hard. DJ keeps up with his pace as he watches him make a meal out of me. I'm so close, but once again, words refuse to form. My pussy tightens around Matt's tongue. My thighs tremble and try to close around him, but he pushes them wide apart.

DJ continues his masterful stroking of my clit. Just when I think they can't possibly take me any higher, DJ gives me a wicked grin. I have no time to make sense of it before I feel two fingers slide into my already soaked, tight, and uncontrollably pulsing pussy.

"Ah!" I scream. My hips buck up hard. I arch completely off the counter. DJ thrusts hard, deep, and fast. Matt continues slamming his tongue into me, matching DJ's intense pace. "Matt! DJ! I can't... Ah!" I scream again, erratically arching into them with each thrust they give me.

"Come, baby. Come for us," DJ rumbles as he watches me.

"Ah!" I wouldn't be able to hold back even if I wanted to. I come for them. Hard. "Matt! DJ! Fuck, yes! Yes!" My pussy clenches around Matt's tongue and DJ's fingers so tightly, I don't think either of them would be able to move.

Thankfully, they don't. I spasm around them as I come. My hips jerk into them both. DJ keeps rubbing my clit, making the orgasm so much more intense and fierce. After it's finished, my entire body goes limp. I collapse on the counter, panting.

My body experiences aftershock after aftershock as I lay there. As my pussy contracts, my body seems to jerk slightly. I feel DJ slow his rubs and gently pull his fingers out. Matt slowly licks me before pulling away. Through my lust-filled haze, I see DJ lower himself between my thighs. His tongue gently finishes licking me clean, but it's Matt sucking me off of his fingers that nearly makes me come again.

Matt and DJ help me up. Matt slides my panties back on while DJ gives me soft kisses. When he has my panties to my thighs, Matt wraps his arms around my waist and gently lifts me off of the counter. He steadies me while DJ pulls them up the rest of the way.

"Time to head to that meeting, baby," DJ says as he kisses my forehead.

I slump slightly and look up at him. "I wanted to return the favor...," I whisper. "Isn't there some time?"

DJ shakes his head and cups my cheek. "We need to eat dinner quickly and head out." He leans in and kisses me.

"Mmm..." I close my eyes and melt into his kiss. "I'd rather eat you instead," I murmur against his lips as he pulls away.

Matt laughs as DJ grins. Matt kisses me softly. "I'll take you up on that offer later. First thing, though, is taking care of our girl. Now, be good, and go get dressed."

I pout, but do as I'm told because I am a good girl. Their good girl.

But as I get dressed, the apprehension of meeting the people going into that club with me starts gnawing at my stomach again. I'm not looking forward to this at all.

✮ ✮ ✮

"Ready for this?" Matt asks as he brushes his lips against mine.

I look up at the giant house in front of me with a sigh. "As I'll ever be, I guess. What is this place?"

"Uh, it's… the vacation home of a very powerful man. One of them anyway. He has many," DJ begins a little hesitantly.

I tilt my head. The house is huge. It sits on the outskirts of Gainesville and seems to go on for miles. There's nothing else around it, really. It's set away from everything, but I'm starting to think that's intentional. The wrought iron gate that we were buzzed through by a guard dressed in a black suit was definitely a first clue.

I knew the moment we drove up that we are about to speak to someone extremely powerful who probably has a lot of sway or something. I'm thinking Governor. Or perhaps a State Representative or Senator. They have enormous houses, don't they? But something about the way they're acting has my mind flashing to more outrageous potentials. I shake off the thoughts because they would never put me in danger.

"So, is he a House Representative or something?" I finally ask when neither of them says anything.

Matt chuckles and glances at DJ. "I think he probably owns the House of Representatives."

I swallow a little harder than I intended, but those words make my heart jump into my throat. DJ leans over and kisses my cheek before he opens the door to Matt's truck. He helps me down. His hands on my hips warm me and calm me almost instantly.

I look up at him. "You realize you're scaring me."

He nods. "I know. And I'm sorry. But please trust us. We'll never allow anything to happen to you." He looks up at the house. "And this is a way to guarantee that. It took us a week to get this meeting with him."

Matt climbs out of his truck as DJ closes the door. He walks around the truck and meets us at the front of it. I look up at him then DJ

68

again as they lead me to what I'm starting to think might be my doom. Again, though, I shake the thought away. Whatever is going on, I trust them. Even still, I can sense their nervousness. They're both usually so confident and sure.

"Do you even know this person?" I nearly whisper.

"We know of him," Matt says. He squeezes my hand.

"That… does not make me feel better," I mumble as DJ knocks on the door.

"He was recommended to us by a highly trusted and respected officer. One in our inner circle and yours," DJ says. That does make me feel a little bit better, but not by much. I can feel the panic starting.

I'm between the two of them. Both are holding my hand. I take an involuntary step back, though. I don't know what's waiting on the other side of the door. For all I know, it's the boogeyman. Or maybe a mass murderer. I can't imagine we'd be walking into a murderer's lair, but at this point, I have no idea what's happening.

When the door opens, my heart seemingly leaps out of my mouth. I flinch and squeeze both of their hands. I am hardly aware that I'm trying to pull away, and that they've moved closer together. I'm effectively hidden behind them. It should make me feel safe, but I think I'm past the point of that.

I'm panicking.

Way past the point of stopping it. It could be Duchess Kate behind that door, and I'd still want to throw up and run.

"How can I help you?" a large man wearing blue jeans and a navy blue dress shirt with no tie asks. He's as tall as he is muscular. The top two buttons of his shirt are undone. His eyes are dark and filled with something that I can't place but makes me shiver. I don't know how, but he seems somewhat familiar.

I'm sweating.

I don't sweat.

I let out a small whine of terror. My palms feel like they've turned into a sticky mess. I try once more to pull away.

Run.

DJ and Matt don't let me, though. They probably have no idea, but they're the only things keeping me from passing out.

"We have a meeting with Mr. Crane," Matt says confidently. I don't think he feels it, though. I can feel a slight tremble in his arm. "I'm Lieutenant Chance." He nods to DJ. "This is Captain Rens. Our girl is Lyric. Mr. Crane is expecting us."

Crane? It can't be who I'm thinking of. He should be in Chicago with his family. Last I heard, they had something big going on in their businesses.

No. No, it's not him. It can't be.

The guy looks him up and down and nods. "Follow me." His eyes meet mine. I shiver again.

Matt follows him, leading me and DJ. I glance around the house. It's clean. Modern. I'd admire the architecture, but I'm too scared. So, I drop my eyes back to the hardwood floor. It's so quiet, I'm not sure there's anyone else in the house at all.

The man stops outside a door and knocks before he pokes his head in. "GPD is here, Ry."

"Send 'em in," a deep voice rumbles from somewhere behind the door.

I furrow my brows because I know that voice.

And that nickname.

The man stands aside and gestures for us to enter the room. I swallow even harder than I had before. I keep telling myself that I'm being crazy, but my stupid mind refuses to listen to all reason. I'm doing all I can to keep my focus on the two men at my side who I know would never hurt me. Never let me get hurt.

My eyes widen as they fall on the man rising from behind his desk. He's wearing jeans and a black dress shirt. Like the other guy, the top two buttons of this man's shirt are undone, but he's taller. The shirt looks like it could rip in half if he flexed too hard. He's not much taller than Matt or DJ, but he looks like he towers over them. Or maybe it's just me he towers over. His hair is a dark brown. His eyes almost look like coal. His facial hair is as dark as his hair. I can see a dusting of lighter coloring through it, though. The crinkles near the corner of his eyes sort of makes him a little bit less fearsome.

The biggest shock is that I know that face. I spent a lot of my time recovering from the miscarriage around him and his family. My breathing picks up as I try to process everything. I know I'm failing.

"Ryan?" I ask in a squeak. My voice is high in my shock. I wasn't expecting to see Ryan Crane in front of me. I thought we were meeting informants. My mind races as I try to figure out what is going on.

Ryan extends a hand to Matt as Matt eyes me curiously. "Hey. Ryan Crane," Ryan says.

Matt lets go of my hand long enough to shake his hand. He looks between us with furrowed eyebrows. "Matt Chance."

DJ steps forward and shakes his hand also while Matt takes my hand back in his. "DJ Rens."

Ryan smiles down at me. "Well, if it isn't Lyric Sharpe. I wasn't expecting to see you until later."

"Hi, Ryan." I just blink at him confused. I try to focus on the smooth circles DJ's rubbing over my hand. My breathing is starting to become a little erratic. Everything is becoming too much. My mind won't calm. I try desperately to focus on Matt and DJ's colognes.

"Wait. You know each other?" Matt asks, confused.

"We do. We can explain how later." Ryan smiles down at me, reassuringly. I know he can sense my anxiety. "Okay, guys and girl. Take a seat. Tell me what brings you to my doorstep."

DJ takes a breath. "I know you don't know us from Adam. You don't work with people you don't know and trust. I'll be honest. Neither do we. Coming to the mafia for help isn't something I ever thought we'd do."

I squeak as I shoot up, barely hearing a word going on around me. I can't do this. I have to get out. It's too much. The constant ball of anxiety I have had in me all morning bursts inside me. I need to breathe. I rip my hands out of DJ's and Matt's. I have to get air. I can't breathe. I slip around Matt when he reaches for me and flee the office. I sprint towards the door.

"Shit. Lyric!" Matt calls. I know he's behind me. I sense him. I hear DJ and Ryan both call my name on top of his call.

But I can't think of anything but air. I claw at my t-shirt. It suddenly feels too tight. I pull the collar away from my neck as I pull the door open. I don't even get two steps before I run into what feels like a hard, brick wall. Two strong hands grab me and keep me from falling.

"What the... Lyric?" A deep, baritone voice comes from above my head. It vibrates through the chest I'm pressed against.

I look up into two piercing blue eyes. Eyes I know but didn't think I'd be seeing today. "J-Josh? Wh-what are you d-doing here?" My voice sounds unnatural and high-pitched even to my own ears.

"What the fuck? Get your hands off her!" Matt growls. His arms wrap tightly around my waist, but it's DJ's chest I'm suddenly collapsing against.

"Shh… Baby, shh…," he whispers as I take gulp after gulp of the air filled with his scent. "Shh…" He sways with me. He tangles his fingers in my hair and hugs me so tightly to him that I feel surrounded completely. I may not be outside, but I know I'm safe.

"I don't understand… I thought we were meeting your informants…," I whisper. "Why is Josh here? Why is Ryan?" My mind is racing so fast, it could rival a Formula One race car driver. I breathe in their scents as I focus on them to combat off my panic attack the way I was taught to.

I'm not scared about the mafia part. I trust Matt and DJ. I trust Josh and Ryan. I know they are mafia. They wouldn't do anything to put me in danger. That's not what caused my anxiety to overflow. It was the unknown. Too much to process at once.

Josh.

Josh Lucinio.

My ex.

My best friend.

Josh didn't hold back when he told me what was going on with him when we were together. I know he and Alex, his twin brother, teamed up with Ryan to take down their father, Matthew Lucinio. He told me he is the leader of the Lucinio Mafia. He told me Ryan Crane is the leader of the Crane Mafia. He told me how powerful both mafias are.

He told me about the abuse he suffered at his father's hands. About how his mind had been affected by a serum his father was injecting him with. He thought I would be disgusted with him and his actions. And there were a lot that he wasn't proud of. I wasn't disgusted at all. I know what it's like to be put down by someone who is meant to build you up. Not tear you down. We became stronger because we were truthful. We stayed together for about five years.

I met Ryan and his family just after my miscarriage. Luca couldn't get time off of work to keep an eye on me. His boss was an asshole and refused even after learning why he wanted time off. Josh flew out to Gainesville when Luca called to tell him I was in the hospital having a miscarriage. He and Alex arrived within a couple hours. He refused to leave my side. Alex stayed to support us. Before I was released, it was decided that I would head back to Chicago with them and take some time away to recuperate.

It wasn't until a few years later that we realized while we loved each other deeply, we weren't in love. It wouldn't have been fair to either of us to stay together when our perfect matches were waiting out there for us. We're still best friends, even though we were no longer together. Josh still texts every day and calls every week to check in. He visits as often as he can.

As I listen to DJ's heart and grip Matt's waistband, I know we made the right choice. I found my perfect matches. He will, too. I know it.

"Shh…," DJ whispers against my ear. "I can't answer about your friend, but I can about the informants. We decided against using them. Not only did we not feel comfortable putting you in their hands, we knew you didn't either. You tried to put a brave face on, but I know you were terrified at the thought of being on your own near them. While we were looking for other options, we got word that Ryan Crane was going to be in town. Mariah has never worked with him, but her ex-boyfriend does. He recommended him and told him about us. Ryan agreed to meet us. We had no idea you knew him. We didn't connect until now that your friend Josh is the Josh that leads the Lucinio Mafia and works with Ryan."

He runs his fingers through my hair and sways with me. I keep my ear pressed against his chest, listening to his heart. My hand gripping Matt's hand and waistband slowly lessons its grip as I slowly come down. Matt runs one of his hands soothingly up and down my back, calming me further and further.

"I'm sorry we blindsided you. We should have said something. I didn't because I thought it would be easier that way. I should have seen you were having an anxiety attack, baby. I'm sorry." Matt murmurs, leaning in and kissing my neck. I relax even more as my heart rate goes back to normal. We've only been together a short time, but their scents have become a lifeline for me. I'm able to calm almost instantly.

"I might not know much about mafias, but I know there are a few legit ones that help people. I know Ryan's is one. I know Josh's is another.

I know Ryan helps Josh and vice versa. I spent a lot of time with them when Ryan first got married." I whisper into their necks as I breathe in their scents. "I stayed with them all for a while after…," I trail off and shake my head.

They both look down at me as I look up shyly. I don't need to finish the sentence. I can see the understanding in their eyes. I take another deep breath and focus on nothing but DJ's earthy scent and Matt's spicy one. Their arms wrapped around me. Their lips against my neck.

"I'm sorry I ran. I got overwhelmed. I couldn't come down even after seeing Ryan and knowing it was okay. I wanted to be strong. I have to be strong to do this," I whisper after a few moments.

I feel Matt wrap his arms tighter around us both. I'm held so tightly between them and feel safer and safer. "No, honey," He whispers in my other ear. "We should have told you. You're the strongest woman I know. You don't need to pretend you aren't afraid to prove that."

"Sweetheart, even the strongest of people need a team behind them. You're not a one woman show. We're a team. We wanted to bring you here and control this whole thing. We shouldn't have. You're part of this team. We should have treated you like that. We intended to bring you here to meet the guys who will be going in there with you, but we neglected to tell you where your team is deriving from. Granted, we didn't know that you knew them, but that was still wrong of us. I'm sorry, baby."

Matt kisses my neck softly. "We're sorry, sweet girl. If you don't want to do this, we'll come up with a different plan. I do think he is our best option to not only keep you safe, but also to get justice for all of the women who were killed."

"I want justice for them. For Alice," I say resolutely. "I'm sorry I panicked. It was just too much at once." I look up at DJ and Matt apologetically and see that we're alone outside the office in the hall.

DJ kisses me softly. "You have nothing to apologize for," he whispers.

"Nothing at all," Matt whispers just before he kisses me. His breath tickles my lips as he pulls away. "Forgive us?"

I smile. "Of course I forgive you." I nuzzle their jaws lovingly.

"Good," DJ says, relief evident in his voice. "So, that was the guy? The ex? Josh? The one you ran into?"

My eyes widen at the reminder, and I look towards the office. "Joshy! Get your butt out here! You have answers to give! You're meant to be at a merger!" I know both Matt and DJ are looking at me in shock at my outburst. It's not often I speak out like that, but Josh never told me he was going to be here. I thought he was at a merger for one of his businesses.

A few moments later, Josh opens the door and gestures for us to come in. Like Ryan, Josh would be considered tall, dark, and handsome. He's got muscles in all the right places. I always feel safe when I'm with him. He closes the door behind us. I watch as he walks to the pretty black leather chair that matches the couch Matt leads me to. He and DJ sit on either side of me, keeping my hands in theirs as Josh settles in the chair.

"He's the one you were talking about," DJ says. "The only one you've been with." He chuckles and kisses my forehead. "Right?"

I nod a little. "I always knew that no matter what it was, I would be safe with you. With both of you. I'm not sure I understand why we're here. Mariah sent you? I didn't know she knew them." I blink at all of them as I play with my fingers in my lap. DJ and Matt take my hands and link their fingers with mine.

"Because your boyfriends called me," Ryan says. "I expected. Your friend, Mariah, used to be in a relationship with one of my associates. She's still very close with him. I don't know a lot about the case. That's what this meeting was for. Josh and I were here for business."

"You got the merger?" I squeak out excitedly, unable to stop myself. "I'm so proud of you! I know how much you wanted it." Josh had mentioned it during our last Skype chat. I'm so pleased. It sounded like something incredible. It would help a lot of people.

"I did." He chuckles at my reaction and nods his head with a smile. He leans back in his chair.

"Wait." It takes me a second to catch up. "Your merger was with Ryan? You never told me that! Nor did you mention it was going to be in Gainesville when I asked." My eyes widen, and I mock gasp. "You distracted me with ice cream!"

Ryan chuckles and continues as if I hadn't interrupted. "We planned on leaving today after we had stopped by to surprise you. But when I got the call, I asked Josh to stick around for the meeting." He folds his hands on the desk and looks at us seriously. I straighten slightly in response to his dominating aura. "So, why did you call me for this meeting,

Captain Rens? Why did one of my close friends tell me that I needed to make time for this?"

"Well, Mr. Crane," DJ begins. "I mentioned on the phone when we spoke that there has been a rash of murders in our city. They've all been linked to a pretty high-end club. Sapphires has an incredible five-star restaurant, but it also has a club that's... uh... pretty secret."

Ryan nods. "A BDSM club."

My eyes widen a little because not a lot of people call it a BDSM club. I clear my throat. "That's... not all it is." I hadn't intended to speak, but I feel like I need to defend the club that's become important to me. I've met five out of the few people in the world I care about there.

His eyes meet mine. "Oh?" he asks curiously. I sit a little straighter when I see the approval in his eyes. He always did tell me I didn't need to be afraid to speak up.

"It's... more of..." I tilt my head as I try to explain. I nibble my lip and glance at Matt and DJ. I quickly release it when I see the warning looks on not just their faces, but on Josh and Ryan's too. "I guess a place where people can go to be themselves. Where they don't have to fear being ridiculed or looked down on for being who they are," I say hesitantly. "And hopefully find someone who fits with them. Not everyone is into BDSM. At least... not the... traditional sense of the word." I wrinkle my nose and shiver.

He nods slowly. "So, more of a place where people with both extravagant and specialized tastes can go. You're a natural submissive. I've known that since we first met. These two are dominants. Your dominants. But judging completely by what you said, I'd say that you don't like whips and chains and ball-gags. You just need to be with men who can make you feel less out of control by making sure you're taken care of."

DJ chuckles a little at what must be a surprised look on my face. I had forgotten Ryan knew that. "In a manner of speaking," DJ says as he squeezes my hand. "Anyway," He shakes his head and gets back on topic. "We have a plan in place to go in. The problem is the cops we'd trust on a taskforce would be easily recognizable by the other cops who attend the club. Cops we haven't seen there. They show at different times than when we go there, and we've found out from one of them that we interviewed that if he sees any other vehicles in the parking lot he recognizes, he leaves. I can't say DJ and I haven't done the same. We've ruled him out as a suspect because DJ and I know him and Lyric, who has seen him at the club, told us not only is he fairly shy, but he's also a submissive. He's the only one of those she's seen who is."

"You mentioned the rest of them are on your list of suspects when we talked," Ryan says.

Matt sighs. "We came to you because we aren't comfortable putting in our contacts with our girl. Drug dealers and gang members. People we're using to get us bigger criminals. I might trust their information, but I couldn't force myself to trust them with her. Even with us watching, the thought made me sick. We don't know who in our department we can trust. There are a couple on that list who I considered friends. After what Lyric said about them? I'm questioning my own instincts."

"We've heard about you," DJ continues. "Mostly through Mariah, as you know, but also… we lost someone a few years ago to a mafia we later learned you took down. Matt and I became curious. We know your brother has a branch of his company here. We've done our research." He looks at me with a loving smile before looking back up at Ryan. "And seeing how at ease our girl is with you, it eases our mind more and solidifies our thoughts. You're one of the good guys. And I think you might be the only ones we can trust to help with this. If it were another cop we were putting in there, maybe I'd be less… protective. Well, still protective, but not as much."

"But this is your girl." Ryan nods with a smile. "Believe me. I understand. Doubly so because Lyric is family to us, too. And it's reasons like this that we do what we do. You were right to come to us." He looks at me. "Though, why you didn't call us before you came up with this plan, I don't know." He gives me a stern look. I duck my head because I honestly hadn't thought to. All I thought about was getting justice for those women. For Alice. He turns back to Matt and DJ. "So, why don't you tell us what you need."

"Men we trust who will be unrecognized and can play dominant men," Matt blurts out. "I can't put other cops in there, and I won't trust her life with people I wouldn't trust with my own. I know you have cops working for you. I know you've done a fuck of a job of cleaning up cities you have a foothold in. We need that right now."

Ryan looks at Josh before looking back at us. "I have two men here I can give you. I have several more who work for me, but I'd prefer to give you more… higher-ups, if you will. Not because I don't trust my guys, but because I think you'll feel better if you have men who work closely with me. I can't put myself forward because my face is all over the tabloids. People know I'm married."

"I can think of two more men I'll put forward. I trust them with my life, and I would trust them with Lyric's," Josh says firmly. "One of them is Alec, Mariah's ex. I'll also be one of the men going in with her. I would pull Alex in, but he's too well-known."

Matt nods and looks down at me. "I think you'd feel better having someone you know with you."

I lean into him and nod. "I would."

"I need a day to get them here and brief them," Ryan says. "How about we meet here tomorrow for dinner? I'll make something. The three of you can meet the men we'll send in with you. Lyric already knows most of them. We can discuss the plan in more detail. A little less formal than in an office." Ryan gives me a gentle smile. "I know you'd prefer that." He smiles when I smile shyly. He knows me well.

"Thank you, Mr. Crane. We really appreciate your help with keeping our girl safe." DJ says, picking up on the dismissal, and stands.

"Please. Call me Ryan. You're with Lyric. She's family. Mr. Crane was my father, God rest his soul." His smile turns a little sad, and I suddenly remember Josh telling me what happened to his father. "Be here at six tomorrow."

"Sounds great." Matt follows DJ and stands, pulling me up with him. "We appreciate your time. You don't know what this means to us. I'm sure you understand we'd like to keep this away from the department."

"Oh, I know the amount of trouble it could cause. Don't worry. They'll be none the wiser." Ryan stands and shakes both of their hands.

"Thank you," I whisper into his chest, hugging him tightly when he pulls me into him. He kisses my head and nods with a smile when I pull back.

Josh shakes their hands as well and then turns to me. He wraps his arms around me and hugs me tightly. I hug him just as tightly. I've missed him. I swat the back of his head lightly. He chuckles as he kisses my forehead and smiles down at me. With that tap, he knows he's forgiven for not telling me he was in town.

As we leave the mansion, I find my heart has not only dramatically slowed, but that I've calmed considerably. It's not only that I feel good about what we're about to do. It's that a part of me feels like Matt and DJ will also have protection. That if anything goes down, they won't be in the fight alone. I feel like they've focused solely on me and my safety while neglecting their own.

I'm sure it wasn't hard for Ryan and Josh to see how important Matt and DJ are to me. I didn't need to say a word. I've told Josh about them both. I know that with Ryan and Josh involved, not only will I be safe, but so will they.

Since they've become my entire world, the loves of my life, I want nothing more than to make sure they're also defended.

I smile softly to myself as Matt drives. It's only been a few weeks, but I'm in love.

I'm heels over head in love with the two men beside me.

And I wouldn't change a thing.

Chapter Seven

☆ Matt ☆

"Lyric. Stop it." I run a thumb over her lip and hold it up so she can see the blood on it. "This is why I told you to stop biting your lip. You're hurting yourself. I don't like it. Do it again, I'm taking you over my knee. Understand?"

Her eyes widen when she sees the blood, and her thumb immediately goes to her lip to stop the bleeding. "Sorry, sir," she whispers.

I lean down and kiss her softly, licking at the blood. When she smiles and giggles, I grin. "There's my girl."

"Vampire." She teases with a giggle. I chuckle and kiss her again.

I hug her close to me as DJ grabs our food. Ryan truly outdid himself today. I never thought the guy would go to such lengths to make Lyric feel comfortable with this entire situation, but here we are. I'm sure Josh might have had something to do with it, but I don't care. She's happy.

We're sitting in his backyard around the pool while he grills. Not like he couldn't pay someone to do it. I know the guy is worth billions. Yet, he's grilling and has brought down several of his family members, including his own wife and kid. Lyric, while still nervous at the amount of people here, has calmed considerably. It helps that she knows almost everyone. Pretty sure I'll never be able to thank him enough for this. Fuck. For any of this. He didn't have to accept our request, but he did.

"Why did he say he'd take a grown woman over his knee?" a quiet voice asks.

Lyric and I both look up to see a girl who can't be any older than fifteen standing on her tiptoes in front of Josh with her hands lightly gripping his shirt near his stomach for leverage. I chuckle a little because I can see very clearly that she's infatuated with him.

"I'll explain later," he says just as quietly with a wink to me and Lyric. "Much, much later."

I look down at Lyric after the girl takes off. "I think he has an admirer," I whisper in her ear.

She smiles. "I think she has one, too." She nods her head to Josh, who is watching her with a torrent of emotion playing across his face. After a moment, he seems to visibly shake himself and walks into the house.

"I'm staying out of that," I whisper.

"I'm sure he'll talk to me about it when the time comes," Lyric giggles as she stands. "I'll be right back."

I raise an eyebrow and watch her walk towards the young girl as DJ comes back with plates. He hands me mine and puts Lyric's down on the pool chair between us.

After a few minutes, Lyric punches something in the girl's phone. The young girl gives her a shy smile and quick hug before she runs towards the group settled near the other side of the pool. She sits and curls into the side of one of the men. He looks down at her with an amused smile as she talks animatedly. Judging by the glance he makes towards Lyric, she's telling them about their talk.

DJ sits and watches her as she walks back to us. She pauses by Josh when he walks back out and towards Ryan. She says something too low for us to hear before continuing back to where we sit.

"What was that about?" DJ asks.

"Uh. I'm pretty sure that girl has a crush on Josh. I threatened a punishment because Lyric bit her lip and drew blood. She overheard and asked Josh what I meant, but I don't think she realized we could hear her. Lyric, I think, just decided to give her her phone number."

DJ chuckles. "Our little princess."

Lyric smiles as she takes her plate and sits down. "Her name is Dallas. She's the younger sister of one of the guys here. Alec. I think it must be Mariah's ex. Josh helped rescue Dallas from something bad. I didn't ask because she looked like she was going to cry. But I told her if she has questions about things he does that don't make sense, or she just wants someone outside her circle to talk to, she has my number. Day or night, I'll answer."

DJ leans over and kisses her temple. "You're adorable."

She blushes. "I see myself in her, and I know how overwhelming it can be to embrace your true nature. To be yourself. I didn't have anyone I could talk to who was a submissive like me. Now, when she reaches that stage, she does. Not just that, but a lot of the family around her can be intimidating. Even the women. Arianna is one of the sweetest women I have ever met, but I struggled to approach her at first. She may be tiny, but she can be just as intimidating as Ryan when she wants to be."

I smile. "A submissive knows a submissive when she sees one."

She blushes again and focuses on her plate as she starts picking at her food. "I appreciate Ryan for all of this, but I really just want to meet the people I'm going into the club with. It's like this dark cloud above my head that still needs to be discussed for it to dissipate."

I reach over and rub her thigh. "We'll get there, baby. I think this is a good idea. You might know almost everyone here, but we're getting to know everyone, too. We'll know that when you're in the club with them,they'll protect you. You'll know they have your back while we watch you both. And it's pretty cool to see that the big bad mafia bosses are still just regular guys." I nod towards Ryan grilling, and Josh having a water balloon war with a couple of the kids and, who I assume, are their dads. I shake my head as I realize everything I said is selfishly for my own benefit, but I hope it also helps ease her anxiousness.

Our girl, though, has come to know us both far too well. She squeezes the hand I have on her thigh and leans over to me. She kisses my arm. I can't help but chuckle because she knows that just that small gesture will ease my nerves immensely. I kiss her head just to reassure her that what she's done worked.

Lyric has spent most of her life being told she's stupid. She was bullied beyond belief in the United Kingdom. As soon as she and Luca turned eighteen, they started working on moving here. It took a couple of years to get everything in place, but they did it. It's been about ten years since they put down their roots here, but it was only a few years ago that Lyric felt comfortable enough to venture out of the bubble she'd created for herself.

For many years, the only places Lyric went was to work and home. Those were her safe places. It took a lot of coaxing for Luca to get her to even attempt Sapphire's. And he only got her to go there because he said it was where Kieran was celebrating his birthday. Then she met Josh. And she came out of her shell more and more. She had a setback when she went through the miscarriage. It's only been in the last year that she felt comfortable enough to venture out again. Luca confided in us that it was because Alice was badgering her into it. She mocked her for not wanting to go out. Lyric ended up giving in because she didn't want to disappoint anyone.

But as I sit here and watch her, I can't believe how far I've seen her come in such a short time. She's gaining a confidence that both Luca and Josh have pulled me aside and told me they've never seen in her. Not even Mariah has. I'd never say it, but knowing I'm a part of that bolsters my ego.

"Shit," DJ says, interrupting my thoughts. "I need to take this. Chief is probably pissed off that I haven't given him a list for the taskforce yet."

"Tell him you're working on it," I say with a low growl. "Things are delicate."

"Tell him I said to calm down, or I'm telling papa he's been betting again," Lyric says softly. "He should know you're doing the best you can."

DJ chuckles as he stands. "I don't think that excuse is working anymore. You know how much he cares about Lyric. He wants to know she'll be safe." He puts his phone to his ear as he walks inside where it's more quiet.

"I'm going to get another water," Lyric says as she looks up at me. "Want something?"

"No, baby. Thank you. I still have the bottle of Coke I got earlier."

"I'll get you a lemonade." She kisses me as she gets up. How it's possible for her to make my dick spring to life with just a kiss is something I'll never understand. It's something only DJ has ever managed.

I adjust myself and watch her walk towards the cooler Ryan has set up by the grill. I chuckle at how she's always looking after me and DJ. It's both adorable and sexy as hell. She laughs when she sees Ryan chasing his wife with a water balloon and dodges out of the way when he throws it, missing his wife completely when she ducks.

But she's precariously close to the pool. My eyes widen when I see Josh with a Super Soaker duck behind a chair. "Lyric, look out!" I call. But it's far too late for her to heed my warning. I'm already on my feet.

Lyric screams when she gets soaked to the bone by Josh's stream of water. She flails and falls right into the pool before I can reach her. Josh cracks up and moves on to stalk his next victim. I scoop up a water balloon and launch it in his direction in retaliation. He laughs as he dodges. I kneel down next to the edge of the pool.

Lyric pops her head up. "Josh! I will get you back for that, you asshole! I don't have a change of clothes here!"

"The Florida sun does wonders for drying clothes!" he yells from somewhere behind me.

I grin and hold out my hand to her. "That was a pretty epic fall. Grace and style."

She pouts as she swims to me. "I heard you tell me to look out, but there was no saving myself from that one. He's like an assassin." She takes my hand.

"In all fairness, considering who he is, you're probably correct."

She swats me after she's out and giggles. "I need to dry off. I wonder if Ryan would let me use a towel."

I push her hair behind her ear. "You're so beautiful," I whisper. She blushes and ducks her head. I kiss her forehead and look at Ryan. "Hey, Ryan! Do you happen to have a bathroom available that she can dry off in?"

He grabs his wife, Arianna, around the waist before she can pop the water balloon she has in her hands on him. She squeals as he wrestles the balloon from her. "Yeah, you can head in the house. Go through the kitchen. First door on the right is a bedroom with a private bathroom. There's a washer and dryer in a closet in the bathroom." He pops the balloon against her chest.

"Ryan!" she screams as she wiggles to get away.

I laugh as Lyric giggles. I lead her into the house. DJ is leaning on the counter in the kitchen with his eyes closed. He's pinching the bridge of his nose and shaking his head. He opens his eyes on a sigh and meets my eyes.

"I get it, Chief," he says, defeated. "I'll have it to you by the end of today, but I'm standing by my decision. I'm not taking other cops in on this. Oh. And your beautiful goddaughter said to let me handle this my way, or she's telling her dad you're betting again." He hangs up after getting the last word in and looks at Lyric. The scowl is instantly replaced with a grin. "What happened to my girl?"

"Josh soaked me with a stupid water gun, and I fell in the pool." She pouts so adorably, and stomps her foot, it would be impossible for DJ to not walk to her and kiss her. She moans into his mouth and rubs her thighs together. I watch with a grin as she nips his lip.

DJ, never one to miss anything, notices and smiles even wider. "Why don't you tell Matt what a good girl you've been? I bet you he'd love to reward you while I be a good boy and attend to my Captain duties." He nods outside, but keeps his eyes on her. "I need to talk to Ryan and Josh and get this thing moving. Chief isn't a fan that we've been taking so long." He leans over and kisses me just as hard as he did Lyric before he hurries outside.

We both watch him for a moment before I continue leading her to the room Ryan told us about. "I wonder how hard he laid into him," I say after I close the door to the room.

"I hope not too much... I know Uncle King is worried, but DJ has been trying to cover all of the angles he can." She sucks her lip into her mouth, but immediately thinks better of it as she looks around the room. "Holy fuck. This room is giant." Her eyes land on the bathroom. She beelines for it.

I look around the room. She's right. I doubt it's the Master bedroom, but it's bigger than our bedroom at home. Even the bed seems far larger than our King size. The room is light and airy. It's truly impressive. The walls are white, but there's a blue accent wall. The blankets on the bed are a patterned blue and white.

I sit on the edge of the bed and groan at how comfortable it is. "We need an upgrade," I say to Lyric when she comes out in nothing but a towel.

She tilts her head shyly as she walks towards me, sashaying her hips. "Are you in love with the room?"

I grin. "No. I'm in love with you. The room, though, is a nice perk we get to take advantage of while your clothes are drying." I grip her hips when she's close enough and tug her to me with a playful growl.

She squeaks when she hits my chest and stares at me wide eyed. "You… love… me…?"

I tighten my grip and hug her closer as I look up at her. "I do." I hadn't meant to say the words. Not yet. I don't want to scare her by admitting my feelings so quickly. Now that the words are out, my heart seems to stop while it waits for what she's going to say or do.

She runs her fingers through my hair and lets her hand trail down my jaw. "I love you," she whispers.

My breath whooshes out of me. I shift and pull her down on the bed. She squeaks and laughs as she wraps her arms around me. I pull her closer to me and cover her mouth with mine. I let my hand slide up her thigh, under the towel I wish she wasn't wearing, to her perky ass and squeeze.

She moans into my mouth and shifts so she can cuddle closer. She wraps her arms around me and presses tighter. She hooks her leg over mine with a soft moan as I deepen the kiss. The towel slides up further. She rubs her pussy over the zipper of my khaki shorts, and all resolve I have melts away.

"Lyric, I'm trying to be good here, baby." But I don't stop kissing her. I pull her even tighter to my body than she already was, so she can rub herself over me more. I kiss down her jaw to her neck and push my dick against her with a groan.

"Maybe I don't want you to be good." She nips my lip and tries to push me on my back. I let her, but only because I can't think of anything right now but her riding me.

It's not that we haven't done this. Lyric has gone all the way with both of us individually. We've all been together individually. We've hesitated being with her at the same time. We're easing her into that. Getting her used to us individually before we take her all the way and let go. We're going with what feels right. But I've never fucked her in someone else's house.

I'd never deny her what she wants, though. She straddles me and throws the towel on the floor. I groan again and let my hands wander over all of the curves I've already committed to memory until I reach the perfect swell of her tits.

"You're beautiful." I can hear the raspiness in my voice, but I can't help it.

She blushes a gorgeous pink and shivers. I sit up and pull my shirt over my head. As I kiss her, I feel her hands fumbling to unbuckle my belt. I tangle my fingers in her hair and let her. When she gets it undone, she unbuttons them and carefully unzips them. She shifts and tugs them down along with my boxer briefs. I kick them the rest of the way off and deepen our kiss.

I moan when she nips my tongue and sucks, but I don't give her control for long. I tilt my head just a little and plunge my tongue into her mouth. I begin the familiar dance with her. Her hand grips my shoulder. I groan when she rubs the tip of my dick along her pussy to her clit and back to her pussy.

"Matt…," she moans into the kiss. Giving me absolutely no warning, she drops herself down onto my cock, hard, taking all ten inches of me until I'm buried inside her balls deep.

"Holy fuck, Lyric!" My eyes roll back in my head. I let myself fall onto the bed, but I keep my hands on her hips.

She lets her head fall back and braces herself with her hands on my stomach. "Oh God, I'll never get used to how big you are."

I grin and watch her head fall slowly forward. "I think you get used to me just fine."

She smiles shyly and slowly starts moving back and forth. "Mmm…"

"Lyric… Christ. You're so tight…" I let my eyes fall to her pussy when she leans back, bracing her hands on my thighs. My dick jerks when she clenches. "And you're fucking soaked."

"For you." And without another word, I get my wish. Lyric rises slowly and slams herself back down on me.

Hard.

"Fuck, Lyric!"

My sweet little submissive gives me a wicked smile and lifts herself off me again. I try to make my eyes rise because I love watching her expressions during any kind of sexual act we're involved in, but I can't. I can't look at anything more than her pussy taking each and every inch of my dick with every bounce. It's like she's mesmerized me. Cast some kind of a spell on me. Something I'm positive she has no idea she's doing. Lyric goes by what feels right in the moment. A quality I'm beyond thankful for.

As I grip her hips, the dominant part of me is screaming to take control. To lift her and slam her down on my cock. To control the pace. The entire show. I wish I could say that's the part of me I'm listening to because it would be fun, but that is not how this is going. I push that voice down. I don't want to push her too fast. She isn't ready for that side of me. I've dominated, but never fully.

Her moans and soft whines hit my ears and send shockwaves through my entire body. When I can't take anymore, I thrust up into her, meeting her halfway. The move drives her over an edge I didn't realize she was near. It's like she loses complete control. She bounces faster and harder. Her nails dig into my abs. In my lust-filled haze, I hadn't noticed she had shifted position.

Lyric is a small girl, but she has some wicked curves. Her tits are large. Disproportionate to the rest of her, but they drive me crazy. When I'm finally able to move my eyes up her body, I'm rewarded with those beautiful, round, soft, orbs bouncing with her.

"Oh... Matt... Yes, yes, yes!" She clenches tight purposely around me with every bounce. She twists her hips as she clenches tighter around my tip then slams back down, taking every inch of me.

"Oh, Christ, baby girl." My dick gets thicker and thicker with each and every thrust.

She gets tighter and tighter. Wetter. Her pussy pulses erratically around me. I'm so close, but I won't come until she does. I've never left anyone unsatisfied by coming and being done before they get their satisfaction, too. No matter how much I need it; how close I am to tumbling off that cliff of desire. Only with DJ do I let myself come before he does. His dominant side wouldn't allow anything less.

"Matt... please... I need..." She lets out little whimpers and moans that go straight to my cock.

So, I allow myself to listen to that dominant voice, though only a little. I sit up and move my hands to her ass. I start moving her back and forth over my dick while letting her ride me as hard and fast as she wants. Her eyes widen at the new depth and sensations coursing through her pussy, and I know I'm hitting the elusive G-Spot. Her pussy immediately tightens and pulses even more erratically around me. I feel her get even wetter.

"You know what you have to do, baby. What do you need?" I rumble, not letting up on my pace, keeping it matched with hers.

"Please! Please, Lieutenant! Please, sir, let me come!" She keeps bouncing as I move her back and forth. "I need to come for you! Please, sir!"

"Good girl. Such a good girl for me," I praise. I slap her ass. She moans and jerks into me. "Come, baby. Holy fuck. Come. Come for me," I command with a low growl.

"Ah! Yes, sir! Yes! Matt!" she screams as she comes hard, soaking my cock.

"Fuck, Lyric!" My dick, thick and ready, jolts inside her as she releases. I fill her with hot streams of come as my hips jerk against hers while we both ride out our orgasms.

Lyric collapses against me, still connected to me in the most intimate of ways. I hold her close, laying back on the bed, and rub her back soothingly as she buries her face in my neck, catching her breath. I kiss her shoulder and hug her as tightly as I can.

"I really do love you," I whisper in her ear.

"I really do love you," she whispers back to me.

I smile and hold her close, relishing in the peaceful feelings washing over me at having the love of the greatest man and woman I've ever had the pleasure of knowing. I don't know how I got so lucky, or what I did to deserve them, but I'm never letting either of them go.

Chapter Eight

☆ DJ ☆

"I think we need to move, then," Ryan says after I tell him what Chief King said in our conversation.

I rub my forehead. "Part of me wants to find more ways to stall. I don't want Lyric anywhere near any of this."

He chuckles. "I really don't blame you. But I also think her argument is right. She's a submissive person by nature. I could send in any of my brother's wives, but it wouldn't be the same. They simply aren't at the level she is. She doesn't need to put on an act. It's just who she is. And dominant men are attracted to that. Some of us, while dominant, don't need a full submissive." His eyes land on Josh. "Some of us do. Those that do are the type that attend those clubs." He looks back at me. "Sending in a woman who isn't fully submissive will never fool a man who is as dominant as you are. Or Matt, even."

I sigh. "I've been going there myself. Investigating on my own. Interviewing. I'd rather just keep doing that, but I don't think I'm getting anywhere."

"No man worth anything wants to put his significant other in danger. I won't lie to you and say there's not a huge amount of danger for her, but I can promise you that she'll be protected. Every single person I've pulled will make sure she's safe. She's family. Has been ever since the day Josh flew into Chicago with her."

I let out a breath and rest my elbows on my knees. "I just want this all over with."

"Well, then you made the right call. We'll introduce you both to the guys going in with her. Good news is she knows most of them, which will set her more at ease. And both of you as well. I'll be doing surveillance with you and Matt. There will be lots of guards there. We're replacing the owner's security with my guys. He should be here soon to discuss that and meet Lyric, as well." Ryan pats my back when he hears the doorbell. He stands up. "That's probably him now."

As he walks into the house, Matt and Lyric walk out. Both of them look far less stressed, which goes a long way in making me feel better. He sits next to me. I raise an eyebrow because he knows that's where Lyric had been sitting, but she crawls into my lap, straddling me, instead. My arms automatically wrap around her waist, as if they've just been waiting for her so they can claim their rightful place.

She takes my face gently in her hands and presses her sweet lips to mine in the softest kiss I think she's ever given me. The pureness of it steals my breath. When she deepens it and swipes her tongue across mine, I shiver. Everything feels different. It's like she's pouring her entire soul into the kiss. All of her love.

She pulls away slowly and runs the pad of her thumb gently over my lower lip. "I love you," she whispers.

Fireworks explode where my heart should be. My stomach tenses. I feel the smile breaking across my face. And damn if my dick doesn't get hard underneath her. I hug her closer and tighter to me. I kiss her a little harder than she had me, but with just as much intensity and passion. A quiet moan escapes her lips as she closes her eyes and melts against me.

When I pull away, I can feel Matt watching us both with a huge grin on his handsome face. No one exists to me right now but the three of us. My head is spinning with her declaration. It's not that I couldn't feel it. Hell. I've felt the same for a long time. But the words falling from her lips are the only thing in the world I need or want to hear in this moment.

I tangle my fingers in her hair and kiss her nose. "I love you, too," I whisper.

Her beautiful eyes light up. She smiles so wide that I'm sure her face might crack. She leans in and hugs me hard, but the nuzzle to my neck when she buries her face in it is gentle and sweet. Matt leans over and kisses us both as he hugs us.

With just those three words spoken between us, I feel stronger. More complete. Like our little unit is bonded. Sealed in one of the most intimate and final ways. What I did to deserve the love of these two amazing beings is something I'm sure I'll never know, but whatever it was, I hope I keep doing it. I kiss Lyric's forehead.

We stay like this for a few moments before I notice her hand moving around behind us. She grips something, and in a sudden flurry of movement, is straddling my lap facing the pool. She aims and hits Josh straight in the face with a jet of water that makes him jump and sputter.

We all burst out laughing as she cackles and dances triumphantly. "Gotcha, asshole!"

I groan and still her hips.

"Good shot." He chuckles as Dallas tosses him a towel so he can dry off. When he finishes, he folds it and sets it down on the chair next to us as he looks at Lyric approvingly. "Those lessons have improved your aim."

I can't see her face, but I can tell she's smiling brightly at his approval. "I never thought those shooting lessons would ever come in handy, but…" She shrugs with a giggle.

"Glad that my lessons in protection and defense are working." He chuckles as he sits on the end of the chair Dallas is laying on.

I kiss Lyric's neck and wrap around her as we settle, watching as the kids run around the backyard. It doesn't last long, though.

Matt nudges me. "He's ready for us."

I glance at the door where Ryan is standing, then look at Lyric. "Ready to see the men who are going to try and steal you away?"

She giggles. "They don't stand a chance." She stands and tilts her head and gives me a teasing smile. "Well, maybe Josh."

Matt laughs and slaps her ass. "Not even he could take you away from us."

"I'd simply have to kill him," I say with as straight of a face as I can.

Lyric smiles wider and pokes the corner of my mouth. "I'd believe you. Except you're about to laugh."

I do just as she says as I take her hand and lead her in the house. "You're too observant for your own good."

"I just know my man." She squeezes my hand.

I groan because it sounds just as possessive as I sound towards her. I kiss her hand. "Yours."

We follow Ryan through the house until we reach a conference room near the back of it. Of course the guy has a conference room larger than the one in our Headquarters building located in his damn house. I can't help but laugh a little as I take a seat. Lyric settles next to me. Matt sits on the other side of her.

Ryan moves behind us. "You all know why you're here, so I won't get into semantics. For the couple of you who haven't met her before, this is Lyric." He puts his hands on her shoulders and squeezes gently. I watch as she relaxes slightly under his reassurance. "She's the one going into the club. We'll be protecting her at all costs." He gestures to me. "This is Captain DJ Rens." He gestures to Matt. "And this is Lieutenant Matt Chance. They both work for the Gainesville Police here in Florida. They came to us on the recommendation of both their colleagues and close friends because we're their last option. They don't trust their CIs with the woman they love. I don't blame them. I wouldn't either. They can't use the officers they work with. They're too recognizable."

Josh leans against the wall across from us. "This is time sensitive. A rash of murders have been happening in this area, and all are linked to Sapphire's, a club owned by Cooper Hayden." He inclines his head to the tall, well-dressed man next to him who I know very well. He's from Chicago, but he and his wife own the club we frequent.

"I've been in close contact with Matt and DJ regarding this issue," Cooper begins. "But even I know this is out of their hands. A lot of the people they know and trust also frequent the club. Usually at different times, and not all frequent the upstairs portion of it. Either way, they are all very recognizable, as Ryan said. There are also other police officers who were brought to my attention recently that attend the club. I've never received a complaint against them, but given what I've found out, they will not be frequenting the club after this is done, even if they aren't involved."

Lyric ducks her head, knowing she's who brought them to our attention. She knows we went directly to Cooper. I squeeze her hand, reassuringly.

"You've all been briefed, so I'm not going to sit here and bore you with all of that shit again," Ryan says. "You're here right now because Lyric, Matt, and DJ need to know who Josh and I are sending in. Each of you will take one night with her. Your job is to make it look real. You're interested in her. You leave the club like you're taking her home. Only you'll be taking her to her apartment where you'll stay with her until Matt and DJ get there. We need to watch and see who reacts. We'll have our guys stationed throughout the club. I want our guys to replace his security, but Cooper said that might come off as too suspicious. I happen to agree, so instead, we'll place them as customers. He brought in the Head of Security from his main club to oversee security while we're there. He trusts that he can handle the added workload. He'll keep his eyes on the room at all times from the inside. We'll be looking through their CCTV cameras. Every inch of the club will be covered."

"Lyric has told us that each of the women murdered were known to her," Matt steps in. "Not that she was overly friendly with them, but she knew who they were. We couldn't find any kind of a commonality among the women except the club until she told us that each and every single one of them typically went home with a different guy each night."

"They were each considered a submissive slut," I say. I squeeze Lyric's hand when she flinches slightly at the word. She hates the word slut. "Those aren't our words or Lyric's. They're the words of a couple of people I interviewed who work at the club. Apparently, there's a hierarchy. We've been going there a while, but we never really paid attention to that. We minded our own business. But there's the shy submissive. She's the one who sits by herself and observes. Sometimes, she goes home with someone. If she does, she's not seen for a while. She's considered the top of the hierarchy. Desired because she doesn't put herself out there. Also known as a natural submissive. They're the most popular in the club. Lyric is in that category. She's a natural submissive." I squeeze her hand when she leans into my side.

Matt continues where I left off. "Then there are the slut submissives. You'd think they'd be on the bottom, but they aren't. They're in the middle. These are the women who are submissives. But they aren't shy. They know what they want and don't hesitate to go after it. They're looking for the dominant they fit with and won't hold back about going back to the club to find him if the one she left with doesn't fit."

When he pauses, I continue. "The bottom tier are the fakes. The fake submissives are the ones who want to be dominated but aren't submissive in the slightest. You'll discover a few fake dominants in the club, too. Their tastes run along the same line. They're the ones who like it extremely rough. I've recently been informed that a fair few of them have extreme fantasies, like the kidnap or the rape fantasies."

"I still can't believe that's a thing." Cooper shakes his head. I'm with him on that. I will never understand what they like about it.

Lyric visibly shudders. I pull her chair closer, wrapping my arm around her. Matt moves his chair so she's pressed into both of our sides and takes her hand, kissing it. Ryan squeezes her shoulder again.

"There are a lot of different types of people who frequent that part of the club," Josh says. "It's where I met Lyric." He smiles down at her. She smiles shyly up at him.

"From what we've discovered through our interviews, it seems like the girls who are victims were popular among the dominants," I say, bringing us back on topic.

"Sounds to me like someone is jealous seeing all the girls go home with someone and they aren't," one of the guys at the table says.

"That or someone is jealous the girl didn't pick them to go home with," another says.

I nod. "We have a few theories. Each of the victim's fit in the submissive slut category."

"Actually…," Lyric interrupts quietly then silences herself, biting her lip.

"Lip, little girl." I rumble, dominantly. I smile approvingly when she releases it instantly. "Did you want to add something?"

"Um… Alice… she… she fit more in the fake submissive category. Though, she went home with men almost every night." She says quietly. She blushes when she notices all eyes are on her.

"She was?" Matt asks her. We hadn't known that. We assumed she was in the same category as the others.

"Yes, sir. She would always mock the submissives when she wasn't in the club. She called them weak, feeble, and meek. That they had no personality. She would say that there was no way she would let a man have control over her. That while it was sexy in the bedroom to be taken rough and hard, but outside in the real world, she didn't need him. The only one she was submissive with in the slightest was the one I told you about who she didn't really talk much about with me. All of the rest were, though. Just… not her." She lowers her eyes to our hands. "I'm sorry I didn't say something before."

"Nothing to apologize for, little one." I lift her chin so she can see that I'm not mad.

She smiles shyly, leaning into my side. I glance at Matt over her head. That's something we'll have to amend in our investigation. I don't think it occurred to Lyric to mention it before now. I shake my head and get back on topic.

"Thank you for telling us, baby girl," Matt smiles at her, kissing her cheek. She smiles shyly up at him.

"We think it's either a guy who asked the girl to go with him. She refused and went with someone else she felt like she fit better with. When it didn't work out and she found herself back at the club the next night, he probably asked again and got turned down again. We think he's someone who is tired of being shot down. We have a couple of suspects I think Ryan shared with you all. Our other theory is a little out of the box." I look down at Lyric with a chuckle.

"A little Brit thinking." Lyric giggles.

"I still say you're more American than British. Even when you were still in the United Kingdom, you preferred US foods to what you could get there," Matt chuckles.

"He's got a point there," Josh nods with a chuckle. "I always did say you were born in the wrong country. Your accent is more American than British. Even back when you first moved here."

I look down at her with a grin. "See? Matt and I aren't the only ones who believe that. Even he knew it." She smiles shyly, nuzzling my jaw. I kiss her softly. I can't help it. She's beautiful when she smiles.

Ryan chuckles. "You said you had another theory?"

She blushes with a giggle. "I think it's a good theory."

I chuckle and look back up at the guys in the room as I squeeze her thigh. "It is a good theory. Lyric thinks the suspect is a female who is jealous they aren't getting picked by anyone to go home with for the night.

I say out of the box because we do have evidence that the suspect is tall and strong enough to easily overpower the woman. Not to say a woman can't overpower another woman, but it's unlikely. I've been working as a cop for almost twenty-five years. The number of times I've come across a case where the woman was the killer can be counted on one hand, but the times they've been a serial killer? None."

"Again, though, not to say it can't be. We have suspects who are both male and female. Just unlikely. I don't know that I would have put much value in the theory, but I respect Lyric and how she got there," Matt finishes.

"With that," Ryan says as he walks to the head of the table. "I think it's time your boyfriends meet the men who will be taking you home." He gives her a teasing smile and a wink that makes her both blush and giggle.

"Okay." She leans back in her chair and doesn't quite make eye contact with anyone. I know my girl, though. She's studying everyone.

"Starting to my right." Ryan sits. "You know them, Lyric, but Matt and DJ don't. This is Luke Massena. He's my second in command. Next to him is his husband, Robby. Robby is a tech genius. He'll be helping with surveillance. Not going in, but I want you both to know who will be watching your girl's back. Robby also happens to be the best fucking sniper I've ever met. He's saved my life more times than I can count. Next, I have Gavin Vandenberg. He's Josh's second in command. Then, Alec Cassidy. He's a close friend of Josh's. He's the president of a motorcycle crew called Viper's Venom. He's also the one your friend, Mariah, was talking about. They dated for a long while back before any of us really knew who Alec was. Next to him is Tyler Legend. He's Alec's second in command, or vice president. You know Josh will be going in. If we need more, I have two others." He nods to the end of the table. "Trey works with Cooper. And Ryder is also part of Viper's Venom. And if we need more than that, I have a lot of other people I can call in, but I don't think we'll get to that point. I know that Josh has asked others to be on standby, as well."

Lyric's hand grips mine a little tighter. I run my fingers through her hair as I lean down. I kiss below her ear. "You okay?" I whisper.

She squeezes Matt's hand and leans into me. "Just nervous. I know all of them except Alec and Tyler and Ryder. It's not that. Just nervous about it all."

"I'm still holding out hope of talking you out of this. Or going all fucking dominant and forbidding it all together because I know you'd never disobey a dominant's order."

"You wouldn't dare. I may be your submissive, but I'm not your doormat," She says the words quietly, but I can hear the attitude.

I chuckle at her sass and tug her hair. That sass is one more thing I love about my girl. "But I won't because I respect you and love you."

"I think it would go a long way with Lyric if we could go over the plan," Matt says. He soothingly rubs his thumb over the back of her hand. "It will help ease the anxiety she is feeling. Maybe even that DJ and I are feeling as well."

I keep my fingers tangled in her hair as I sit back. "Probably a good idea."

"Well, first thing is I'll wire you," Robby begins, looking at Lyric. "You and the person you're with that night. It won't be that gaudy shit you see in the movies." He holds up two tiny pieces of something and leans over the table to show her. "This is your camera and audio. Everything you do will be seen and heard. If you have to go to the bathroom, then just say something. A lot of things can happen in a bathroom, so I'm sorry to say, but audio stays on. I will shut the camera down, though."

Lyric wrinkles her nose. "I think I'll just refrain from using the bathroom." She hands the equipment back after we look at it.

Robby chuckles. "Understandable. But if you need to, you need to." He shrugs with a reassuring smile. "If it happens, I'll have DJ sing to you."

Lyric snorts out a laugh that causes everyone at the table to laugh right along with her. "I love him, but he can't sing."

I don't know why, but I laugh harder. "I'm serenading you every time you go to the bathroom now!"

"God, please. No," Matt says as he laughs. "He may look pretty, but he sounds like a dying cow."

Everyone laughs harder. The brief break in the seriousness of this situation loosens us all up more and more. Lyric comes out of her shell just a little bit. She's blushing and throws me an apologetic look since the humor is at my expense, but I give her a wink to let her know it's okay. She smiles brightly and sits up straighter. I give Robby a small nod in thanks. He gives me a subtle one in return.

"Now that we got that out of the way," Josh says with a half-smile. "The rest of the plan. We're sending in Alec with you first, Lyric. Of everyone in this room, other than me, he'll be the one who can ease your mind the most. He's the most dominant. He'll be the best fit with you. I'd do it myself, but I want to make sure everyone is in place. I want to get a layout of the club and take a bit of time to observe the people."

"Okay." She nods confidently, and I can't help but be proud of my girl.

"You and I will just talk," Alec says before he looks at me and DJ. "I know how hard it will be for the two of you, but there's going to be touching. It won't be anything too intimate, but we need to make it look real." He looks back at Lyric. "After a respectable amount of time, we'll leave, but not until I know that we have eyes watching us. I want to make sure that we get attention. That's another reason I need to touch you in at least some manner, and you'll have to pretend you like it. It won't be believable otherwise."

Lyric nods. "I understand. I can do this."

Alec smiles. "You can ask me anything you want to. We can talk about ourselves, or about any of the other guys going in with you. I'll tell you all about me and your friend. Our relationship. How she got here. I'll be happy to answer anything you want. Anything to make you more comfortable. When the time comes, I'll take you home. I'll stay for a couple of hours. DJ and Matt will be back at the club a little while longer observing everyone. They're looking for someone who is paying too close attention to us. Specifically, you. I don't think a move is going to be made until whoever this is sees you leaving each night with someone else."

"We'll start tomorrow," Ryan says. "Chief King called DJ today. He was pretty pissed that DJ has been investigating on his own and hasn't given him a taskforce yet. DJ was able to talk him into the end of the week. I don't know how, but it worked. I'm hoping we're done by then because DJ's concerns are valid. We don't want Lyric going in with anyone that could jeopardize this. But we also don't want to see anyone else dead either. Lyric, you might hate me for this, but you can't drive to the club with DJ and Matt. I'll need them to set up each night with me so we're prepared for when you do get there."

She takes a breath and nods. "I understand."

"We'll have a different guard pick you up in a different vehicle each night. He'll drop you at the club. It will look like you've taken an Uber," Josh says. "You'll take out your phone to make it look like you're clearing the ride as you walk in. I'll make sure the guards who drive you are ones you know. That will reassure you more."

"It would. Thank you," she says softly. She gives him a shy smile.

"You've thought of everything," I say, rubbing Lyric's neck soothingly.

"I'm sorry you're all stuck with me," Lyric says quietly to everyone. She looks down and sighs before stealing herself and looking back up. She squares her shoulders, but I can feel her tense. "I know you could all be out on dates with someone much more beautiful and in your league rather than having to watch over me."

The entire room falls silent. All eyes land on her, including mine and Matt's. I can't believe those words just came out of her mouth. Not after all we've worked on over the past few weeks. It's like it all just fell at the wayside with every word that fell from her lips.

Lyric shrinks into herself when she sees all of the men in this room giving her their very own dominant stares. But it's mine and Matt's that make her wilt. She slumps, realizing what she said and immediately drops her head.

"If they don't spank you for that, Lyric, I swear to fuck I will," Josh growls. "I've done it before, and you can be fucking sure I'll do it again. I spent years with you, helping to build your confidence. You've come a long way since then. I sure as hell won't let you fall back into bad habits and talk about yourself like that now."

"I'm sorry," Lyric jumps at his tone but keeps her eyes lowered. "I didn't mean it like that," she whispers. "I just meant that I… don't think I'm not pretty. I just have a hard time believing that two amazing men like Matt and DJ like me…"

"Love," I correct with my own low, dominant growl. "We love you, Lyric." I stand and pull her up gently with me. She blushes, but I can see her smiling at my words.

Matt follows, but takes it one step further than I had. He bends and throws her over his shoulder. She squeals. "You have our numbers." He nods to Ryan. "Let us know when you want us." I see Ryan murmur something quietly to Josh that he nods to. I'm sure it's something to reassure him. He hates hearing Lyric talk down about herself just as much as we do. It's pretty obvious just seeing his reaction to it.

Neither of us say another word as we leave the room. Matt carries a wide-eyed Lyric out to his truck. He helps her in. We both climb in behind her. As we pull out of Ryan's driveway, I know Lyric knows she's going to get a punishment for her words, but she says nothing.

After a few moments, though, I can't go on letting her think the thoughts I know she is. "Lyric, you're incredibly beautiful, and we love you more than words could ever say. One way or another, you're going to realize that."

She nods, and as Matt drives home, I make a decision. She spends all of her time with us, but she still lives with her brother. I don't want things to move too quickly because I don't want to scare her, but there's one thing I know she's ready for that we haven't done. And after what we just heard, I think it's about time we show her not only how beautiful we know she is, but also show her how serious we are about our relationship.

How much we love her and want her.

How much Beckett adores her.

It's time we bring our girl home.

For good.

Chapter Nine

☆ Lyric ☆

"Ready to go, Ms. Sharpe?" the burly man in the driver seat of the Cadillac Escalade I'm in asks me. I recognize him. I know he's one of Josh's personal guards.

"As I'll ever be," I say quietly.

He smiles at me in the rearview mirror. One of the many men who work for Ryan Crane. Mafia boss. Billionaire. How the hell did I end up involved with the mafia? I shake my head. I need to remember that one of the people closest to my heart is a mafia boss himself.

I take a breath and close my eyes. The truth is, I'm not ready for any of this. I'm terrified out of my mind. The only reason I haven't backed out of my crazy beyond belief, hair-brained idea is because I really want to help get justice for the women who lost their lives.

For Alice.

I lean my head against the window and sigh. Alice wasn't really the greatest of friends, but she was still a person. She had her flaws, but she didn't deserve to die. Not like that. It was gruesome. It sometimes keeps me awake at night. She had to have suffered immensely before she died. She was strangled so hard, her trachea was snapped. It makes me sick to think about. What kind of disgusting individual does that to another human being?

I take another deep breath and wipe my eyes. As soon as this is over, I'm determined to change that fact. I sit up a little straighter. It's time I start to live again. For myself and for my family. Both blood and chosen. For my loves.

"Ms. Sharpe?"

I jump slightly and open my eyes. "Sorry. I was lost in thought." I blush and lower my eyes.

"It's okay. We're here. Don't forget to take out your phone and make it look like you're finishing the ride on your app."

I nod shyly. "Yes, sir."

I open the door and step out as I take out my phone from the back pocket of my jeans. I take a deep breath that does nothing to steady my racing heart. I unlock my phone as I close the door of the vehicle and act like I'm opening an app to finish the ride. As he's supposed to, the driver pulls away.

I look up at Sapphire's and walk in the front door. Something I've done so many times before. This time, though, it seems wrong. I already found my dominants. My home. I have all I want in DJ and Matt. I don't need to be here anymore. I only came here to look for the other half of me. Now that I've found it, I don't need the club anymore.

Only I do. I need to be here. I need to do this. So many women like me, even though they couldn't seem to find the one that fit with them, lost their lives because of who they were. That thought is so scary to me.

"If you can hear me, put your phone in the back pocket of your jeans and hug yourself." Matt's deep, comforting voice in my ear helps to ease my fears so much.

I smile and put my phone in my back pocket. I hug myself as I walk up to the counter. "Lyric Sharpe," I say quietly. "I'll be on the red list."

The hostess, who I've seen a handful of times, smiles brightly. "Yes, ma'am. Follow me."

I follow her to the familiar hallway. She opens a door that leads to the secret elevator which will take me to the top floor. A ride I've taken many times before, but never alone. I think for the millionth time that this idea is terrible. I never should have thought of it or pushed to go through with it. I can't help thinking I'm going to fail with spectacular ferocity.

I let out a breath and close my eyes. "I'm scared," I whisper.

"You don't need to be. Alec is already there," DJ says. "He's sitting in a booth near the back of the club within eyesight of the elevator. I need you to make eye contact with him just like you did me and Matt the night we met you. Lauren is the hostess. She'll lead you to the table we sat at that night. She's the only other person other than Kieran who works there who knows what's happening. She's looking out for you, too."

"What if she's the one?"

"She's not, baby," Matt says. "I promise. Kieran and Lauren are safe. Cooper and his wife are both safe. And there are a lot of other people up there looking out for you, too. You're safe, baby."

I nod and let out a breath over the lump forming in my throat as the elevator doors open. I like Lauren. Being reassured she isn't the one doing this is helpful. I step off quietly with my head slightly lowered, but mostly to make sure no one can see the tears in my eyes or terror on my face until I can compose myself.

"Hey, Lyric," Lauren says quietly. I'm always so happy when she's here. She's so nice. She always makes me feel at ease. She gently squeezes my arm. A show of support. She'll never understand what it means to me.

"Hi," I say just as quietly.

"Right this way. Do you want a menu?"

I shake my head. "No. Thank you. Not right now anyway. I'm too nervous."

"Chef has some incredible soup on the menu tonight. Chicken noodle, but it's so amazing."

"Maybe later." I smile softly as she nods.

As DJ told me to, I find Alec. I smile softly, feeling the blush creep into my cheeks, even though I don't mean for it to. I quickly look away after he nods with a barely perceptible smile. He's dressed quite nicely tonight. He's wearing jeans and a black button down shirt. His sleeves are rolled up to his elbows. He's nursing an amber drink, though I don't know what it is.

It's a starkly different Alec than yesterday. That Alec was dressed in ripped jeans with a few stains that looked like grease. It was hotter than hell yesterday, but Alec had a black leather jacket over his dark t-shirt, and he was wearing heavy boots.

Tonight, he's replaced the boots with tennis shoes that look brand new. The black shirt looks expensive. His hair is styled to perfection. He looks like he belongs here. It was something I worried about yesterday when I initially saw him.

"Do you want something to drink?" Lauren asks after I'm seated.

"Just water, please. I'm so nervous."

"Maybe a Ginger Ale would be better. I'll bring both."

"Lauren," DJ says quietly. "Soup, please. She needs to eat something."

She nods and doesn't give me a chance to argue before she strides away from the table. I didn't know she was wearing an earpiece. I take a breath and do what I usually do. I observe everyone here. The usual servers are around. I'm surprised to see a different manager on duty. That's unusual, but nice. The other one was a jerk. I don't think any of the servers really liked him. Maybe he got fired. He was the one taking half the tips from the servers.

A lot of the usual dominants are around, too. Most of them are doing what I am. They're observing. Some of the girls are watching the shows going on with friends. I don't usually pay attention to them. Most of the things that happen inside those individual little rooms are things I'll never in my life do.

I flinch when I hear a whip against skin. Sadism. No thank you. I lower my eyes and focus on the water and Ginger Ale with the soup that Lauren just put on the table, but I don't miss the looks I'm getting from a lot of people, guys and girls alike. I'm in an area where anyone can see me. I'm usually in a far more private booth. Especially after Alice finds her hook-up of the night. Somewhere I can watch and not be seen. I don't like being in the open.

But I have to be tonight. Everything I'm doing tonight has to be seen. I quietly eat, knowing DJ wants me to. He's right. He knows me very well. I haven't eaten much today because my stomach has been upset, but I am kind of hungry.

At least I don't see any of the asshole cops who come here. Or the whore of a secretary. Maybe they've chosen to stay away tonight. Maybe

I'll get lucky and have a night to get used to this. Not having Matt and DJ at my side is killing me slowly. I'm sure of it.

"Mind if I sit down?" a smooth, far too cocky, deep voice asks just as I finish the soup. It's a voice I wish I'd never heard. A voice that sends a shiver of terror down my spine.

I look up into the cold, calculating eyes of a Sadist. The cop who gets off on punishments. I swallow. Hard. "U-um…"

His smile makes me sick and doesn't reach his gray eyes. "Well, aren't you just a gorgeous creature. I've seen you a few times."

I tremble and do all I can not to show it. "I -"

Thankfully, Alec slides into the booth next to me. He looks up at the Sadist and drops an arm over my shoulders. "We're good here, thanks."

"The fuck do you think you're doing?" the Sadist cop growls. I wish I knew his name, but I never bothered to ask DJ or Matt if they knew who he was by the description I gave.

Alec doesn't flinch. "If you wanted her, you should have sat down. You didn't. I am. You missed out. Better luck next time."

"Cocky motherfucker, aren't you?" He slams his hands on the table.

I jump and squeak. Every fiber of my being is telling me to run, but I can't. I'm frozen in place. Instead, I close my eyes and pray he goes away. I dig my nails into my thighs and hold my breath because if I don't, I'll hyperventilate.

"Lyric. Baby, you need to breathe for me," Matt whispers in my ear. "Turn your head towards Alec. Act like it's him you want to be with. Act like it's me or DJ if you want, but you need to show him that Alec is who you're choosing for the night. He'll leave. I promise."

I do what Matt says and turn my head towards Alec. I keep my eyes squeezed shut and let myself breathe him in. He smells masculine. My brows furrow when I recognize the scent. It's what DJ wears. The earthy cologne. I can't help but smile softly. It was intentional. They know how much their colognes help soothe me. I feel the tension ease out of me little by little.

I hear a chuckle. Alec tightens his grip on my shoulder. After a few moments, I'm calm enough to actually look up. I'm thankful that the Sadist is gone, but he's left a lasting impression. All eyes are on us. No one seems to be moving, and the Sadist is storming to the elevator. I don't move until the elevator doors close behind him.

"Well, that was fun," Alec says with a teasing grin as he looks down at me. "Want to do it again?"

My eyes widen at him as my mouth falls open. I push him, but he's like a tank. Of course he doesn't budge. "No. No, I do not."

He laughs and releases his grip on me. He rests his arm on the back of the booth. "Sorry I wasn't here right away. I wanted to see what he did. How he responded to you. I wasn't about to let that fucker sit down, though."

I let out a breath and rub my head. I suddenly have a massive headache. "That was the Sadist Cop. I don't know his name. I can't remember it, anyway. I used to know it, but I started calling him the Sadist Cop."

"That was Antonio Rodrigues," DJ says. "He's an asshole, but we've ruled him out as a suspect. He has an alibi for every single murder."

"How?" I ask quietly, genuinely curious.

"Well, you're not going to like it, but he has a daughter who has a crush on me." DJ chuckles. "I may have exploited that. Matt and I took her to lunch the other day and questioned her."

Alec shakes his head and looks down at me. "Your boyfriend has a death wish."

I raise an eyebrow. "The question is who's going to kill him. Sadist Cop or me."

DJ laughs. "You can punish me later."

"I'll have Matt spank you. I'd be a bawling mess if I did. Or I'll have him do that thing you do to me."

Alec covers a laugh with his drink. "I'd pay money to see little Lyric take you on."

"Back to work, you asshole," Josh says with a chuckle.

"I do feel better with all of you over the earpieces," I say quietly. "It helps my confidence level. And don't think I don't recognize the cologne Alec is wearing."

"We're right here, baby. Just remember that," Matt says. I can hear the chuckle in his voice at the cologne comment.

"Do you recognize anyone else?" Alec whispers in my ear. To anyone watching us, he'd look seductive.

I shake my head and lower my eyes. "Not yet. He was the only one. The others are all regular people who come here, but no one who has ever raised any kind of suspicion. Regular servers. Regular doms. Regular subs. None of the fakes are here. But they will be, I'm sure. They always are."

Alec twists my hair around his finger. "Slide closer to me. You need to act like you're into me. Not too close yet, but closer than you are."

I obey and inch closer to him as I had with DJ and Matt the night we met. "Sorry," I whisper.

"Don't be. I know this has to be uncomfortable for you."

I smile a little. "It is. But I want to help."

"We got this." He glances around the room as his thumb grazes my neck. He grimaces. "What the fuck are they doing?" He raises an eyebrow.

I follow the direction he's looking and giggle. "That's dominance and submission."

"She's dressed as a fucking dog. Complete with a collar and tail."

I bite my lip and tilt my head. "There are a lot of different types of this. Some like leather and collars. Some like roleplay and dress up."

He grimaces. "She just barked." He looks down at me. "Is that the shit you like?"

I giggle and shake my head. "No. I'm not that type. There are extremes. I would consider that an extreme. Most submissives, like me and your sister, Dallas, are natural submissives. It's just…" I shrug a little. "It's who we are. We need the order a dominant brings to our lives to combat the chaos of our minds."

He tugs my hair softly and bends his head a little, so it looks like he's whispering in my ear. "You think Dallas is submissive? I think she's a fifteen-year-old brat."

I smile and scoot a little closer. I turn my head towards him and duck it slightly, so it looks like I'm whispering back to him. "A submissive knows her own kind. Dallas is…" I nibble my lip as I think of the right words.

Alec tangles his fingers in my hair and tugs. Not hard enough to hurt me, but enough to make me look up at him. The look he's giving me is powerful and dominant. If it were Matt or DJ, I'd have soaked my panties.

"Stop biting that lip." He dips his head so he really is whispering in my ear. "Matt warned me about that shit."

"Sorry, sir," I say immediately at his tone and release my lip.

"Good girl."

I blush and duck my head. "Um… Dallas… She's, well, definitely attracted to Josh."

Alec chuckles. "I can't even deny that. I think she'll grow out of it."

"Maybe, maybe not… But it still isn't going to change who she is. She's attracted to dominant men. I'd bet you all of the money I don't have that she keeps lists and is very ordered. And I'd bet she gets very bratty but ends up rather calm and almost peaceful for a while after a punishment of some sort. Like grounding. Or even spankings. I guess I don't know if your family does that."

He shakes his head with another chuckle. "Well, I don't. At least not with her. All of that is right, though. So, how do I deal with a submissive teenager?"

I smile softly. "Encourage her to be who she is. Don't tell her that her feelings or actions are stupid. Stick up for her if she can't find her voice. Give her boundaries. She'll push them for sure. But it will help her in the long run. And for the love of Loki, don't ever make her feel like a freak for doing her lists, or organizing her belongings more than once in a week. And don't let others either. I gave her my number so we could talk whenever she needs an ear." I pause and hesitate. I don't want to offend him. A lot of people would get upset if you suggest they speak to someone else about family.

"Go on," Alec says. I peek up at him and relax when I see him smile.

"I would also suggest you talk to Josh. Whether or not her crush disappears, he knows how to treat a submissive. To build them up. To help guide them. He's been helping me for years. He kept helping me even after we broke up. Whenever I was having a spiral of panic and anxiety that Luca couldn't bring me down from, Josh wouldn't hesitate to fly in from Chicago. I don't know what I would have done without him. He's my best friend. Even if he is a butthead for knocking me into the pool."

"Brat," Josh growls. But I can hear the teasing tone behind the words. "Stop telling Alec shit that he'll kill me for. There's nothing between me and Dallas. She's far too young. And not legal."

"Doesn't mean you can't be friends," I counter.

"Stop it. Fucking matchmaker. Get back to work," Josh commands. Alec laughs.

"So, tell me about you and Mariah. Mariah said it would be a good conversation for us while we're here."

He grins. "Mariah. Well, long story short, we were expanding our territory a bit. It was before we were totally legal. So, we were running drugs and shit. She lived in Duluth, Minnesota, at that time. We wanted to stake our claim there. There's a huge shipping industry in Duluth. It helped us expand our business quite a lot. Anyway, I was up there. I was at a bar near the docks. Pretty nice place, but I could tell it was a place where shit went down at night. Tourist attractions galore by day. Not a good place to hang out at night."

I wrinkle my nose. "We have places like that here."

"I think everywhere does. I met Mariah that night. I was drunk off my ass. I was just about to climb on my bike when I heard crying behind some bushes." He tangles his fingers in my hair and grimaces. "I may not be one of the super good guys, but I have my morals, and I'd never leave anyone in distress. To her credit, she was trying to be strong. She'd left her husband that night. Dropped divorce papers on him and walked away. He was an abusive motherfucker. Emotional and mental. Really fucked her up. She'd planned on grabbing something to eat and driving anywhere other than Duluth. But she realized that she didn't have anyone. She had nothing. Very little money. And her car had an engine issue. She didn't know it, but a field mouse had gotten in there. When she turned over the ignition, the mouse blew up."

"Eew."

"Yeah. Not pretty. It was also cold. So, she thought she was going to have to go back. She had nowhere to go. Nothing. And her car was broken down. She didn't have the money to fix it. As soon as I saw her, though, that was it for me. I wanted to take care of her, but what was more? I wanted to show her that she's worth the effort it takes to pull off a relationship. She wasn't the type of girl who would let me take her back to a shitty cheap motel in downtown Duluth, though. And she didn't deserve that anyway. So, I got us both a room at one of the nicer hotels not far from where we were. I got her her own room. We talked a lot through the night. By the next day, we had a plan. We'd leave her car. I'd take her home to

Chicago with me. I'd help her reach all of her dreams and goals. And most of all, she wouldn't have to do it alone."

"She said she was a cop in Chicago for a little while."

He nods and smiles. He's still close to me and still speaking low. "It was a couple of years after I took her home, but she worked with the department for about a year after she was hired. She hated it. And she hated that there was a taskforce specifically set up to take me down. By that time, Mariah and I were dating. Pretty seriously. But things happened in our lives that made us both realize that while we'd always love each other, we weren't each other's perfect matches. She needed to spread her wings, and not be torn between protecting me from the cops she worked with. And I needed to know she was safe. She was recruited by Gainesville Police Department after a huge bust she was involved in. Gainesville begged for her smarts and assistance. They had no idea that the bust happened because I told her about it. All they knew was they had the type of problem she appeared to be good at handling. We were good friends at that time. I encouraged her to take the job. Gainesville and Chicago are worlds apart. Mariah took the chance. When things get out of control, she quietly calls me in to help."

"Are you still close?" I really hope they are. Mariah doesn't have many friends in her life. She has a very close circle. Just like I do.

"Very. Much like you and Josh, actually. We still talk all the time. Not just when she needs my help."

"I'm glad." I nod.

He grins. "She's just as much of a brat as you. I can see why you get along."

I can't help but laugh, but it dies on my lips. I sigh instead. "The whore from Whickamore Lane is here. Lock up your men, she's a come a prowlin'," I say in my best Southern accent. I smile at the dual groans I hear but say nothing.

"Well, that didn't take long," Alec says when he spots her coming towards us. I scoot closer to him until I'm plastered to his side. I'm attempting to show I'm staking my claim and hoping she keeps walking.

I'm not that lucky.

"Well, I've never seen you here before," she says in the fakest Southern belle accent I've ever heard in my life. I expect her to take out a paper fan and start fanning herself. "I'm Carmen. What's your name, sugar?"

Alec looks her up and down as he rubs up and down my arm. "Not sugar."

She doesn't take the hint. I knew she wouldn't. She never does. She giggles and sits down next to Alec, sliding as close to his other side as I am. He looks down at her with as much disdain as possible, but when she grabs his thigh, I'm pretty sure he might actually shove her off him. He surprises me when he doesn't, though.

"Do you often interject yourself into private conversations and plaster yourself to strange men?" he asks her with a raised eyebrow. He doesn't move or even flinch.

"Only the ones I like."

Even though I know he's here with me, I can't help but lower my eyes. I feel silly for feeling insecure next to her. But I've seen her play this game before. She doesn't care what the dominant's sexual orientation is. She just sits at the booth for quite a while before she's sent on her way.

Usually, the submissive of the dominant she's flirting with is the first to leave when she sees the dominant's attention has turned on to Carmen. They know right away that he is not their dominant. If he were, his attention wouldn't stray. It isn't long before someone better comes along for those submissives anyway.

I remember once I was at the bar with Kieran waiting for him to finish his shift. I had only just started coming to the club again, and I didn't want to be alone. I sat in the corner where I could observe without being spoken to much.

There was a male submissive sitting at a table with a dominant, and Carmen interjected herself. It wasn't long after she sat down that the male submissive got up and moved to the bar. Kieran and I watched in disbelief as the dominant pulled her into his lap and started making out with her. If security hadn't intervened when they did, they probably would have fucked right there. The dominant was banned from the club for false representation. I wish they would have banned Carmen that night, too.

The next time I came into the club, Kieran told me that Ashton, the male submissive, had actually found his dominant that night. They met while at the bar. I was happy to hear that. Josh might tease me about it, but

I do want to see everyone in a happy and healthy relationship. He says it's the sap in me.

Alec watches her for a moment before he reaches down and grabs her hand. He pushes it off his leg like she's nothing more than a fly. I can't help but bite my lip to keep myself from laughing. Judging by the look on her face, I don't think she's used to being rejected so quickly.

Alec, though, says nothing more to her. He turns to me. "It's time for you and me to get the hell out of here, pretty girl." He brushes his fingertips along my cheek and leans down. His lips brush my neck as he nudges me out of the booth. "There is way, way too much whorish desperation in the air. I came here for a beautiful, submissive woman. I lucked out and got the cream of the crop with you, baby. I'm done here."

I blush and look up at him through my lashes as I slide out of the booth. I wait for him to stand. He takes my hand, twining our fingers together, and I follow him submissively. I grip his arm with my other hand because I know it looks far more natural than him simply leading me out.

When we get into the elevator and turn, Carmen's arms are crossed over her chest. I can't even describe the look on her face as a pout. It's more a vicious glower coupled with a furious glare. She's shooting daggers at us.

As the doors close I notice something else that makes me step closer to Alec.

She's not the only one…

Chapter Ten

☆ Matt ☆

(Three Days Later)

"Thank you, Lieutenant. Thank you so much for getting justice for our little boy." Mrs. Hurley hugs me so tightly that I question where the tiny as hell woman gets her strength from.

I wrap my arms around her and hug her back. "You're very welcome. I'm just glad the school cooperated with us. That's not the case a lot of times when something like this happens. They know they're partially responsible and don't like it."

I feel her deflate a little as she lets out a breath. "It's so very sad that things like this are allowed to happen."

"Well, your lawsuit against the school should bring a lot of awareness to the situation." I pull away slightly when she looks up at me. "Thanks for waiting to file that until we were able to bring the bullies themselves to justice."

She gives me a watery smile. Her husband puts an arm around her and draws her close. He holds out a hand for me to shake. "I wish we had a way to arrest that useless principal," he grumbles.

I smile and shake his hand. "I think your lawsuit will definitely help. You know you have our full support. I'll give you all my case files if that's what it takes. I'm just sorry it took a month to arrest the little delinquents."

Mr. Hurley nods and drops my hand. "If you want my honest opinion, I'm just glad you were even able to arrest them. As soon as we found out who their parents were, I expected nothing more to be done. A lot of cops back down when powerful people are involved."

I shrug and grin. "I've never been one to back down from a fight. I'm a Marine, through and through. Mayor's kids or not. I promised your son I'd get justice for him. I wasn't going to quit until I did. I'm lucky Chief King isn't one of those higher-ups who bow down to the city. He's actually rather strict on the subject of bullying and abuse. His goddaughter was a victim of it. So, he gave us his full support. I didn't know him well, obviously, but your son was a good kid. Grant didn't deserve what happened to him. I hope he can rest a little easier now, though."

"His death will not have been for nothing," Mrs. Hurley vows. "I'll move mountains to have laws changed if that's what I need to do."

"I believe you will. And I'll happily stand by your side and help." I smile and wink at Mr. Hurley. "You've got quite the spitfire on your hands."

He laughs. "Don't I know it!" He smiles as he turns to leave my office. "Thank you Lieutenant. For everything."

"You're welcome." I close my office door behind them and let out a long breath before walking back to my desk to gather my notes.

It's just after nine in the morning. Almost one month ago to the day, I watched a bright, young fourteen-year-old kid jump to his death. It's one of many memories that haunt me. No cop likes when they have to go to a call dealing with kids in a crisis. For me, though, this one hit close to home. Way too close to home. It makes me thankful every single day that Beckett is okay and hasn't seen the kind of bullying at school that Grant did.

At least not that I know of.

I finish gathering my stuff and look up just as DJ opens the door. "Ready to go?" he asks.

"Yeah. I guess." I scrub my hands over my face.

"Thinking about Beckett?"

"Yeah." I shake my head. "No." I sigh. "Fuck. I don't know. All I know right now is I need to get to the high school and talk about bullying and the very real consequences it has. I'm not looking forward to it because I don't get to actually show the images from that day."

"Well, at least not all of them. You can still show some. I think the ones you chose for the presentation get the point across."

"That's just it, DJ. I want those kids to see Grant laid out on the sidewalk. All the blood. His brain matter splattered next to him. I want them to see all of that. And then the other part of me doesn't want anyone to ever see the horror we did that day."

"That doesn't even touch the legalities of the matter, Matt. You know showing images too gruesome without parental permission would result in you losing your shield, and the department getting sued."

I sigh again and run my fingers through my hair. "I know. Fuck, I know." I walk towards the door slowly. "The mood I'm in, though. It might just be worth it."

DJ chuckles and cups my face in his. He kisses me softly. "You have to take all of the positives out of this and do what you can to move forward. You got justice for him. The department is fully backing the Hurley's case. And you're about to deliver one fuck of a speech to both the school and the other kids who think bullying is cool and gives them some kind of power over others."

I smile and hug him. When he wraps his arms around me and hugs me back, I feel so much tension drain out of me. Suddenly, a lot of the strength I felt had been depleted returns. I let out a long breath and hug him tighter, savoring him for a few more moments.

I kiss his neck just before pulling away. "Thank you."

He pulls me closer and smiles. "Feel better?"

"Yeah. I do. Definitely."

"Good. Because I've been looking forward to my man putting the school and its bullies in place all damn morning." He leans in and kisses me, deepening it on a moan.

I smile as my cock stirs to life and pull away with a chuckle. "As much as I'd love to keep kissing you, we need to stop. We'll never make it to the high school in time if we don't."

He looks over my shoulder. "That desk looks pretty inviting."

I laugh. "That desk is probably sick of seeing us naked." I open the door he closed when he came in and push him out of my office.

"Nah. But I bet it's tired of our dicks slapping against it," he says quietly with a smirk.

I laugh harder as we walk to the garage where my truck is parked. After a few moments of driving, I sigh and look over at him. "I wonder how Beckett is going to take this."

DJ raises an eyebrow. "Matt, half of your speech was written by Beckett. You don't need to worry about that kid. He's got a good head on his shoulders."

I fall quiet again. I know DJ is right, but I toned back my speech so much because I was thinking of the sensitivity of these kids. Maybe I shouldn't have done that. Then again, I did have Beckett and Lyric look over my speech after DJ did. I haven't looked at the notes since then because I haven't had time, but I trust my family. I'm sure the speech is great. I'm not even sure I'll be using it much. I've always spoken from the heart.

This isn't the first time I've led an assembly at the high school. It wasn't that long ago we had a rash of parties and a lot of drinking. Some kids died because they drank far too much after being dared to do it by their friends. I'll never understand the thought process of teenagers. I have a great nephew, but even Beckett confuses me sometimes.

I pull into the high school and create my own parking place near the door. The sign that says loading zone only can go fuck itself. I jump out of my truck and grab my notes and laptop. DJ follows and chuckles when he sees where I decided to park.

I look at him with a raised eyebrow. "Pretty sure they ain't going to tow a cop."

DJ laughs. "I don't know, babe. I might have you towed just because of the blatant disregard for the sign."

I grin. "But you won't. Because I learned that shit from you."

"Do as I say. Not as I do."

"Lead by example," I counter.

He laughs. "Okay, okay. You got me." He opens the door to the school for me. "Ready?"

"Yeah, I'm ready. I wonder if everyone is seated."

"Doubtful. I'm sure the parents haven't even arrived, if they decided to show up at all."

"I still don't understand the assembly scheduled for the middle of the morning. Why not do it at night when parents are off work?"

"Because then we can't get them to consider it mandatory. It's voluntary. Doing it now ensures we get the kids to show up."

"That's not all of who the message is for, though. I want parents to understand that this shit is just as much their fault. Raise your fucking kids better."

DJ chuckles and rubs my back soothingly as we walk through the empty halls. "The fact that you care so much is part of what makes you such a good man."

I smile as we enter the main office to check in. After they give us our visitor passes, the secretary leads us to the auditorium. She shows me where to set up my laptop so that it projects over the large screen behind me for everyone to see.

Once I'm set up, she looks at me. "You know, I hope your speech is direct. Gruesome, even. I hope you're showing photos of Grant after he jumped." Her eyes fill with tears. "I hope you put the fear of God into those kids. The little shits deserve it. Barely a handful of them tried to help him. I did what I could. Gave him a place to hide in the administration office during breaks. I spoke with the principal. I called his parents. I called the bullies parents. I was the one who reported some of the bullying. At least what I knew about. But it wasn't enough. Give them hell. For Grant."

I glance at DJ. He raises an eyebrow. I clear my throat when I look back at her. "I can only go so far, Ms. Sanders. I'm already treading in a dark gray area."

She shakes her head, but doesn't break eye contact. "This stack gives you permission." She taps a pile of paperwork beside her.

I look down at the stack of papers she indicated sitting on the podium. "Permission slips?"

"Like I said. Give them hell."

I just look at her, dumbfounded. "You made parents sign permission slips?" I crack a half smile.

"Damn right. You have full reign, Lieutenant. And you can thank your pretty girlfriend for the idea."

"Hang on," DJ cuts in. "When did you talk to Lyric?"

Ms. Sanders smiles. "When you had her come to get Beckett when he was sick a couple of weeks ago. She stopped in my office and said it was something she'd been thinking about since you'd mentioned the assembly to her. She didn't go into details, but I got the sense that this was important to her. She said getting justice for these bullies was like getting a modicum of closure for what she went through back in the United Kingdom. So many don't get the justice they deserve. She said she wanted to make sure that Grant did. That it could have been her son, or the son of her heart. Beckett. And she wants to make damn sure that it never happens again. She was very passionate about it."

"She was bullied when she was a kid," I say quietly. I shake my head with a smile and look at DJ. "Leave it to her to make me even more fucking emotional."

DJ and I wait as each class is released for the assembly. I watch as students fill the seats, and am quite surprised when several parents walk into the auditorium as well. But it's when news crews start coming in and setting up cameras that I look at DJ with a little more nerves than I typically would feel.

DJ smiles encouragingly. "Don't worry about it. I'll cover you with Chief King, but I really don't think he'll be upset. He's just as pissed as us. Anyway. He can't really get too fucked up about this. We didn't call them in."

"Ladies and gentlemen," the principal of the school begins. I hadn't even seen her come in. "Thank you all for coming. I know you students didn't have a choice, but your parents did. I'm pleased to see so many of you here. As you all know, one of our students recently lost his life due to bullying. We've had a few assemblies regarding this issue, but we've never actually had a student who committed suicide because of how horrendous it was. I have spent countless hours with Grant's family. A lot of you have spent time with our guidance counselors. And just last night, Grant's bullies were arrested on a very strong case put together by the incredible officers at the Gainesville Police Department. Today, two of those officers are here. I'd like to introduce Lieutenant Matt Chance and Captain DJ Rens to you all. They'll be leading today's assembly. So, without further ado, Lieutenant? I hand them all over to you."

I stand from my chair and walk to the podium. My eyes immediately seek out Beckett. I smile when I see him sitting next to Lyric. Layne, friend, is beside him. Mariah is on the other side of Layne. Luca stands at their backs with a hand on each shoulder. Beckett gives me a small smile and nod of his head. Layne smiles encouragingly. A sign to give them all I have.

"I'm Lieutenant Matt Chance. Captain Rens will be running our slideshow today. I want to begin by saying something that is going to sound ridiculous. I'm going to get a lot of eyerolls. But bullying, like drugs, is bad." I give a teasing smile. "Let's get the eyerolls out of the way." I grin when several students do just that. "That's it? I only get about a quarter of everyone in the room to roll their eyes? You can do better than that."

"Dork," DJ chuckles from behind me.

I shoot him a wink after almost everyone gives me an eyeroll. I turn back to the people in front of me. "Okay. Time to get serious. We're here for one reason. Bullying. It's a huge problem. It's been growing over the years. How many of you in here have been bullied? And I include the adults in that question."

A few people raise their hands, Lyric being one of them. I wait a few moments as more and more hands go up. A couple of teachers and more parents raise their hands.

"Now I want you all to look around the room. Almost three quarters of the people in this room have been bullied, including several parents and a few teachers. Bullying is not something that just affects teenagers. It's something that is very wide-spread. It can happen in the workplace just as much as it does in the halls of this school. It can even happen in your own home. Now, how many of you have been bullies? And again, I'm including the adults in this question."

As I suspected, not a single hand goes up. No one wants to admit to being a bully. Especially not to a cop.

"Really? No one in this room has been a bully? I'll tell you what. I'll go first." I raise my hand and look at DJ.

He slowly raises his hand, keeping his eyes on Lyric for her reaction. "Where are you going with this, Matt?" he growls out of the corner of his mouth.

I say nothing. I just wait as more hands go up in the room, including Luca's. Lyric glances at Luca as he raises his hand. I catch the apologetic look he shoots her. She dips her head then looks back to us. Her eyes widen when she sees both our hands raised. She bites her lip and lowers her eyes. I watch as she takes a deep breath before looking back up at us.

Beckett furrows his brows and crosses his arms over his chest. Layne looks at him concerned. Neither of them know what I'm doing. Fuck. I don't either. I'm going by feel. And it's working. Several other students and parents raise their hands.

"That's better. Now, look around. Statistics show that one in every five people have been bullied. But those statistics just count those who have reported it. I'd say those numbers are a lot higher, considering what we just saw here. And as you also saw, bullies can be anyone. My story? I was a cocky as hell quarterback in high school. I didn't care about much of anything other than football and who was going to be my next conquest. It wasn't until the kid I was making do my homework came to school one day with bruises all over himself that I got to thinking about my own life. Here this kid took shit from me when he was getting his ass kicked at home on a nightly basis. In that moment, I made a decision. I made amends. Changed my life around. Became a cop to help kids like him. Now, I'm not saying everyone's story is like mine. I've seen it all. What I am saying is that we all need to start thinking of the consequences of our actions."

I take a deep breath and meet Lyric's eyes. They're shining with tears, and I hate myself for just telling this entire school something I've never told her. Even when she opened up to us and told us she'd been bullied. She never said who, but given the look I saw pass between her and her brother, I'd think he had something to do with it.

When she lowers her eyes, though, I know instinctively just how hurt she is.

But I battle on.

I grip the podium. "When I apologized, he confided in me that he had been contemplating killing himself that night. His dad was a drunk who beat on him and his mom. Then he came to school and had to deal with me and a lot of my friends. It wasn't just homework I was making him do. I did things like push him around. I knocked his books out of his hand. I berated him if he got me anything less than a B on my assignments. When he told me that, everything changed for me." I pause. "I could have been the one to cause him to take his life. His blood would have been on my hands."

I pause again and let my eyes roam across the faces of the students in the room. Seeing Lyric hug herself so hard, though, squeezes at my heart. She's destroying my soul. I glance at DJ, but he can't even look up at her.

Discreetly, he wipes his eye. He feels the exact same feelings from her that I do.

She feels hurt.

Blindsided.

Betrayed by the men she loves.

I look back out at the kids. "And that is where we find ourselves today." I glance towards the side of the stage. "Can I get the lights out please?" I pause while Ms. Sanders turns them down. I turn towards the screen. "A few weeks ago, Grant Hurley committed suicide." I glance down at my speech and see the entire thing has been completely rewritten. I chuckle and nod my head a little. "I had intended to make this whole thing a little easier for you all and not show you a lot of the things we saw. But I'm not going to do that."

DJ puts the first image up while I glance down again at my speech. There are a lot of gasps throughout the room. A few shocked sobs. A few muffled screams.

"This image is of Grant just after he jumped off the roof of his house. As you can see, he jumped headfirst." I look out at the faces in the auditorium. I can't see a lot of them in the dark, but I can imagine they all look as horrified as I was. "Grant told me a lot of things that had been going on while I was trying to talk him down. Things like how he'd been left in a locker overnight in the locker room after gym class. How our patrol officers couldn't get anyone to come to the school and unlock the doors to check for him after his mom told them that this has happened before. How when he was found by the police at almost three in the morning after they broke into the school, he'd soiled himself and wet himself. How humiliated he was. And how students somehow found out what happened and started calling him names like Poop Stain and Pissy Grant."

I look down at my hands, still gripping the podium, to compose myself. I swallow down the lump in my throat. After a couple of moments, I look back up.

"Grant told me he'd been beaten so severely, he wasn't able to attend class. Now, you might be asking yourself the same questions I was when he told me this. Were all of these things reported? Was anything done? The answers to both of those questions? Yes and no. Grant didn't want repercussions. He knew that if he said anything, things would be worse for him. So, he said nothing. He didn't tell anyone names. Not even his parents. Everyone knew he was being tormented, but no one was able to do anything. Even if they did report what happened, we couldn't get far because Grant wouldn't give up names. And the reasons for that? Well, it was because he had tried to tell someone. He told his favorite teacher. He was told that boys will be boys. Suck it up. It will stop eventually. Toughen up. And after telling him his story, Grant was beaten up again in retaliation. He was threatened. He was told that his parents would be murdered in a fire if he said another word. So, he didn't."

I pause a few more moments. I can hear people crying. I don't need to see her to know that Lyric is one of them.

"Grant took the beatings. He took the bullying. Until one day, he just couldn't." I gesture to the picture behind me as I finish my speech. The picture of Grant's brain matter and blood splattered all over the sidewalk. The picture I intentionally left on the screen the whole damn time. "Until one day, Grant couldn't take the torment anymore and ended it the only way he knew how. And as I stand here and look at that, I can't help but wonder. If I hadn't apologized to the kid I tormented, would his blood have been on my hands? Would this image you all see right now have been him?" I pause once more and gesture for the lights to come back up.

My heart clenches again when I see Lyric with her head in her hands and Beckett rubbing her back. Layne is kneeling on her other side. Luca has moved behind her.

But I soldier on.

"This is real. This actually happened. And it happened because two students decided to bully this kid until he felt like he had no other options. His blood is on their hands. And if I have anything to say about it, my case and my testimony will put them in prison for a long, long time. You guys, this shit is not okay. It's not. If this image doesn't affect you, then we have bigger problems. Come talk to me. I'll get you into a program that will scare the shit out of you. I also want you to know that if you or anyone you know is a part of bullying someone else, I will be coming for you. And if you are someone being bullied, come talk to me. I'll be your advocate. I'll get you justice. Grant was never able to see his killers, and yes, that's exactly what they are, he was never able to see them brought to justice for what happened to him. But I made him a promise that day. I told him that I would help him. I told him I would do all I could to help him. I did just that. And I'm here today to tell you all that this shit will not be tolerated. Not by the police. It should not be tolerated by teachers, parents, or any of you. Don't be afraid to speak up."

The entire auditorium erupts in whispers, which quickly turns into yelling. I glance at DJ. He raises an eyebrow and shrugs. We both watch the room, though I'm not sure what for. Maybe because we think someone is going to throw a punch.

But just as I'm about to say something to quiet everyone down, a soft but steely voice cuts through the chaos, silencing everyone instantly.

It's not the voice I was expecting in the slightest.

"Enough…!" Lyric's voice echoes through the room as she stands. She didn't even need to raise her voice, though she did. The tone is enough to send a chill down my spine. "None of you seem to grasp just how serious this is. A child is dead. Do you not comprehend that? *A. Child. Is. Dead.* I don't give a damn if you are a student, a parent, a teacher, or the principal. You are all responsible."

"Lyric?" DJ whispers as he catches her eye.

She takes a deep breath as her eyes trail over the students. "Most of you students stood by and did nothing. You laughed when he cried. Called him names. Joined in on the jeering, and made him suffer even more than he already was. All because you thought it was cool. You know who you are." More than a few heads lower when her gaze travels over the students. She turns her attention to the adults in the room, and her voice turns cold. "Parents who ignored when their children came to them with their concerns, hoping that they would be able to help. Only to be told to stop lying. To stop overreacting. That it was none of their business, and to stay out of it. Going by the reactions of a few students in the room, that is exactly what happened."

"She's not wrong," I whisper to DJ as I watch everyone. Some look very ashamed and guilty.

Her voice turns even icier as her glare focuses on the staff. "The teachers and faculty who turned a blind eye to the bullying. Because there is no way that none of you knew what was happening. I know that for a fact because I know someone in this room called the police and told people who worked. People who should have been able to help. Locked in lockers after gym class? I don't know how the hell you gym teachers wouldn't have known he was in those lockers. As far as I'm aware, the teachers always go around the building making sure windows and doors are closed or locked if necessary. And as teachers, you should never leave the building before *all* students have left. I know teachers didn't leave before all of us when I was in school."

Her gaze falls on the principal and turns glacier. "The principal. The one person who is supposed to always know what goes on in their school. You never followed up on any of the accusations of abuse. Never asked any questions as to why the GPD had been calling you back to the school on multiple occasions to help a student who had been locked in." She shakes her head in disgust, turning away from the principal to face the room. "None of you did a damn thing to make that boy's life any easier. And now you want to bitch and whine because you're being called to task about it? Grow the fuck up because that child will never have the chance to."

"Well, damn," DJ whispers, proudly.

I watch as she visibly calms herself before she continues. "Now, the students who stood by can't exactly be punished. But the teachers and faculty sure as hell can be. Even the principal. You all were negligent and abusive. Towards Grant. Towards any other student being bullied at this school. And after the show of hands earlier, we know Grant was and is not the only one. If I had my way, you all would be fired and under a criminal investigation for manslaughter because every single one of you led that poor child to his death. And I'd have you investigated for corruption." Her eyes trail over every adult here. "Because I would bet the little life savings that I have, that more than half of you have seen a hefty increase in your bank accounts."

Several eyes fall to the ground. A few shoot glares at her and cross their arms over their chest. The principal stares at Lyric with her hand over her mouth. Beckett and Layne look up at her like she's their hero. Fucking hell. She's my hero. I couldn't stop the pride radiating off me if I tried. Looking down at DJ, I know he agrees.

She's ours. That beautiful as hell Goddess is all ours.

But when she lowers her head and wipes her eyes as she turns and flees the auditorium with Luca hot on her heels, my heart drops once more. My stomach clenches. My chest tightens. The entire room is silent, but I can hear the roaring of my heartbeat in my ears.

She might not be ours anymore.

After what she just found out about us, we may have just lost her.

And fuck if my heart doesn't shatter at that thought.

Chapter Eleven

☆ DJ ☆

I prop my head up on my hand as I lay on my side in our bed after our shower and rub Matt's back. I've been waiting for my strong Marine to lose it like this for quite a while now. It's been almost a month since Grant's suicide and since we met Lyric that very night. Over the month, Matt has made a lot of arrests and solved several cases, but he's worked tirelessly on two things.

The first is Grant's case. Matt and I both have insomnia, mostly stemming from our time in the military, but Matt has gotten far less sleep than he usually does. He told me over and over again that he wasn't going to rest until that kid got the justice he deserved.

And he did just that.

The second is our relationship with Lyric. It's been both the easiest and the hardest thing we've ever done, but I think it's been even more difficult for Matt. He takes everything on his shoulders. All the stress. All the chaos. Even though he knows I'm here for him, and that I'll shoulder just as much as he does, he never allows it. He constantly tells me that I deal with enough.

So, when it comes to our relationship with each other and with our girl, Matt puts it all on his back. Even if things are going just fine, he stresses himself out by making sure it stays that way. He knows he doesn't have to, but he does it anyway.

"When are you going to learn you're not the only person in this relationship? This isn't all on you, Matt. I kept that part of myself away from her, too."

"Don't lecture me right now," he mumbles into his pillow. "I'm doing it enough for both of us."

I slap his naked ass. Hard. He looks at me with a low growl and glares. I raise an eyebrow and growl in return. "Do I have your attention?"

He sighs. "Fine. Yes. You got my attention."

"Good. Because you're doing it again. That same bullshit we've talked about countless times over the years. That thing where something happens, and you take it all on yourself. The blame. The stress. Literally everything."

He turns over and lays on his back. He links his fingers behind his head and stares up at the ceiling. His shirtless torso ripples with perfectly cut ridges I've run my tongue over many times. The small patch of hair that disappears underneath the blanket he's pulled up to his waist leads to his long, thick cock that's filled my mouth and ass more times than I can count.

Matt is irresistible to me. Hell, he's irresistible to many. Men and women flock to him. He's so easygoing and naturally gorgeous. I can't really blame them. I'm just glad I get to call him mine. All mine.

But it's the heavy emotion swarming in his eyes that shreds my heart. I'm just as upset about what happened at that assembly as he is. I watched Lyric's eyes as he talked. I couldn't take my eyes off her. She texted me not long ago and asked me to explain what my story was. She had heard Matt's. Now it was my turn. I told her because I'd never intended to keep that from her. It's not that I didn't want to tell her. I just didn't think it was important. It was in the past. I'm not the same person. Neither is Matt. We both moved on from that part of our lives and atoned for our sins.

We didn't think it mattered, but now I know that it matters to Lyric. She told us she'd been bullied severely in school. She said she'd been pushed down stairs. Shoved against lockers. She's had her shoes stolen before lessons started. Her books and homework were violently slapped out of her hands. She'd been beaten up. Kicked. Hit. Taken advantage of. She even told us about the sick bet she was a target of that a boy in her year had been a part of. She never said what Luca's role in all of that was. I'll ask one day, but not today. Today is about fixing this.

All of it.

Starting with Matt.

"The way she looked at us, DJ. I can't get that hurt out of my head. The betrayal. I knew right then that, even though I didn't mean to, I lied to her by omission." He looks at me. "We both did. We blindsided her. Unintentionally, but it destroyed her. We did the one thing we promised her we'd never do to her. What kind of fucking partners are we?"

"Matt, come on. Mistakes happen. You're being too hard on yourself. Was it wrong for us to not say anything? Yes. It was. But neither of us thought about it. I know I didn't. I was too busy focusing on her and her story. I was too busy comforting her as she spoke about one of the most painful things she'd ever gone through. I wasn't thinking past making sure she was okay. And I know you. I know you weren't either."

He closes his eyes tight when the tears shining there threaten to fall. "And look where it got us? She's gone."

I shake my head and let my hand trail up his rock hard stomach to his steel chest before cupping his cheek. I turn his face towards me with a stern, dominant look. "Matt. Look at me. Now." I wait for his eyes to open before running my thumb under his eyes to wipe the tears away. "She's not gone. She needs time. Time to think. Process. Do I want to be with her? Fuck yes. But she has Luca. She has Mariah. She has Josh." I ignore his low growl. "Stop it. She's not alone. And if you want me to be totally honest with you, she needs to get her head in the game. Unless she tells us she's not going to Sapphire's tonight to help us finish this shit, which won't happen. I know her. But unless she says she's not going, she has to get her mind right and focused on tonight. Give her time, Matt. She's meant for us. And you know damn well, we're not letting her go without a fight."

"I never should have let this happen, DJ."

I raise an eyebrow again. "You? I'll give you one chance to fix that since I love you."

He smiles a little. "Fine. We. We fucked up."

"Yep. I'll give you that. Do you think maybe it's time for you to get out of your head and get back into this case tonight? It's been a couple of days. Time for people to wonder where she is. We need to keep Lyric safe out there. Even if she isn't talking to us."

He chuckles sadly and looks at his watch. "We still have time for me to wallow in self-pity and doubt."

I shift and straddle him. I lay down, pinning him underneath me with hands on either side of his head. Heat pools low in my stomach and matches the intensity in his eyes. I lean down and kiss him. It's slow at first, but it quickly deepens, becoming hungry and fierce.

I spear his short hair with my fingers and grind down into him when he pushes up into me. His tongue fights me for dominance, but I know him. He doesn't need the control. He needs to let it the fuck go and feel.

His arms wrap around me as he groans, gripping my ass. I tug his hair when he squeezes. I deepen the kiss, nipping at his tongue and sucking. The groan I get makes me grin. I nip his lip as I pull back slowly. His eyes darken with lust.

"You need to get your head in the game," I say. I lean down and nip his jaw before kissing down to his neck. I let my teeth scrape across it and grind my hardening cock against his. I grin again at his groan.

I slide my hand down his ribcage and lick his neck. When I reach his hip, I dig my fingers into the flesh of his muscular ass and pull him closer to me. Skin to skin, I feel Matt relax more and more. He comes back to himself inch by inch. His breath, warm against my neck, comes out smoother. His lips against my neck feel less hesitant. His body slowly starts to come to life underneath me.

"DJ...," Matt whimpers against my shoulder. He shivers and jerks slightly. "Fuck. I need you..."

I kiss down his collarbone to his smooth chest. I stop at his already pebbled nipples and flick my tongue over them with a low, possessive moan. His cock twitches against my stomach while he watches me. I nip them before kissing down his abs to his throbbing, and very tasty, hard as steel dick.

I fist his length and look up at him. "I'm going to get you out of your damn head if it's the last thing I do." With no warning, I take him in my mouth and suck. Hard.

Matt arches into me. "Holy Christ, DJ!" He tangles his fingers in my hair and tugs.

I grip his hips and hold him down as I bob my head up and down his length. I lightly scrape my teeth along the vein running up his shaft and swirl my tongue around his already swollen tip. As I expected he would, Matt struggles a little against my grip, but I don't let him move.

I move my mouth off him with a hard suck and a pop that makes him jerk. "Grip the headboard."

"Fucking hell, DJ. Come on." He attempts to push my head back down.

I growl in warning. "Headboard. Or I'll stop."

He glares and slowly does as he's told. "You'd better make this worthwhile."

I raise an eyebrow. "Don't I always? Don't let go. No touching, or I'll stop."

"DJ…"

I watch as his arms tremble in anticipation. His stomach tightens. His dick jerks. I give him a long, slow lick. He lets his head fall back as his eyes slowly fall closed on a moan. I smile and reward him with another long lick that has him gripping the headboard tighter.

"There's what I was looking for," I rumble against his dick.

It causes him to jerk once more against me, but he keeps gripping the headboard and gives up control a little more. I reward him again by taking him in my mouth. I bob my head up and down fast, sucking hard.

"Shit… DJ, I'm gonna come." He trembles and clenches his stomach muscles. I hold him down against the bed, though, so he can't buck into me.

I pull off his dick with a last hard suck and nip his tip. "Not yet."

His eyes meet mine. He whimpers as I grin wickedly and shift to my knees. I grip his hips and tug him down as I lift just enough so the backs of his thighs are braced on mine. The head of my thick, throbbing cock meets his ass, but I don't give him what he wants.

Not yet.

I wait until he relaxes even more. Until the tension I see in his arms subsides. Until his stomach muscles unclench. Until his eyes, which are begging for release, burn with desire instead. But it's not until he closes those eyes that I finally give him what he wants.

Slowly, ever so teasingly, I push the head of my cock into him. He groans and damn near melts. A person looking in might think I haven't fucked him in years, or that it was our very first time. The truth is, this is how Matt loses his grip on the control and domination he strives for. Letting himself go here, in this bedroom, with me, is how Matt is able to just be. In here, there is nothing that he needs to control. Nothing that he needs to concern himself with. He can trust that I have him. That everything he's struggling with can be released.

Matt lets out a breath. It's one more sign that he's finally allowing me to catch him as he falls. So, I push in further and further until I'm so deep inside him that I don't know where I end and he begins. Matt sinks deeper and deeper into the state of bliss I'm leading him towards.

I lean down and kiss him lovingly as I thrust into him slowly. He clenches around me and meets my thrusts. His tongue hits mine and tangles with it in a seductive dance that I lead. I reach down and grip his hip, pulling him into me. I move harder and faster but continue the deep thrusts he needs from me.

"DJ...," he moans into my mouth. "Please... I need to touch you..."

I smile against his lips. "Let go."

He lets go of the headboard. His hands fly to my back. He holds me close and tight, arching into me. He slides a hand down to grip my ass as he wraps his legs tighter around my waist. I kiss down his jaw to his neck once more, holding him just as closely and tightly.

I don't speed up the pace, though. Another thing I've learned about Matt over the years is that, while he'd never admit it, he loves when I make love to him. Slow and deep. This pace. Right here. So, I give him what he needs. I strip away the control with each thrust until Matt's soul is laid bare beneath me.

Matt writhes and clenches around my dick. "Oh, fuck...," he moans. "God, yes, DJ! Fuck, baby, yes!"

I crush my mouth to his again and thrust hard and deep while upping my pace just a little more. I roll my hips and slam into him again and again until he's squeezing my dick so tightly I know I won't be able to hold out much longer.

"Christ, baby," I rumble against his throat as I kiss it. I shift back to my knees and plunge into him as deeply as I can. I grip his dick and stroke it to the same rhythm of my thrusts.

"DJ, fuck... I need to come, baby. Please." He looks up at me as he scrambles to grip anything he can. He meets my thrusts and moans with grunts of his own. When he whimpers and whines, I know he's reaching his breaking point. His hands finally settle on holding onto my thighs. "I can't... Fuck! Baby, please! I can't hold on!"

I smile wickedly and continue pounding into his ass. I roll my hips against him again and again while I stroke his thickening cock fast. I squeeze it with the perfect amount of pressure and watch him as I rotate my wrist.

"You're still refusing to give up that last shred of control, baby. Give it up. Let go. Give me what I want. Come. Now."

"Fuck!" He thrashes underneath me. He tightens so much, I have no chance of moving.

So, I don't. I bury myself deep in his ass, rolling my hips. I jerk my dick inside him as I stroke his cock even faster. "Let go, Matt. Give me what I want. You're not coming when I do. You're going to come when I want you to. Which is now."

"Fuck, baby! I'm gonna come!"

I feel the exact moment he finally lets the control completely go. His body, which had been holding on, waiting for me to come, untenses even as his ass clenches tighter around my dick. He comes hard. He pulses around me with each spurt of come that lands on his stomach and chest.

I pump his dick through his release and come just as hard, deep inside him. "Fuck, Matt..." My hips jerk against his while he moans.

"DJ... Holy Christ, baby." He collapses against the bed while my dick pulses inside him.

"Fuck...," I moan. I let my head fall back as I slowly stop stroking him. My hand is covered in his come. So is he. "Fuck me, baby." I pull out slowly and fall next to him while we both pant heavily as we come down.

"I'll admit it. I needed that."

I chuckle. "If you think I didn't know that, you haven't learned anything."

He laughs as he sits up. "We should clean up quickly and get going. We might end up being late."

I look at the clock on the nightstand and groan. "I'm not looking forward to this. Seeing Lyric is going to cut me wide open."

"I just hope she'll talk to us. That she's had enough time."

"Me too."

I follow him to the bathroom and quickly clean up. We get dressed and grab our gear on the way to my car. I can sense Matt feels far less tense and stressed. At least he can think past the pain we caused our girl, but I can't. All I can see right now is Lyric's face and how hurt she was to find out something about the men she loves that we had every opportunity to tell her but didn't. She has to feel like her trust in us was misplaced.

I only hope we can earn it back because we've both worked hard over the month we've been with her to gain it. I'd never go so far as to say everything in our relationship was perfect because it wasn't. Yes, we knew quickly that she belongs with us. We know damn well we love her and she does us. But that doesn't mean our relationship doesn't take work and balance. We're all still trying to figure out the dynamic of our new relationship. It might not have been perfect, but it was close.

I park my car in a private parking garage owned by Ryan's brother and get out of my car. Matt follows. We walk the half block to the van Ryan has set up with surveillance located out of sight of the club but close enough that we can be right in the thick of things if we need to be. I knock on the door.

It opens moments later to a very angry looking Josh. "You're late."

I raise an eyebrow, then narrow them. "We're three minutes early."

"Get the fuck in here. She just got to the club and is already seated." Josh slides back to his place.

Matt glances at Ryan. "What did I miss?"

"Something about you both being muted so you can hear what's going on but can't speak to her." Ryan holds up his hands when we both snap our glares to Josh. "It's out of my hands."

We climb into the van and take our seats. Josh hands us earpieces but keeps his eyes glued to the screen in front of us. Robby gives us both a small shrug nodding towards his controls. I can very clearly see we're both muted.

"Does this have to do with the assembly?" My heart feels like it's being squeezed by a python. "Because she hasn't returned texts or calls. We texted after the assembly and apologized. We called and apologized.

Other than her text today asking me for my story, and then the thank you I received after I told her, we haven't heard anything. We know she'll respond when she's ready. We wanted to give her the space she needed to get in the right mind frame for tonight."

Josh gives Robby a look. He quickly mutes him. Josh sighs and scrubs a hand down his face. "Yes. It does have to do with the assembly. Lyric is struggling right now and asked me to keep her focused. When she told me what happened, I wanted to pull you both. She begged me to allow you both to be here and listen, but she asked me to keep you muted. I already had to quiet the chaos of her mind more times than I can tell you since that assembly. She needs to focus. She can't do that if she hears you both."

Every possessive fiber in my being is very suddenly rising to the surface. I know Matt is feeling the same way because he suddenly coils like he's about to strike. I put a hand on his thigh and shake my head. I tamp down both my anger and hurt while soothingly rubbing his thigh. Matt just shoots Josh a vicious glare.

"If that's what she needs, we'll do whatever it takes," I say to Matt. "At least she still wants us near her. That has to count for something."

"You both fucked up." Josh levels us both with a stare. "But it's fixable. She just needs time to think. You may not be happy with me helping her the way I know you both want to, but I will do whatever she needs me to. Nothing fucking sexual about it, since I know that's where your minds just went."

"This coming from the guy who dated her for how long?" Matt asks with raised eyebrows.

Josh just glares for a moment. "I know you're hurting as much as she is right now, so I'll let that go. That has nothing to do with this. I helped her because she needed me. And if you had just told her in the first place, it wouldn't have been necessary. You kept it from her, even after she opened up to you. A mistake on your part, but it still hurt and blindsided her."

As if ending the conversation completely, Josh nods to Robby, who unmutes him. I scrub a hand down my face and lean back in my chair. Matt takes quite a while longer, but he finally relents when I shoot him a look. I'm grateful he reads it correctly and leans back in his chair.

It doesn't matter if it was Josh who helped her when we couldn't. He knows there is nothing more than friendship between them, regardless of their past. And with everything they have been through together, I'm not surprised that he didn't hesitate to help when she needed it most. All I care about is that she's okay. And despite his frustration, I know Matt does, too.

We both focus on the screen. Seeing how sad she looks brings tears to my eyes, but I fight them off because I know she needs this. I know our girl. I know she needs to think everything through and process it. I know she understands us not telling her about our pasts wasn't us trying to hide it from her, but I also know her mind.

She's fighting with herself right now. The logical part of her is telling her over and over again that it was in the past. That we didn't intend to hurt her. That we love her. That she's safe with us. But that other part of her is scared. She found out that the two men she's fallen so deeply for were bullies. Were just like those who tormented her. She's fighting the part saying to fight for her love for us and the other part saying to run. Run fast and far.

"You look like you've seen better days. Mind if I take a seat?" Luke Massena asks her as he walks up to the table. She nods. He takes a seat.

"You look like you're about to cry, honey," Josh says. "You need to take a deep breath and focus on the task at hand. One step at a time. We talked about this."

Lyric sniffles and nods. She tries to smile, but it fails. She looks down. "What if it was all a prank? What if they're just like those boys when I was in school? What if they just wanted to get in my pants, and then toss me aside? What if I was a target for them?"

"Shit…," I whisper. I grip Matt's arm when he tries to get up. I look directly at Josh. "You need to tell her that's not true."

He holds up a hand and shoots me a withering glare, but I don't back down for a second. "Lyric, honey, you know that's not true," he says.

Luke reaches up and takes her earpiece out of her ear, but I can still hear her through him. She lets out a small squeak of surprise. Robby shuts her audio off when he gets feedback. Josh growls in warning. Ryan puts a hand on his arm and shakes his head.

"Lyric," Luke says quietly as he leans into her. "I'm not going to pretend like I know everything about what's going on. Josh only gave us the basics when he told us about the mics being muted." He pushes her hair behind her ear. "But I can tell you that I don't think for a second that everything was just an act. I don't know what you went through. I don't know you that well, but I do know love when I see it. Those two love the hell out of you. And I know damn well you feel the same way for them. There's no way they'd do something so stupid as toss you aside. Was it idiotic of them to omit a part of their past like that and blindside you with it? Fuck yes, it was. But I do not for a second think it was intentional."

She sniffles and looks up at him. "You don't?"

"No." He shakes his head. "I think you're far too pretty and way too sweet to think that men wouldn't be drooling over you. And I think you're way too smart to ever believe something as silly as them targeting you only to hurt you. It's been what? A month? And in that month, they've done all they can to show you how much they love you." He lowers his voice. "They didn't know about Josh at the time or that you knew Ryan. The girl's may kick his ass if he keeps telling them they can't fly down right now. You know how much the girls care about you." He chuckles. I close my eyes when I hear her giggle almost silently. "Lyric, the point is, they approached the leader of a mafia to make sure you were safe. They listened to a friend when she said he could help. All they knew was that their girl would be in danger, and they wanted to do everything in their power to keep you safe. Ryan was the result of that decision. And they did it because they love you."

"Luke, you have people watching you," Josh says quietly. "You need to make it look more like you're flirting and having a less serious conversation."

He leans his elbow on the table, shielding her from view slightly. He plays with her hair with his other hand, lightly tugging it. "I know you're hurting. I know you'll need time to think. But don't for one second think that they don't love and adore you. I've only known them for a short time. I can see how much they do. They look at you the way I look at Robby. They made a mistake. All men do. We're only human, after all. It won't be the last mistake they make. Life is full of them. It's how we learn."

"I miss them," She says quietly as she nods and sniffles, but she plays her part well. She leans into him and turns her head like she's interested in him. He subtly puts her earpiece back in her ear when he starts playing with her hair again. I watch as she wipes her eyes and straightens. I smile. There she is. Our brave, beautiful girl. "Land-ho!" Lyric whispers. "The hoe's a come to shore!"

Luke chuckles and drops his hand to Lyric's thigh. I let out an inadvertent low possessive growl at seeing another man's hand on my girl. It's Matt's turn to grab my arm, bringing me quickly down so I can focus on this being all an act.

"How has that girl not been banned by now, Cooper?" Ryan says, incredulously. "She's gotten more and more aggressive these past couple of nights."

"Because she hasn't technically done anything that goes against the rules of the club, Ryan." Cooper's deep baritone comes over the earpiece from his place in his office. "Until she does, my hands are tied."

Lyric sighs. "Here we go again."

"Luke has this, honey," Josh says. "Trust him. Focus on your assignment. You're trying to show everyone in that club that you're at the top of your game. Every dominant wants you. Everyone else wants to be you. I need you to be our strong little girl, Lyric. You can do this."

"You're just here snatching up all the hot men, aren't you? Yet, you can't seem to keep one," Carmen, the Chief's assistant, says snarkily. Even I can hear the viciousness behind the words. I don't need to see the glare she shoots her. Lyric bites her lip and looks down.

"Lyric," Josh says dominantly. "You need to get out of your head. She's saying shit to hurt you. Keep doing what you're doing because it's working for what we're trying to portray, but don't you dare let her words get to you. Or I'll take you over my knee before the night is over. You know better."

I let out a breath and give him a nod. He'll never know how grateful I am right now that he's spent enough time with her to know her like that. It doesn't take much for Lyric to think down on herself. Those words were enough to send her to her dark corner.

Luke doesn't flinch. He doesn't even look at Carmen when she sits down. He keeps his focus entirely on Lyric. He leans into her, tangling his fingers in her hair and shifting his body just enough so Carmen can see his hand on her upper thigh, incredibly close to a place I don't want anyone but me and Matt to touch. Luke leans in closer so his lips are just a breath away from Lyric's.

I chuckle. "He's really fucking good. If I didn't know he was gay, I'd be worried. Carmen looks like she's about to fucking explode."

"He's pushing her," Ryan says. "I told him if she shows up to really push her. See how far she'll go until she freaks out."

"Clever," Matt says. "I'm curious to know who she'll complain to tonight."

I smile. Last night and the night before, Carmen glared after Lyric with her foot tapping on the floor and her arms folded over her chest. She watched the club a little bit before she got up and stormed to the bathroom. After a few moments, she went to both security and Lauren about how rude the guys with Lyric were to her. How they should be kicked out of the club.

We put Alec back into the club last night and had him visibly talking with another woman. Carmen has no idea the other woman was someone else we planted. We did the exact same thing with both Tyler and Gavin tonight. Both were with Lyric the past couple of nights. Carmen has shot them both pretty vicious glares. It's quite interesting, though, how she's focused on the guy Lyric is with and isn't going back to them.

Luke continues to ignore Carmen completely. His decision to say nothing to her and not even acknowledge her seems to be working like a charm because Carmen is visibly becoming more and more upset.

Carmen runs her hand down Luke's arm. "How about you let me show you what it's like to be with a real woman? I know how to satisfy a man like you."

Luke rumbles low and dips his head so his lips are against Lyric. "I know a really good restaurant down the street. They serve the best burgers I've ever eaten. How about you let me try to be that dominant you're looking for?"

Lyric smiles shyly and follows his lead. She leans her head on his shoulder, giving him more access to her neck. I groan a little when he kisses it, but tamp down the jealousy. I have no reason to be jealous. I know this is all an act. Even though she's upset with us, she'll always be ours.

As we watch her leave the club, I'm filled with a renewed determination. A sense of hope. We'll make this right. And we will come out the other side stronger than ever. I know we will.

I can't survive without her. We. We can't survive without her. She has woven herself so deeply into mine and Matt's heart that neither of us would ever be the same if she left us. We need her at this point more than we need air. We'll fight for her. We will show her how much we love her. We're not complete without her.

But, and it hurts my heart just even thinking about it. If she chose to walk away, she'd take our hearts with her. Because whether she realizes it or not, she is the only woman for us.

There will never be another.

Just her.

Our Lyric.

Chapter Twelve

⭐ Lyric ⭐

(Two Days Later)

"I'm sorry I took you away from your date night with Mariah," I whisper into my brother's chest as he hugs me.

Luca chuckles. "Date night can be any night and anywhere. You didn't take me away from anything. You needed me. You know I'm here for you. And if it wasn't for his meeting, you know Josh would be, too."

I sniffle and nod. I shift and draw my knees up to my chest on the couch we're sitting on in our apartment. Is it ours? I furrow my brows. Most of my things are still at home. Is it even my home anymore? I don't feel like I belong anywhere else. Home is where Matt and DJ are, but I haven't spoken to either of them since two days ago.

"I'm just struggling so hard with this. I mean, I told them about what happened to me. I didn't hold back. Why didn't they tell me what they did? Wouldn't that have been the perfect time?"

Luca sighs and puts his feet on the coffee table in front of us. "You know I feel like you're thinking far too much into this." He keeps his eyes forward. "People change, Lyric. They were dumb kids. They grew up. They're nothing like how they described themselves in high school."

I glance at him as I nibble my lip. "I guess." I rest my head on my knees, but I feel the exact moment he looks at me.

"Lyric, I changed, didn't I? I'm not the same person I was all those years ago. I did the same things that they did. Worse, because I let my friends do it to my sister. I stood back and let it happen. Did I get one hell of a wake-up call when I found out about Oscar's bet to get you to sleep with him and then dump you after you fell for him? Yes. Hell, I kicked his ass for it. But before that, I was the same as Matt and DJ. Matt told the whole assembly what his wake up call was. He saved that kid's life in a way. He turned himself around and made himself into the man he is today. I don't know DJ's story, but I would think it's something similar. You won't know that until you talk to them. If you don't, you're going to continue on the downward spiral you are now. The what-if's that are racing through that mind of yours. I don't want you to miss out on what could be the greatest love in your life because you're scared to take that leap with them."

"I just felt so blindsided by it. Is that wrong?"

He shakes his head. "No. It's not. I can see why you'd need to think things through. Josh told me about the last two nights. How you had him mute them so they couldn't talk to you. I understand why you did, but, Lyric, you can't avoid them forever. I don't want you to do that again when you go back tonight with Josh. As upset as you are, you focus better when you have them in your ear. You struggled more because you didn't have that connection with them. As safe as you felt with Josh in your earpiece and Luke with you in the club, and then Ryder last night, you would have felt more confident if you hadn't blocked that connection. While you knew they were there watching, you didn't have that... reassurance that you get when you hear their voices in your ear."

"I know," I say quietly.

"Have you asked anyone how they're doing?"

My eyes widen. "No..."

"You know they're hurting just as much as you are. They love you, Lyric. They look at you like I look at Mariah. Like Alex looks at Raleigh. You've told us so many times in the past that you want a love like theirs. Like ours. I don't think you realize that you could have that with them. I believe you already do. Not many people meet their person in life. You fall so hard and fast that it steals your breath away the first time you lock eyes with them. You told me that you felt an intense connection with them the moment you met. Doesn't that tell you that you have something worth fighting for?"

I chew my lip. "I know I need to talk to them," I whisper. "I really do love them."

"If you don't release that lip, I'll tell on you." He warns me before he continues. I release it immediately, not wanting a repeat of the last punishment Josh gave me for splitting my lip open. "Go get dressed, Lyric. And tell them. Talk to them. It's time. Your relationship is never going to work unless you all put in the effort. I won't let you keep this up. This can be avoided with a few simple words and actions."

I nod as I stand. I head to my room and quickly get dressed. The driver taking me to Sapphire's is going to be here soon, if he's not already. I slip on a pair of black shorts that I created from skinny jeans that I grew out of and a white tank top. I throw my hair up into a messy bun and grab my phone.

Mariah arrives just as I'm leaving. "Hey, beautiful girl." She smiles at me and fixes something with my hair. "Ready to head out?"

"Mmhmm." I try to smile, but it doesn't quite reach my lips.

"Oh, honey." Mariah hugs me. "Everything will be okay." She kisses my forehead. "I promise. Just talk to them, sweetie. Matt and DJ are truly some of the greatest men I know. And you know me. I don't say things like that easily."

I smile softly. "I know." I sigh as I turn for the door. "Have fun, you guys. Love you!" I close the door behind me and hurry down the hall to the elevator.

I didn't realize how late it has gotten. I need to be at the club soon. I don't doubt what I'm doing. I know it's the right thing. I wouldn't change my decision to do this. But I am getting tired. I'm tired of going and having the same thing happen each night. I get hit on. Carmen the Whore shows up. We leave.

I step out of the building and look for a black vehicle. One of them flashes its lights, the signal that it's one of Ryan's men. I hug myself and head for the vehicle. I quickly climb in the back and put my seatbelt on as I let out a breath.

"Your earpiece and camera, honey," Nick West says. I smile a little knowing Ryan has him to be my driver today to put me at ease. He and Josh have given me men in their teams that I'm most familiar with as drivers the last two nights. Last night it was Damon. I'm happy that tonight is one of Ryan's brothers.

I reach forward and take them. I quickly put the camera on. It's located somehow in the charm on a necklace. I don't know how, but that's what Robby told me. I put the earpiece in and take a deep breath as I close my eyes.

"You with us?" a deep voice in my ear asks me.

I smile softly. "I'm here," I say quietly. "I just got in the car."

"Good girl. Josh is already in the club. Alec and Tyler are heading in right now. Luke and Gavin found tables already. Just a heads up, Carmen is already there. It looks busy tonight."

"Yippee," I whine softly.

Ryan chuckles. "Don't worry about her. Josh will handle her."

I sniffle and nod. "Are… are they with you?"

Ryan pauses. He clears his throat. "They are. But I have orders to keep them muted."

I lean my head against the window. "Those w-were my orders," I whisper. "C-can I rescind them?"

He chuckles low. "Lyric, this is your show, sweetheart. Josh might think he can give me orders and make them stick. I'd listen for the most part, but essentially, the choice is yours, honey. If you want to unmute them, Robby can do that. I will say this, though. They're practically bouncing out of their seats with their prospect of getting to talk to you."

"I miss them…," I whisper as I sniffle again.

There's another pause before a voice that both fills the cracks in my heart and nearly makes me cry fills my ear. "Lyric?" Matt whispers.

I close my eyes against the tears. I feel the car slow to a stop after Ryan gives a quiet command. "Matt…"

"I'm so sorry, baby girl. When you were telling us what happened to you, the only thing on my mind was making sure you were okay and felt safe and protected."

"Loved," DJ says. "We were trying to make sure you felt the love you deserve. I didn't even think of saying anything about my past because all that mattered was you. I -"

"As much as I know you need to have this talk, now isn't the time," Ryan interrupts us quietly. "You need more time than we have for you to reconnect. Right now, Lyric needs to wipe her tears and straighten her spine like the warrior we know she is. She needs to focus. I had Nick pull over so she could have a few moments to compose herself."

I smile a little brighter. Just having Matt and DJ in my ear and helping me makes me feel so much better, even though I know we have a lot to discuss. Hearing their voices and their reasoning for keeping something like that from me, though, helps to ease my heart.

Nick starts driving once more. He looks in the rearview mirror at me. "Doing okay, honey?"

I nod. "Yeah. Just feel a little… apprehensive, I guess. When I stayed at Ryan's last night, I mentioned to him that I think something is going to go down soon."

He nods. "He pulled me and a few other guys in. You know I work with the Chicago Police Department, and I'm Ryan's and Josh's brother, but you don't know how far Ryan's reach is. You're family, Lyric. When he told me he thought your boyfriends could use a little backup from some trusted cops, since they have no idea who they can really trust and can't, I didn't hesitate. I'll be staying close tonight. Dane, Taylor, and Cole will also be here. We pulled in a few others who have worked with Ryan in the past. Most are from my team. Some are from Josh's."

"I… don't really know why…, but that makes me feel better." I say softly. I met Taylor around the same time I met Ryan and the rest of their family. I met Dane and Cole a little later. I know I can trust them to keep me and them safe.

"We're good, baby girl. You're safe," Matt says. "That's all DJ and I care about."

"Well, thanks. We love you, too, asshole." Alec's voice comes through with a sarcastic lilt.

I burst into giggles. Nick laughs. The earpieces erupt in laughs and quips.

"You can suck my dick, asshole." Matt shoots back in between laughs.

"Fuck no. That's mine." I subconsciously let out a possessive rumble, then squeak in embarrassment.

145

"Damn, little girl. I didn't think you had that in you." Damon, one of Josh's people, chuckles.

I never thought I would ever say it, but I am so grateful Matt and DJ brought Ryan into this. That Mariah has a connection to them. If I could go back and change my decision to do this, I wouldn't. It never occurred to me to reach out to Josh for his help. It should have, now that I've had time to think about it. He has never hesitated to come when I needed him. I know Ryan and the others feel the same. I got close with all of them when we were in Chicago during all the chaos. We've kept in touch since, but it's been nice to see them all, despite the circumstances.

Though, I may still hold Josh not telling me about being here for his merger over his head. Maybe Alex, too, since I know he knew. With everything else he told me about it, he never mentioned it would be in Gainesville, nor that it was Ryan he was merging companies with. Even though I spoke to him the night before. The fibbing fibbers who fib. All of them. Wives included. Raleigh, Alex's girlfriend, gets a free pass because I adore her.

I blush furiously. "That's it. I'm going home."

"As long as home is with us where you belong," DJ rumbles just as possessively as I had moments ago.

My heart beats a little faster and lightens a little more at the thought that he still wants me. "Yes, sir."

"Good girl," he says.

"Pulling up now," Nick says. He turns his head slightly. "Make sure you take out your phone. Act like you're clearing the ride. There's a lot of us here tonight. Ryan put a few more in the club because of how busy it is."

I nod as I get out of the car. I take out my phone and act like I'm clearing the ride as Nick drives away. When I enter, I nod to the hostess and give her a quiet smile. She's been here each of the past nights I have been. I'm pretty sure it's something Ryan and Josh set up. She quickly excuses herself from the people she's waiting on and guides me to the private elevator.

I take a breath when I step inside and the doors close behind me. "Promise after tonight we can talk about everything?"

"Baby, if we could do it right now, we would," DJ says. "But we can't. Ryan is right about that. So, yes. As soon as we get home, we'll talk about everything. You can ask us whatever you want. We'll answer you honestly. Neither of us ever intended to keep anything from you, beautiful. We didn't mean to blindside you like that. Neither of us even realized that we hadn't told you until the second we saw your reaction."

I blush and look down. "I know," I say softly.

As soon as the elevator doors open, my arms immediately wrap around myself. On any other night that was this busy, I'd tell Alice I wanted to leave. Kieran would lead me to the office where I'd stay until either Luca came to get me or he was done with his shift. On rare occasions, Uncle King would come and get me. But I can't do that this time.

So, with a deep, shaky breath, I step off the elevator and force myself to be strong. I immediately scope out as many people as I can who I recognize. Josh is back in a corner booth. Alec is with a girl near an empty table. Gavin is also with a girl on the other side of the club. Luke is sitting at the bar with a very shy girl I don't recognize sitting extremely close to him. Tyler is sitting near the kitchen with a girl. So is Ryder. They're all playing their roles well, but their eyes are all on me.

There are a couple of tables with a few guys dressed in business attire. To anyone else, they'd look like friends who want to hang out after work or something. To me, though, I know they're more people to help in case things go down. I truly feel like things are escalating, so I'm happy to see that Ryan has taken my concerns seriously.

I whimper almost silently when I see that more than a few of the doms I pointed out as dangerous are also here. Including that Will guy. I quickly look away before they notice my eyes on them and take it as an invitation. I don't need more trouble from them than I already feel.

"Shit, Lyric," Lauren says. "It got so busy in here that I had to make sure I saved you a table. I don't have any idea why everyone and their mothers are here. Don't worry about me." She flits her hand in the air. I love that she knows I'm already worried about her and everyone else. "Mr. Hayden spoke to me before my shift started. He told me to stay near Kieran at the bar whenever I can."

I say nothing, but I feel like I know exactly what's going on. Instincts are screaming at me that this is the night. Everything has escalated so much the past few days.

Lauren leads me to the only empty table I see in the entire club. The one near Alec. I give her a soft smile after her attempt to reassure me of her safety. She heads to the bar to grab me a strawberry lemonade. I love the way Kieran makes it.

Before she comes back, though, the hairs on the back of my neck stand straight up. I look up just as Will sits next to me. He doesn't say anything right away. He just watches me. I inhale sharply after forgetting completely to breathe.

"What are you doing here? I'm not stupid. I know you're with Rens and Chance. What the fuck are they planning?"

"Wh-what?" I try to keep from hyperventilating as I stare at him wide-eyed. I shy away with a whimper when he leans closer.

"Where are they tonight? Huh?"

"Fuck… What is he doing there? We didn't see him come in on the feed," DJ says.

"Tell him we're not together, baby," Matt cuts in.

I shiver at the threatening tone Will uses. "W-we're n-not t-together a-anym-more… N-not s-since a f-few d-days b-before t-the as-assembly at the h-high school." I take a deep breath to combat my stutter.

"Seriously? You're going to fake a fucking stutter? I know damn well you were together at the assembly. I saw you there, little bitch."

I sniffle and flinch at the name. "I-I w-went to s-support m-my b-brother and his girlfriend. I s-stayed by his side the w-whole t-time."

"Good girl, baby. Stay strong. Let him talk," DJ whispers. "You got this. We're all here. He won't hurt you."

"You're not a very good liar," he growls. "I know they put together some fucking taskforce, but no cop will tell me if they are or aren't on it."

I give him my best clueless, innocent look. "A w-what? I d-don't k-know what t-that is…"

He raises an eyebrow and laughs. "Bullshit. You think I didn't see you last month in a meeting with the Chief?"

"U-Uncle K-King…?" I tilt my head slightly, adding to my innocent look. "H-He helped m-me and my b-brother move here… He was my father's fr-friend. I gr-grew up around him. I v-visited him after I l-left my phone at h-his house when I s-stayed the night after b-babysitting. I've b-been to his office m-multiple times. H-he has me w-wait there if I n-need a ride h-home." I reach up and pull my hair over my shoulder as I subtly wipe my eyes. I lick my lip nervously.

"Good girl," Matt praises.

Will watches me, obviously deciding if I'm telling the truth or not. After a few moments, though, his eyes darken. He grabs my wrist and leans into me. "Fucking lying bitch. I've only seen you a couple times. I would have noticed if you were there more often.."

"I-I don't see w-why you would… I'm not exactly beautiful…," I say quietly, lowering my eyes as I try to pull away from him.

"Don't try pulling that shit on me. You know you're gorgeous." His grip tightens.

I look at him confused as I slowly stop trying to pull away. "What…? No, I'm not. I have never thought I was gorgeous…" I blink up at him as innocently as I can, trying to make it look like I'm thinking about his words.

He yanks on my wrist, pulling me towards him. I let out a startled yelp. The tears I had been faking start falling for real as he begins to pull me out of the booth. My heart is roaring in my ears. I try pulling away again, but he only tightens his grip more. I whimper softly. I feel like he's going to break my whole arm.

"Hasn't anyone ever told you not to touch a submissive without her permission?" Josh growls dangerously. "Any woman, for that matter."

He towers over Will as I squeak out sobs. I can hear scuffling over the earpiece as if someone is trying to hold Matt and DJ back. At least that's what I think it is if their snarls are anything to go by. And the angry growls and possessive grunts.

Josh grabs Will's wrist hard. "Let her go. Now."

Will growls and glares at him. "How about you go the fuck away? This doesn't concern you."

"She's a submissive woman in distress, if her fucking tears aren't proof enough. A submissive who very obviously doesn't want to go anywhere with you. Let her go, or I'll break your wrist in so many fucking places, the best doctors in the world will have no chance in hell of fixing it." As if to hammer his point home, he bends Will's wrist. His grip loosens enough on mine for me to pull it free. I cradle it against my chest as I fall back into the booth and away from him. "Now move your ass. Leave."

"I'm not going anywhere."

"Oh?" Josh bends his wrist even more until I hear a break that makes Will howl. I flinch and lean into Lauren as she appears next to me, pulling me gently up out of the booth and out of the way. Security runs over to see what's going on. Josh looks at them, still holding Will's wrist. "He attempted to force this girl to go with him. He was being very violent. Rough. Just look at her wrist. I can see the bruises already forming. He was terrifying her."

Security nods and helps Will off the floor as he cries and screams in pain. And it's then that I notice the chaos that has erupted in front of me. I haven't even caught my breath yet and already I'm hyperventilating again. It's like some kind of signal was sent to the men in the room.

Everyone is on their feet.

Women are screaming in fear.

Punches are thrown.

Lauren pulls me back towards the bar. I stumble into a table when I'm shoved aside. Lauren helps me back up and ushers me towards the bar faster. My earpiece must have fallen out because I don't hear anyone in my ear anymore. My hand shoots to my necklace and I breathe out in relief when I feel it still there.

Josh seems to be handling himself well. He's barking out commands to everyone on our team. They all move like a well-oiled machine. Some get the girls to safety behind the bar. Other's jump in to help Josh and those that are fighting. Several of the cops on my danger list are in the thick of the fight.

"Lyric? Lyric!" I hear Alec shout from across the room as he tries to find me in the chaos. "Lyric!" His voice is joined by Gavin and Luke's.

I yelp when I'm knocked away from Lauren and fall to the floor. I know I heard her cry out when she fell in the opposite direction. I scramble up and back out of the way as I look around, trying to find her. To find any semblance of safety in this chaos. I don't see her, but I do see someone who looks like her being dragged into the back near the bathrooms.

"Lyric? Lyric!" I hear my name called from multiple directions.

I don't pause to think about what I'm about to do. I don't even hesitate. I just react. I take a bottle from the bar and immediately chase after her, thinking of nothing other than saving her. I spot Kieran just as I take off from the safety of the bar.

"Lyric! Lyric, stop!" Kieran yells.

But I don't listen. I can't. Lauren's life depends on it. I know it.

"Kieran!" I hear Alec yell in response to his call. "Where is she?"

"She took off! I lost sight of her near the bar!" He yells back.

I pay no attention to them as I run towards where I think I saw Lauren being dragged. I keep the bottle tightly in my hand and ready to hit someone if I need to. I won't let anyone else be a victim. There have been far too many as it is. Lauren doesn't deserve this. No one deserves such a violent fate.

I turn the corner heading towards the bathroom but see no one. I slow down and look around. There's a set of stairs that lead down to the kitchen and outside to the alley. Instincts lead me towards them. I suck in a breath when I see Lauren laying still at the bottom. I can see a pool of blood forming by her head from here. I hurry down the stairs and drop to my knees beside her.

But I don't get even a second to see if she's okay. I can't scream because a hand is suddenly around my mouth. Something sharp is pressed against my throat. The cold of what I think is a blade pricks my skin. I wouldn't scream even if there wasn't a hand stopping me from doing so. I'm too terrified that knife is going to cut me if I don't do exactly as I'm told.

It's the overpowering stench, though, that turns my stomach. Too much rose scented perfume. There's only one person I know who wears that much of the disgusting fragrance.

But when I see the gold, wire-like bracelet that runs from her wrist to her elbow, my suspicions are confirmed.

"No…," I whimper.

"Finally. Finally, I'll be rid of you. Once and for all."

The woman I've suspected since I first laid eyes on her yanks me to my feet and starts pulling me out into the alley. I don't struggle in the slightest. My only prayer now is that someone on our team will see me. Follow me through the camera on the chain around my neck.

But if they don't, I hope I'll be able to see the faces of the men I love one last time…

Chapter Thirteen

☆ Matt ☆

When the doors to the elevator open, I'm not prepared for the chaos. Punches are being thrown. Girls are screaming. Property is being destroyed when someone is thrown into it. Tables are smashed. Shit behind the bar is shattered. Some of Ryan's men are ushering terrified women to the elevator and pushing them in as we're running out.

Despite all of the insanity around me, my mind is on one person. A woman I don't see. "Lyric!" I shout.

DJ is at my back and pulls me out of the way of a body Alec has shoved. Alec overpowers him easily, securing his wrists in a zip tie and shoving him into a chair against the wall.

"Lyric!" DJ yells.

"Wherever she is, it's dark," Lance, one of Josh's people, says over the earpiece. "Could she have been knocked out in the chaos?"

"No. We would have found her by now if she was." Josh comes over the earpiece as he shoves two grappling men face down onto a table. Two of his men quickly secure their wrists with zip ties. They yank them up and shove them into a booth out of the way.

"Where the hell is Robby? Is he tracking the camera?" I ask, frantically searching for my girl.

"I'm tracking it, Matt. Robby is our sniper. He's grabbing his gun. As soon as I find her, he'll be getting in position to take out the person who took her." Lance is calm. Too. Fucking. Calm.

The last I saw before me, DJ, and Ryan all ran up here was that Lyric saw Lauren at the bottom of a stairwell. We watched her rush down the steps and to her side. A stairwell that we don't know about because no one knows where it's located. Cooper isn't answering us, which means the earpiece he was wearing is either not working or fell out. And since I know he came rushing in when the brawl started, I'm leaning towards the latter. We know Lyric's fell out because we heard major feedback that nearly deafened us all when it was stepped on in all of this madness.

Before I know what's happening, Ryan and Josh's guys seem to have everyone under control. People are taken to the ground quickly and cuffed. It's not long before the only people standing are those on our side. But everyone cuffed is still yelling at someone else while we search desperately for Lyric.

Finally, I spot Cooper. "Hayden!" I bark. "Stairs! Where are they?"

"Back by the bathrooms!" he yells back.

DJ and I waste no time. Josh and Ryan are on our heels. I don't need to look to know Luke, Alec and Gavin follow behind them. We take off running towards the bathrooms near a back corner of the room. I see nothing around but doors, though. Doors to the bathrooms. Doors that have cleaning supplies behind them.

Finally, we find it. Between a door for staff to get to the kitchen area and a closet is a door that hides a staircase. We pound down the stairs, guns raised and ready.

At the bottom, Lauren is groaning and holding her stomach with one hand and head with another. "Holy, shit. Lauren!" I drop next to her. Her left eye is swollen. Her lip is bleeding. There's a gash on her head that's gushing blood.

My heart rate accelerates to a beyond healthy level. My head starts spinning. I need to help her, but I have to find Lyric. I reach for my shirt, but the bulletproof vest I have on over it makes it harder to take it off. I have to stop the bleeding somehow.

"Go!" Luke yells. "I've got her!" He drops to his knees next to me and tears the sleeve of his shirt. "Go!"

DJ pulls me up and drags me with him through the restaurant's kitchen and out the exit door. We both look around the alley, breathing hard. Ryan and Josh both appear next to us. We all stand next to each other trying to figure out which direction Lyric would have been taken. I can't fucking think.

"Give me fucking something, Lance," Josh growls. "Anything. What's around her?"

"A trash bin. Blue. It's dark. No streetlights. She was just shoved to the ground and kicked. Come on, Lyric. Turn over, sweetheart. Let me see where you are. Give me a look at the attacker."

"Dark. No streetlights," I mutter to myself. "No way anyone would chance crossing the street with someone that looks as terrified as Lyric would be. She wouldn't be able to hide that no matter if a fucking gun was to her head."

"Blue trash bin. Only place I know around here with blue trash bins is the Blue Stone," DJ says. "They matched them to their blue theme." He points down the alley. "That way."

"Wasn't that where the victims' bodies were found?" I hear Damon's voice come over the earpiece.

Josh curses in realization.

But I'm already running in the direction of Blue Stone. As soon as DJ said it, I remembered where the other bodies were found. My only hope now is that she's still alive. I can't imagine the killings would take long. Blue Stone is still a high traffic area.

I slow when I hear a scream. Purely cop instincts and training because my heart wants me to keep fucking running. To get to her as quickly as possible. I know that if I do that, though, I could do nothing more than get her killed.

So, I take a breath and allow my training to lead me. DJ falls into step next to me. We immediately start talking with hand gestures. I'm surprised Ryan and Josh understand them, but it shouldn't be something that shocks me, considering who they are and what they do.

"I have eyes on her," Robby says in a near whisper. "I don't have a shot. She's got Lyric with some kind of gold wire around her neck. She took it off her arm."

"The fuck? She? Who?" DJ whispers.

"That annoying chick. Carmen," Robby answers. "She's around the corner from where you are right now. Past the bins. Hurry up."

I swallow the lump in my throat and let Josh take the lead. DJ wipes his eyes. As much as I hate not being in control of this situation, we agreed that if anything went down, we would follow their commands. They're in charge. Josh counts us down from three, speaking quietly in the earpiece. When he tells us to go, we don't waste a second. Especially when we hear Lyric choking out a sob.

"Police! Let her go!" one of Ryan's guys commands. Taylor, I think. He's joined by seven other people. Some I've never met, but I'm happy as hell to have them with us.

I hear DJ let out a quiet breath. I swallow hard. Robby wasn't lying. Carmen is holding Lyric against her chest with something that looks a little bit like a long, gold chain, like a necklace, snaking across Lyric's neck. I don't even think my heart is beating anymore.

Lyric not being injured was wishful thinking on my part. I should have known better. Prepared for it. Because all I can focus on right now is the blinding rage that Lyric has been violated in any manner whatsoever. All I see is red. Blood red. When I get my hands on Carmen, I'm going to fucking kill her.

I can't hear anything but Lyric's terrified squeaks.

She's hyperventilating. It's not helping her at all.

The chain is wrapped tightly around her throat. The fingers on her right hand are caught under the wire, as if she's trying to stop it tightening around her neck. Each breath she takes has to be painful. And she's taking a lot of them as she claws at Carmen's hands.

Lyric is crying.

Begging with her eyes for someone, anyone, to help her.

Carmen laughs manically. "Are you joking? I work with the police. I know them all." She points to me and DJ. "You two are the only cops. So, who are the rest of these idiots?"

"Let her go, Carmen. Now," I growl low and dangerously.

"You think Gainesville is the only city with a Police Department? I knew she was a slut, but I didn't realize she was ignorant, too." Nick comments, snarkily. "You heard him. Let her go," he commands.

"What do you all see in her? Huh? What does she have that makes you all drawn to her? She's average looking. Practically obese. And as dull as a rubber."

"A personality," DJ growls. We all growl along with him when we see Lyric flinch and look down. She gives up fighting. "She's fucking beautiful, and so far from obese that the term used to describe her is comical."

"Don't you dare, Butterfly. Eyes up." Josh growls. "You know better than that." Her eyes snap back up at his tone. I see some fire return to them.

I raise an eyebrow slightly at the nickname, but let it go. I know how close they are. She hasn't told me everything that happened with Josh, but she told me what she could. I know she was there for him when he was going through some dark shit. I shake my head to clear it. None of that is important right now anyway. She is.

"Let her go, Carmen. You have no other choice," I say. "I have a sniper aiming at you right now. You're not getting out of this alive if you don't let her go."

"No shot, Matt," Robby whispers. "You have to get her to turn just a little bit to your left. Too much risk with Lyric otherwise."

My eyes flick slightly to my right. I don't know where Robby is, but he has to be to our right if he wants her to move to my left. Carmen laughs again. She tightens the chain around Lyric's neck.

I can't believe I didn't figure it out sooner. She's the only person I know who has a full arm bracelet that is thin and flexible enough to be repositioned and strong enough to strangle someone.

"You have all these guns pointed at me, but no one has taken a shot yet." She smirks at us. "I think I have all the choices in the world."

Lyric manages to get her other fingers underneath the chain. It won't last long, but at least she has some reprieve. She looks at me, then DJ. I expect to see fear, and I see that. I also see the love she has for us shining through. But what I'm not expecting to see is the regret. I don't know what she's about to do, but I have a feeling I'm not going to like it.

Her eyes move from DJ and I to Josh as she sniffles. "J-Josh…," she stutters. "'Member m-my l-last b-birthday… we w-watched that m-movie..? 'Member w-what I t-told y-you… i-if I w-was i-in t-that p-position…"

"Shoot the hostage...," Josh whispers.

"What?" I ask, stunned.

"That's not fucking happening," DJ growls.

"Josh...," Lyric whispers. "You p-pinkie p-promised...," She doesn't look back at us. She keeps her eyes on him.

I'm about to rip his throat out.

"No one is shooting anyone," Ryan growls. "Carmen, let her go. What the fuck is the point of this?"

Carmen's eyes snap to Ryan. She glares. "Because I'm sick of stupid girls getting all the attention from everyone in that club! Look at her!" She pushes Lyric slightly, but it gives Lyric the ability to slide her fingers under the wire more. It digs into her hands, though. I can see the blood. "She's bigger than me! Look at her! She's fat! She's ugly! She has nothing on me! Nothing! Yet she's gone home with so many guys, including the two of you! At the same time!" She pouts and stomps her foot like a child, glaring at me and DJ.

"So, you're killing women who get more fucks than you?" Taylor asks. "Come on. That's the stupidest shit I've ever fucking heard."

"Come on. Move a little more," Robby growls.

"J-Josh... you p-promised...," Lyric whispers.

She breaks my heart with each word. I know how much promises mean to her. Especially pinkie promises. To her, those are unbreakable. I could kill him for promising such a stupid fucking thing.

"They all didn't deserve them! No one did!" Carmen yells.

"So, Alice and all those other girls just lost their lives because guys thought they were more attractive and fuckable than you," Josh rumbles, sarcastically. "Makes so much sense."

She glares harder. "Alice? Please! You think she was a saint?" She practically cackles. "Who do you think brought this bitch to our attention? Most nights, after this whore left, she would complain about how fucking annoying she is. How pathetic she is. How she doesn't understand what men see in her. She's meek. She's fat. She's ugly. And fuck, did she hate that she was British. She's been working with us since we started this!"

Lyric sobs at that. "Please... S-stop...!"

"Don't listen to her, sweet girl. She's a fucking liar who is nothing more than a jealous little slut," I say dangerously.

Carmen laughs again and nods in our direction. "The night she went home with you two, Alice flipped her shit. She'd been trying to get your attention for years! Then, one glance at this whore, and it's like you were fucking enthralled! The threats she came out with that night were delightful. She came up with an entire plan to be rid of her for good!" She sighs mock sadly. "Unfortunately for her, none of what she wanted fit into our plans. So, alas, she had to go."

"So, you're working with Will," DJ says with a grin. "Man, am I going to have fun with him when I get his ass back to the station."

"He ain't getting as far as the station," Josh growls.

"Fuck that," Ryan says with a smirk at the same moment. "I think I'll take a crack at him first. I don't think he'll survive the night. But that's okay, because you aren't either, little bitch."

"J-Josh… Please…" Lyric pleads with him. I can see she's getting weaker. Her hands, while not gushing, are still bleeding pretty heavily. They have to sting. Her legs are trembling. The blood loss is getting to her.

"I still don't have a shot…," Robby's voice comes through the earpiece. "She's moved in the wrong direction. Any shot I take will be fatal to Lyric." He curses under his breath, annoyed at the lack of options. "I can't move from here. She'll see me."

"Please…," Lyric whispers as she looks at us. My heart is shattered right now.

I look at Josh in horror when I see him shift. He lowers his gun a fraction of an inch right before he shoots. Lyric screams as she falls. Carmen screams and shoves Lyric away from her in her haste to cover her ears as she ducks. My vision blackens as I fall to my knees.

"No!" It takes me a few moments to realize the screams I hear are coming from me. I refocus and see Lyric laying on her side. Her eyes are closed, but I don't see any blood.

Another shot rings out before I can process what happened. Carmen's head snaps back. She crumples to the ground. The shot spurs me to action. I crawl to Lyric's side because I'm far too weak and shaky to stand.

DJ runs to her and sinks to his knees next to her. "Lyric! Baby, talk to me. Lyric! Wake up!"

I'm trembling by the time I reach her. Like she was just a few minutes ago, I'm hyperventilating. DJ pulls Lyric into his arms. I wrap around her and him both because I can't do anything else. I feel like I just lost part of my soul. Like my heart has been ripped out of my ass and fed to a wolf.

"Shit, Lyric. Please wake up. Please," I whisper into her hair, nuzzling her like each of my touches will breathe new life into her.

"Fuck, baby. Come on," DJ whispers against her neck. "Please. Please, Lyric."

I don't know when I closed my eyes but when I open them, Josh is kneeling next to me. I narrow my eyes to slits. "Get the fuck away from her! Why would you promise her something like that? You know making a pinkie promise to her is like an oath to her!"

"Matt -"

But I cut him off. "You fucking shot her! You're crazy! Why would you do that?"

"Matt, listen to -" He reaches for her as I shove him backwards. He rocks back on his heels but doesn't fall.

"Stay away from her!" I yell, hugging her and DJ tighter when I feel DJ lose all control. He trembles as he loses the battle with the tears, burying his face in her hair.

"Stop... it... Please stop... fighting...," she whispers shakily against DJ's shoulder. My head snaps to her. DJ lets out a sob as he pulls away enough to look at her. "I hate when people fight..."

"Lyric?" I whisper.

"Fuck... Baby...," DJ cups her cheek. "Tell me I'm not dreaming."

I bury my own face in the other side of Lyric's neck and breathe her in. My eyes widen, remembering that she was just shot. I pull back and tug her back from DJ enough to look her over. DJ, seemingly having the same thought as me, does exactly the same thing.

"Where did the bullet hit, baby?" I ask. "I don't see any blood."

"Because I didn't shoot her, Matt. Fucking hell," Josh said. "I had other options. Robby is good, but he couldn't get a shot. I shot next to her. You can see where the bullet lodged in the wood behind where they were. And just to be clear, little girl," Josh taps a finger against her forehead with a smirk. I chuckle when she goes cross-eyed trying to follow it. Fuck, she's adorable. "I never promised to shoot you. I promised that I would do whatever it took to save you."

She sticks her tongue out at him playfully. "Same thing."

"You're such a brat." He chuckles, tapping her nose. She giggles and wriggles it. "Just wait until mom arrives. She'll pamper you to death." He chuckles again when her eyes widen. She squeaks. He kisses her head and rises. I watch as he makes his way to Ryan. I shake my head and return my attention to my girl.

"Jesus Christ, I am never letting you go." I hug her hard again.

"Never. Fucking ever, Lyric. Do you understand?" DJ hugs her as tightly as me.

"Yes, my heart," she whispers. She melts into us.

As a flurry of activity goes on around us, DJ and I sit on the ground holding Lyric between us. No one says anything. We just feel and allow relief to wash over us. The case has been solved. Justice has been served. Damage was caused that will need to be repaired. Looking over Lyric as we had, that damage is mostly emotional, but I'll take that over losing her any second of the day.

Almost losing her has made me more determined than ever to show both DJ and Lyric just how much they mean to me. How much I love them. This whole case has been a plague in our lives and now that it's over, I can finally see a bright light ahead for us.

I see our future.

Me. DJ. Lyric. Beckett.

Our family.

Chapter Fourteen

☆ DJ ☆

(One Year Later)

"How long do you think you'll be?" I ask Matt. I'm sitting in the garage in my car after just getting home. Matt just called and said he's stuck with some paperwork.

He sighs. "Couple hours? That SWAT call this morning fucked up my whole day. I'll bring home dinner, baby."

I look at my watch. "It's just that I know Lyric misses us both. She's been a little bored today. I expect to walk into the house and see it completely rearranged."

Matt chuckles. "It wouldn't be the first time. I'll grab something at Embers. I can call in our order now and have it ready when I get out of here."

"Yeah, that's fine. I'm game. Just make sure they don't fuck my steak up. When I say medium rare, I don't mean give me a well-done hockey puck. And for all that is holy, don't let them add spice to Lyric's order, or this time, I'll drive down there and let her tears speak for themselves."

"I got it, baby. Be home soon." He hangs up as I'm getting out of my car. I grab my gear and head inside the house.

I'm slightly confused when I don't see anyone in the living room or outside by the pool. I become baffled when there's no one in the den. So, I walk upstairs and put my gear away. I put my gun in its safe and glance around the room. No one is in it. Lyric isn't in the jacuzzi tub.

"Huh," I say to myself. I glance at her calendar on her small work desk. She has no appointments. She writes everything down, including when she plans to go for walks or bike rides with Beckett. I see nothing written for today.

So, I quickly clean up and change into shorts and a t-shirt. As I'm leaving our bedroom, I hear quiet voices coming from Beckett's room. I raise an eyebrow and quietly make my way to his bedroom. I smile and lean against the doorframe when I see Beckett and Lyric sitting on his bed with their backs to the door. They are deep in conversation. I cross my arms over my chest and watch them.

We've come a long way as a family over the past year since Sapphire's and almost losing Lyric. Carmen was killed by Robby as soon as Lyric was out of the way enough for him to get a shot off. I would have preferred an arrest, but I also don't feel bad for a second that Carmen was killed.

We had her brother, Will, anyway. He admitted to everything and told us even more that we didn't know. He wasn't directly involved in the murders at first, but he did help both Carmen and Alice get their victims to a quiet and dark place. Alice was involved that deeply. The murders typically happened quickly and with very little fuss because there were three of them and one victim.

The entire purpose was for Carmen to meet her soulmate while going through every powerful and dominant man in the city. Someone who would please her father while engaging in all of her sexual fantasies behind closed doors. She believed any other female who got in her way deserved to be removed from the equation. They were beneath her. Not even in her league.

Alice went along with her because she was sick and tired of getting the scraps, the men left over after they clamored for Lyric. The men who went for Lyric only went for Alice if they were turned down by Lyric. It pissed her off.

Her revenge on Lyric started after Luca broke up with her. She blamed Lyric. She humiliated her. Brought her down repeatedly. Lyric tolerated it all and believed every word she said because that's what everyone told her growing up. She thought she'd gotten through it, but the more Alice brought her down while pretending to be her friend only made Lyric believe the words more and more.

And she kept it to herself, mostly, because she didn't want to burden anyone. The only one who had any idea of the thoughts that would bombard her was Josh. And that's only because he spent their entire relationship building her up. Proving that those same words that Alice tried to bring her down with were not the foundation her life was built on. That she was and is worth so much more than what Alice made her believe.

After they ended their relationship, he was there to help bring her back from the edge whenever she needed it. We will forever be grateful to him for that. But now... now she has us to lean on. To hold her up when she feels overwhelmed or when those same thoughts try to break her down.

Will became involved because he was tired of women like Lyric turning him down. Despite what he had growled at her that night, he was telling the truth about not seeing her at Headquarters often. On the occasion that he did, she never acknowledged him whenever he tried to get her attention.

According to the Chief, he had made sure to keep her away from the majority of the cops we work with to protect her. I took a little offense at that, but I have to admit, Matt and I can be assholes at times. Though, Lyric has tamed us both. No matter how submissive she is, she doesn't take any of our shit.

It took us quite a while to get her to this point, though, and she still struggles. Sometimes, we catch her looking at herself in the mirror. We don't have to be inside her head to know where her thoughts go. She has a bad habit of picking herself apart.

She's not fat. Not in the slightest. She's rather petite. She's not a size zero and never will be. But she's far from fat and unhealthy. She has curves in all the right places, but those curves make her feel like she's too big.

It doesn't help that we found out Alice was fucking with her scales. She was adding pounds, so Lyric thought she weighed a lot more than she actually does. We discovered that the first time we had her use our scale. She was insistent that it was wrong because hers said something completely different. It wasn't until we had her bring it over so we could compare the two and show her it was wrong that we realized what had happened. Matt and I spend a lot of time showing her the scale we have is zeroed out, so when she steps on it, the weight that shows is accurate. She's starting to believe it.

She's also far from ugly. Carmen kept saying that to her, too. So did the people she grew up with. She has always been told she was plain. The truth is, she's far from that, too. She is truly beautiful. She has eyes a man could drown in. She has very kissable lips. Everything about her is natural. Perfect. No matter what she says or thinks, Lyric is incredible.

All of that is completely behind us now, though. Will is in prison for a very, very long time. Alice and Carmen are no longer a threat to anyone. Ryan and Josh and their entire group of allies and loved ones cleaned everything up nicely for DJ and I. We had no loose ends that we had to deal with. They took care of everything. All we had to deal with were all of the busts of the dirty cops and getting the witnesses to testify. It wasn't that difficult considering we were able to guarantee they'd be protected.

Josh's mom, Rebekkah, flew out to see Lyric. She lectured Josh when he told her there was no need for her to fly out. That Lyric was okay. She could easily use Skype to see her, but she wasn't having any of it. She stayed for a few days making sure Lyric had everything she needed. I had no complaints about her coming. Lyric was so happy to see her. She lit up when she arrived. Anyone could see that they have a special bond. Rebekkah headed back to Chicago after giving Matt and I her own version of a shovel talk. I'll admit that woman might be small, but she's terrifying.

Matt and I are getting used to Lyric's relationship with Josh. He's an incredible friend to her and has become one to us. No one needs to know that we've become close allies of his. It's the least we can do. He saved Lyric's life in more ways than one. He took care of her before she became ours. If I'm being honest, he inadvertently led her to us. If he hadn't paid her membership fees for Sapphire's, we may have never met her. I hate to think how different all of our lives would have been without her.

"Do you think I should tell him?" Beckett asks. "I don't want him to think we're too young. And I don't want to disappoint Matt and DJ. I mean, my dads. That's what they are."

I smile wider at Beckett including me in that statement. He's taken to calling both Matt and I dad since Matt got custody of him from his sister. It probably helped that she didn't put up even a little bit of a fight. She just told him she's happy to give him up and let him go to a home that can love him like she never could. Beckett was in the courtroom that day. He didn't cry a single tear. At least not until he got home. Then he laid with Lyric and bawled his eyes out while she comforted him.

"Well." She tilts her head. "I think it's something you need to talk about in any relationship. For us, it took a little while for me to be ready, but we had to have that conversation. You're still young. You have time. Things like this need to progress naturally."

"But how do I bring it up? What if he's not ready?"

"He might not be. You need to make sure that when you talk to him, he understands that nothing will change if he's not. I think that's what is most important. Even if you're ready, he needs to know that it's okay if he feels that he isn't. As for bringing it up… Beckett, honesty is always the best policy. There's never really a great time. If it's a burden on your heart and mind, though, you should never hide it or keep it in."

"You're right. I just don't want to scare him or make him feel uncomfortable," Beckett says quietly.

"You won't. Because all relationships need honesty to survive. Secrets in a relationship are a burden. They're like a ticking time bomb. They always have a way of coming out. It makes things so much harder when all that ever needs to be done is to be honest."

Beckett looks at her curiously. "Do you have any secrets from dads?"

"No… Maybe? Well, I wouldn't exactly call it a secret. It's just something I haven't spoken to them about yet. I did something that they aren't going to be happy about. But it was something I felt I needed to do."

I watch as she shifts a little, making herself more comfortable. I furrow my brows and straighten slightly. Something she needed to do? That has me curious. She usually tells us everything she does. If she didn't tell us this, it must be something that she doesn't think we'd agree with.

"What haven't you told them?" Beckett asks, quietly.

"Well, you remember when your dads told you everything that happened before I moved in?" She asks softly.

"I do. You were hurt."

"I was. Not as badly as I could have been, thanks in large part to your dads and everything they did to keep me safe." She takes a deep breath. "When it went to trial, a lot of questions were answered. The families of the women who were killed were able to get closure. To know that justice had been served. But for me? I still had questions. I didn't get the same closure they did. Sure, he was behind bars, and the two women involved were no longer around and able to hurt anyone else. But in my mind, I still needed answers."

Beckett listens intently. It always amazes me how much he adores her. "So, what did you do? What didn't you tell dads?"

"There was only one place I could get the answers I needed. So, I made a decision to go and visit Will in prison. To get those answers and settle my heart. I knew that your dads wouldn't be happy if I went alone, so I approached your Uncle Josh. I asked him to come with me. I felt like I needed to know why."

I chuckle when she mentions Uncle Josh. Beckett met him shortly after everything went down at Sapphire's. He took to him like a duck to water. Called him Uncle Josh and dragged him to his room to show off the new Bucs and Dolphins jerseys that Lyric bought him for his birthday. She even had them put his new name on the back of each of them. Josh and Lyric have taken him and Layne to a few of the Bucs and Dolphins football games when we couldn't get time off of work. We felt bad that we couldn't go, but we know they had fun. We've taken them to a few ourselves when we were able to.

He's also taken to Alec Cassidy, Mariah's ex and one of her best friends, his uncle as well. Alec has come down with Josh several times to take the kids to football games. They enjoy it just as much as the kids.

I shake my head and relax back against the wall. I want to be furious that she went to visit Will. That she didn't tell us first. But I can't be. She has the right to know why she was targeted. Why he went along with his sister and Alice's plans. I would have preferred that Matt and I went with her, but I feel better knowing that she didn't go alone. I look back up when I hear Beckett speak again.

"Did you find out? You don't have to tell me. But did you get what you needed?" Beckett asks. He's moved from facing her to beside her.

"I did. I won't keep it from you. We haven't kept any part of this away from you because you're old enough to understand." She takes a breath before continuing. "He told us that he believed he was in love with me. That he went along with it all because he wanted to practice how to rescue me when Alice decided to target me. He got angrier and angrier as time passed. I didn't acknowledge him when I visited Uncle King at the station. Or when I was at the club. He said that the night I went home with your dads is the night it all changed." She shakes her head. "He lost it. He stormed out of the club and met Carmen. He planned to join her and Alice, and help them kill their victim. But Carmen was already angry with Alice. He helped her kill Alice. From there, it was all their anger, jealousy, and rage. He hated that he was always passed over, and so did she."

"That's crazy." Beckett shakes his head.

"It is. And it didn't end there." She wraps an arm around him as they talk. "The first night of the taskforce is when he truly snapped. He saw me leave with Uncle Alec, and he couldn't believe it. He was sure I was with your dads, but if I wasn't, then why wouldn't I look in his direction? That night cemented it in his mind. If he couldn't have me, then no one could. He put all his effort into helping his sister target me. And as each night at the club passed, he got angrier and more possessive until it exploded the last night when I went in with Josh. He couldn't keep up the prince charming act. He became violently possessive." She runs her fingers through his hair. "And Josh defending me was like the signal for the fight to start. In that chaos, they were able to lead me away."

I growl a little under my breath, furious at what he told her. He really was fucked in the head to have thought any of that was rational. It was callous. Manipulative.

"I hate that they hurt you. You didn't deserve any of it. None of them did," Beckett says, passionately.

"You're right. We didn't. And he is going to have to live with his actions for the rest of his life. But us? We get to move on. We get to continue on with our lives. To be happy. To laugh. To love. Something that he will never be able to do. His actions cost him that. What we do now is on us. We get to live our lives the way we want to. To the fullest. Those that they would have targeted after me all get to live their lives as well."

I smile softly at that. She is right. We're going to spend the rest of our lives making sure she knows just how much we love her. We'll live our lives to the fullest. And we'll guide our son through to adulthood and watch as he becomes the incredible man that is already peeking through.

"Ack! Not the hair!" Beckett laughs. I chuckle under my breath knowing she did that to lighten the mood.

"Enough about me and your grumpy dads," She teases. I chuckle again. I'll get her back for that. "I'll talk to them about it tonight. Back to you and Layne. Your relationship is new, but you are best friends. You both believe in honesty. I have no doubt that he might be worrying about the same thing that you are. Talk to him. You both will benefit from it."

Beckett is quiet for a few moments before he nods. "You're right," He turns and hugs Lyric tightly. "Thanks, mom." He kisses her cheek.

"Y-you're w-welcome."

Beckett smiles as he stands. I quickly and quietly take a few steps away from his door. "He should be here any time. We're going to shoot some hoops."

"O-okay."

I quickly text Matt that Beckett's boyfriend, Layne, will be joining us for dinner, then cross my arms over my chest as I lean against the wall. When Beckett leaves his room and sees me, I put a finger to my lips. He smiles even more brightly, staying quiet and nodding as he walks down the hall and stairs. I hear Lyric sniffling, but I stay where I am and wait for her to come out, knowing she won't be long.

After another few moments, I hear Lyric shuffling towards the door. I stay quiet and wait for her. When she turns the corner and sees me, her eyes widen. She nearly screams but lets out an adorable squeak instead and covers her mouth with her hand.

I grin and wrap my arms around her. I lift her and hold her close as I kiss her long and deeply. She moans into the kiss and melts into me, wrapping her arms over my shoulders and legs around my waist. I nip her tongue and suck with a possessive rumble as I turn and walk her to our bedroom.

"How much of that did you hear?" she whispers against my lips when I pull away from the kiss and kick the door closed behind us.

"Enough to know he called you mom. And that you're an incredible mom to him." I choose to leave the rest out because I know she wants to tell us both tonight.

She blushes. "It made me cry. My heart just felt so full of love. And then he hugged me, and I think it burst."

I smile. "My beautiful sap." I walk her to the bed and gently lay her down. I wrap my arms around her. "I love you."

Her smile could light the entire universe. "I love you." She reaches up and runs her fingers over the stubble on my cheek before she reaches my hair. She tugs me a little down to her.

I pull her closer, knowing exactly what my girl wants and needs. I lean down and kiss her, softly at first, but I deepen it and tangle my tongue with hers. I kiss her until we both need to come up for air, then do it all over again.

Just after Sapphire's, Matt and I talked to Lyric about moving in with us permanently. We were surprised that she was planning on asking us about it, but like everything in our relationship, we let it all be a natural progression. Since then, Lyric has slept every single night between me and Matt. We haven't looked back. Our relationship has been perfect. We work on it every day, though it doesn't feel like it at all.

Lyric slides her leg between mine and pushes against me. Her hand snakes up the back of my shirt. She whimpers and deepens the kiss a little more. I smile and tangle my fingers in her hair, pulling her even closer so I can give her the passion she's silently asking for.

As Lyric's tongue slides seductively against mine, I run my hand down her back, pleased that she's not wearing a bra. She hates them. She insists the support in the tank top thing she's wearing is enough for her. I just smile and nod. Then tell her I don't mind because I have easier access to her tits.

Like right now.

I kiss along her neck to her collarbone and down to those supple mounds as I push up her shirt. She pulls it over her head as I take one of her perfect peaks in my mouth. I suck hard on one of them while lightly pinching and rolling the other one between my forefinger and thumb.

She gasps and arches, spearing my hair with her fingers. "DJ... fuck... yes..."

I nip her nipple and move to the other one, lavishing it with my tongue and teeth as I had her other one. Lyric arches into me again and pulls my head closer to her. I slide my hand down to her jean cutoffs and make quick work of the button and zipper that keeps me from her sweet, wet, hot center. I kiss down her stomach to her panty line and tug her shorts down. She kicks them off.

I grin up at her. "No panties either?"

She blushes and shakes her head. "I don't like them, but I also know how much you and Matt like it when I don't wear them...," she whispers, her eyes on fire.

It makes the smile on my face grow wider. I give her pussy a long lick of praise. "Good girl."

She shivers and trembles in anticipation as she watches me. Her breathing quickens. "Oh..."

"You're dripping for me." I dive into her pussy with my tongue because I need to taste her.

"Ah!" she screams out. She arches into me. I grip her hips and thrust my tongue hard, fast, and as deep as I can. She meets my thrusts and rides my tongue. "Fuck yes, DJ! DJ..." She writhes underneath me. One of her hands grips the blanket underneath her. The other tangles as much as it can in my short hair. She pulls me even closer to her pussy.

I bury my face in her and shake my head back and forth so my tongue gives her new sensations. Her moans bring a low growl from deep within me, sending vibrations through her pussy and straight to her clit. Her pussy clenches around my tongue and pulses erratically. I suck hard and nibble. I know she's close, so while I'm enjoying my pre-dinner snack, I set my thumb against her clit. I rub in fast, smooth circles, giving her the perfect amount of pressure. A pressure I've learned so well.

"DJ!" Her pussy gets wetter for me and tightens even more around my tongue. I can't think of anything I want more than her coming all over my face.

"Mmm...," I growl possessively. "Whose perfect pussy is this?" I swirl my tongue inside her, and she clamps down hard around me.

"Yours! DJ, please! Please, let me come!"

I smile. "Mine. All fucking mine." I thrust my tongue faster and faster until she's trembling, and I know she won't be able to hold on any longer. "Come, baby. Now. Show me how much you love my tongue." I dive back into her again and again as I rub her clit at the same pace I'm tongue fucking her.

She arches up and pulls my face closer so I'm buried in her pussy. I slide my hands down and grip the inside of her thighs. I spread her legs wider, burying my tongue even deeper in her pussy with a rumble. She comes hard, soaking my tongue, her pussy, my face, and the blanket beneath her.

"DJ! Ah! Fuck! Yes! Baby! Yes! Yes!" Her pussy spasms as she comes. Her hips jerk up and down as she loses complete control and gives completely into her release.

While I'm leisurely licking her to help her come down, I unbutton and unzip my shorts. I pull my shirt over my head as I slowly pull away from her. I use my shirt to wipe my face and toss it. I push my shorts down and kick them off. I pin Lyric's hands above her head while I position myself between her legs. She looks up at me with a satisfied yet hungry for me look that has my already hard cock begging to be inside her.

"Damn, you taste incredible. I'll never get enough of you," I whisper against her lips just before I take them in a dominating and punishing kiss.

I keep her wrists above her head with one hand and reach down, fisting my dick with the other. I tease her clit with the head of my cock as I kiss her long and passionately. Lyric submits instantly and shudders with each stroke I give her clit with my dick.

She's so wet that when I finally slide my dick into her quivering pussy, I sink balls deep with very little effort. She tightens immediately around me. I grip her hip when she wraps her legs around me and pull her up. I sink even deeper and groan into her mouth.

I thrust hard, deep, and slow. I kiss down to her neck and let go of her wrists as I tangle my fingers in her hair. Her hand instantly grips my shoulders. Her other slides to my ass, digging her fingers in as she tries to pull me even deeper into her. She meets me thrust for thrust and turns her head just enough to give me access to the sensitive flesh below her earlobe. I nibble on her neck and suck hard.

"Oh… DJ…," she moans against my shoulder. She tries to push me onto my back, but that's not how we're playing this game today.

I nip her neck and kiss the mark I left. I slap her ass. "Be good," I growl. "Or I'll leave you a quivering fucking mess."

"Yes, Captain," she moans, submissively.

"Fuck, I love when you call me that." I thrust harder and faster.

Lyric scratches her nails across my back, gripping my ass even harder. She writhes underneath me and arches into me, taking my dick as deep as she can with every thrust. She gets tighter and tighter and impossibly wetter.

I roll my hips just enough to hit the spot deep within her that makes her come undone within seconds. But just because I want to make her lose total control, I reach between us and start rubbing her clit. I kiss up her neck to her jaw and hover just out of reach of her lips.

"Fuck me... DJ... Oh God! Yes!" She bucks into me.

I let loose and pound into her pussy, giving her the hard, fast, deep thrusts she loves. "Fuck... Lyric..." I drop my head and kiss her. "So tight and wet for me," I murmur against her lips before I take them again in another long, hard kiss. My dick thickens, making her so much tighter. I don't know how she takes my thick length, but fuck if it's not something I thank my lucky stars for every damn day.

"DJ... Oh, God!" She rakes her nails across my back again and spreads her legs wider. Her heels dig into my ass as she pulls me as close to her as she possibly can.

I didn't think it was possible for me to sink deeper, but leave it to her to find a way. "Holy shit, little girl." I nip her lip.

She closes her eyes and relishes in the feeling as she keeps meeting every thrust I give her. I give her clit a flick before rubbing it again. Her thighs start to tremble. Her pussy begins to spasm uncontrollably.

"Please, please, baby...," she begs.

"Tell me who you belong to. Who fucks you so good, little one?" I don't stop thrusting. I keep rubbing her clit and rocking my hips against hers. "Tell me whose girl you are."

Her eyes widen at my possessive and dominant tone. It makes her entire body tremble. "You! You, DJ. You! Please, let me come! Please! I... can't... Ah!"

My stomach clenches. My back tightens as an electric jolt shoots down my spine. "Fuck, Lyric. Come for me, sweet girl." I crush my lips against hers and swipe my tongue across her lips.

She opens her mouth for me as she screams. A tidal wave of pleasure rolls through me when her release pulls mine from me. I come hard inside her. My dick jerks as her pussy spasms and pulses around me.

I let my head fall back as our hips slam together. "Fuck, Lyric!"

"Ah! DJ! Yes!" Her nails dig into my shoulder and my ass.

My fingers tangle in her hair and tug lightly. I hold her close to me with my other arm. She pants against my shoulder as she rides out her orgasm. I fill her pussy and moan against her neck. I kiss her softly and lean some of my weight down on her the way she loves us to do. She relishes the feeling of us surrounding her. I bury my face in her hair as we both come down.

After a few minutes, I hear a low chuckle. "Don't you two look nice and cozy."

I smile against Lyric's neck and look up to see Matt standing in our doorframe. "I couldn't help it. She's irresistible. And she was dripping for me."

Matt laughs. "Well, dinner is here. Beckett and Layne are setting everything out. How about you two get dressed and come join your family?"

"Yes, sir," Lyric says submissively as she blushes and hides her face in my neck.

I kiss her chest and slowly pull out of her as Matt groans at her submissive tone. I sit up after pulling out. We both watch Lyric as she slides her hand between her legs and crosses them. To anyone else, it might look like she's being shy. But I know my girl. She loves the feeling of our come inside her. It makes her feel closer to us. She likes the feeling of being full.

I lean down and kiss her before helping her up. Matt smiles as he watches us. As the two of us clean up and get dressed, then follow Matt downstairs for dinner, I can't help but think that our life couldn't possibly be any more perfect.

Chapter Fifteen

☆ Lyric ☆

(One Year Later)

When I was a little girl, I, like so many other kids, dreamt of my wedding day down to the very last detail. I knew exactly how I wanted the table to look. The shape of them. The color of the linen. The centerpieces in the middle of the table. I knew how I wanted the entire venue to look. What my bridesmaids would look like. What the tuxedos the groomsmen and the groom would be wearing. And, of course, what my dress would look like. My hair. Every tiny little detail. I even drew it.

The older I got, though, the more I believed my dreams were just that.

Dreams.

Fantasy that would never become reality.

My family told me I would never make a good wife. My friends, at least those I thought were my friends, told me exactly the same thing. I was too stupid. Too ugly. Too fat. Too meek. Too timid. Too shy. Too lazy. Too weak. Too needy. Too emotionally dramatic.

Luca and my father were the only ones who never said anything derogatory, but they also never defended me from them. They never stuck up for me. At least not until the damage had already been done. Until I believed everything they said to me deep within my soul.

By the time we finished high school, I was so far gone, I'd basically given up. I'd been so used. Mentally and emotionally abused. Even physically. Luca, thankfully, had started to see the turmoil I was in and knew what to do.

It took us a while, with help from our father and his friend, our godfather, Chief King, Uncle King to me, but we finally were able to leave the United Kingdom. Luca, though I told him he didn't have to, made the move with me. I've always thought it was because he wanted to experience new things, but I recently found out that he did it as a way to make up for the years he allowed me to be bullied right in front of him.

It took me a very long time to believe that I ever had a chance of getting married. It wasn't until Josh that I not only understood why I am so submissive and shy away from control, but also felt comfortable enough to be who I am and not hide it. We were together for a long time. He is my best friend. Our relationship may have evolved into friendship and became something even more incredible and amazing, but before that, I could have married him.

Thanks to Josh and Luca, I finally started to believe in myself enough to realize that getting married was possible. That I would and could make an incredible wife to the right person. I wouldn't have been in the right headspace to believe that if not for them. It's something I'll always love them for. One day, it will be their turn. And I'll be there to support them both when the time comes.

So, as I stand here in front of the full length mirror in my wedding gown and hair done just perfectly, it all seems surreal. My dress is exactly like I imagined it. It makes all of the parts I don't like about myself look slimmer. It hugs each and every curve, accentuating all the parts I love. I truly look like a bride. A beautiful, blushing bride.

"You look so pretty, Lyric," Mariah says softly behind me. "I can't believe how far you've come in the two years you've known Matt and DJ. They've made an already beautiful and amazing person into this incredible woman standing here today."

The pink blush to my cheeks turns a lot darker. Mariah is right. Matt and DJ have been an integral part of shaping me as a person. We've been together for two amazing years, and even I can see the change in myself. How much I've grown.

I run my hands down my sides to my hips. I smile softly at the soft satin of my pretty sweetheart neckline, A-line dress. It's light and breathable, though it's long and nearly brushes the floor. Perfect for the outside wedding at Boston's famous Public Library. Matt and DJ surprised me when we got engaged. I not only got a beautiful ring. I also got a written letter confirming the Boston Public Library as our wedding venue. Matt and DJ know I have a serious passion for books and have always wanted to see the famous library. Now, I'm getting married to the loves of my life in it.

"I really do love the way I look," I whisper. There's a glow to my skin that has never been there. If it has, I've never noticed it.

Mariah puts purple gemstones in my hair after she finishes the braid she's managed to make look like a crown. "You're beautiful. Such a beautiful bride. I can't wait until mine and Luca's day."

I smile softly and turn towards her. I hug her hard. "I'm sorry you had to postpone yours."

She shakes her head. "We aren't thinking about that. It's your day. And it's going to be amazing. I'll have mine soon enough."

I nod into her neck and pull away slowly. She's right. They're getting married in three weeks, though it was supposed to be last year. Luca, though, had to go and fall off a ladder three weeks before their wedding while he was on a construction site. He hurt his back and broke his leg. Mariah, being ever so cautious, immediately postponed everything and took time off work to be with him. Luca told her he would be fine, even if he was on crutches, but Mariah was having none of it.

"What do you say we get me married?" I giggle just as someone knocks on the door.

Mariah hurries to the door and opens it. She smiles brightly and hugs her boyfriend. "Finally, you show up. She's ready."

Luca hugs her close and kisses her before pulling away. "Well, let me see her."

I stand in the middle of the room with my hands clasped in front of me. Luca's eyes fall on me. He smiles wide as he walks to me but says nothing. Instead, he hugs me. I let out a breath and melt into his arms, hugging him back just as tightly.

"Doesn't she look beautiful?"

"Incredible," Luca says as he pulls away. He keeps his hands on my hips. "I've been waiting for this day. I always thought I'd be the one to walk you down the aisle, but I'm even more happy that I get to watch you instead."

I furrow my brows. "Promise you're not mad that I asked Josh?"

He grins. "And miss out on being the one to actually give two of the three most dominant men I've ever met a command to kiss their bride?" He laughs. "Not a chance." He kisses my forehead as Mariah lets Josh in. Luca pulls away and takes Mariah's hand as he leaves the room.

"Well, damn." Josh whistles and smiles as he closes the door behind them. "I always knew you'd make a beautiful bride."

I blush. "I don't think I'd be here without you." I smile softly. "Literally. You saved my life."

He shrugs as he walks slowly towards me. "I had a hand in it." He holds out a hand. I take it. He turns me in a slow circle. "This dress… looks incredible on you. I'm glad you trusted Mariah when she suggested you try it on."

I tear up a little as I look up at him. "I honestly bawled my eyes out when I saw myself in it. I had started to believe I'd finally realize my dream of being married, but seeing myself in this dress… It made it so much more real."

"You deserve everything, Lyric. I hope you know that."

I smile shyly as I nod. "I do."

"Good. And if they ever hurt you…" He trails off, but the warning is clear.

"I know."

"Good girl. Never settle for anything less than what you deserve. And remember that what you deserve is the entire fucking world and more. Understand?"

I nod. "Yes, sir."

He smiles. "Now, let's get you down that aisle. They're both waiting very impatiently."

I smile and follow him. He keeps my hand in his. I'm so grateful for that because, while I'm confident in marrying Matt and DJ, I have butterflies. I'm so nervous, but I think that has more to do with how many people showed up for our wedding. Ryan and his entire family. Josh and his entire family. Most of the police department. By the time everyone RSVP'd, we had nearly three hundred guests.

So much for a small wedding.

"Did everyone arrive okay? Matt and DJ forbade me from looking at anything to do with the guests after my last panic attack."

Mariah stands in front of the double doors leading into the library. She smiles. "They did."

When she hears her music start, she plasters a huge smile on her face. She steps through the doors and walks down the aisle. Her pretty purple dress hits mid-thigh. When she reaches the front, the music changes, signaling Josh to lead me down the aisle.

"Ready?" he whispers in my ear when he leans down.

I nod and put my hand on his arm. "Ready," I whisper. Josh walks me down the aisle after everyone stands. I falter slightly when I see my family and the looks on their faces. I grip Josh's arm a little tighter. "Don't let me fall, okay?"

"Never gonna happen, little one," he murmurs as he covers my hand with his.

Everyone's eyes are on me as Josh leads me to my loves.

My life.

My future.

We walk over the purple and white lily petals that Mariah dropped on her way down the aisle.

My eyes are focused entirely on the two men standing next to Luca. Their tuxes are traditionally black and tailored perfectly to fit them. They are each wearing a purple vest that matches the shade of the purple lily in their breast pocket and the petals on the floor.

When I reach them, I see their eyes are just as misted as mine. I don't even hear Luca start the ceremony. All I can focus on is Matt and DJ. Their soft smiles. The love shining from every fiber of their being.

When it's time for us to start our vows, I've already nearly forgotten my name. DJ and Matt haven't taken their eyes off me. Their hands haven't left mine. I don't really even notice anyone else in the room.

"Lyric," DJ begins. His voice is deep and powerful, just as he is. Yet, it's still soft and loving. He pushes a strand of loose hair out of my eyes. "I've loved you since the second I laid eyes on you. I still don't really know how we never crossed paths, even with your uncle running interference, but it doesn't matter. Life suddenly felt very complete with you in it. It will never feel right without you. I was happy before. Content. But now I know what it feels like to be sitting on cloud nine every day of my life. I can't wait to see what our future holds for us. I'm excited to see you grow. Us. To see us grow. Together." He cups my cheek. I lean into his hand with a soft smile and tears threatening to fall at his sweet words. "I love you," he whispers.

"I love you," I whisper back, blinking rapidly to keep the tears of happiness at bay. His hand falls back to his side. He squeezes my hand with his other. Luca motions for Matt to speak his vows next.

Matt leans in and kisses my forehead. "You took my breath away when I first saw you. And you take my breath away each day. I can't wait to wake up in the morning just to see what you have planned for us. Or go to sleep next to you just so I can watch how cute you are when you snuggle into us and fight to stay awake, even though you're exhausted." He smiles when I blush and duck my head. He cups my chin and lifts it, so I'm looking at him. "You fit. No one has ever fit with us. We were okay with that. We had a good life. But then we found you. Suddenly, we knew just how good life could be." Matt lets his hand fall back to his side and kisses my nose as she squeezes my hand.

I blink back the tears again and take a breath as I begin my vows, but Luca holds up a hand. "One more person would like to have his say," Luca says with a wink. I tilt my head as Matt and DJ grin.

Beckett steps in front of me and takes both of my hands, effectively stealing me from Matt and DJ. I look up at him with a smile. He's gotten so handsome. And tall. Seriously. He's nearly as tall as Matt is. I don't know when it happened.

He smiles down at me. "For so many years before Matt got custody of me, I didn't feel like a part of my own family. With my dad not in the picture, Matt was always the person I looked up to for as long as I can remember. The night Matt came to get me and I met you, I couldn't help but think how sweet you were to worry about a kid you never met. You refused to leave before you knew I was okay. I knew you were special for that reason. Matt and DJ have been together for so long. I know they've had other women, but never one they've let me meet. I knew it was different with you." He pauses, squeezing my hands.

"Oh, Beckett," I whisper.

He takes a breath and continues. "You quickly became the mother I never had. You took care of me and my needs. It was a little overwhelming at first, but I wanted you to stay. I fell in love with you. Not like them, but I loved you like a kid should love a mom. And it grows for you every day. You also gave me a little brother. He may not be here in person but he's here," He presses a hand to my heart and then to his. "And I know he is here in spirit. Watching as you marry our dads. We might not be family biologically, but we are in our hearts. We're family by choice. And that is so much stronger." He leans in and hugs me just before the dam of my tears bursts. "I love you, mom. We both do," he whispers, referring to himself and mine and Josh's unborn child, in my ear as he hugs me.

"I love you, too. So much," I whisper back. Matt and DJ both wrap us in their arms. It might be insane, but I swear I can feel a weight on my hand, squeezing and tugging slightly, as if Jaxon was standing at our sides. I'm suddenly filled with a loving and comforting warmth.

I don't know how long we stay like that, but when Beckett finally pulls back, there isn't a dry eye in the house. He hands me a tissue. I dab my eyes as he moves to stand next to Matt. Everyone waits patiently while I compose myself.

Finally, I have the nerve to speak. I clear my throat. "You all have made me a blubbering mess on my wedding day." I smile and giggle a little at myself. I take a deep breath and step back slightly so I'm able to look at DJ and Matt as I hold their hands. "Before I met you both, I felt like I was just going through the motions. I had a routine. If I needed something more than Luca could give, I went to the club. If I needed more than that, I called Josh. After we decided we are better friends, I really didn't think I'd ever find anyone to give me what I needed. Anyone to love. I felt… needy and unlovable. Like I was just too much for everyone. A burden. I took what I needed, but never gave them what they did." I look down as I compose myself once more. A collective dominant growl hits my ears.

"Lyric," DJ warns low as he squeezes my hand.

I squeeze it back as I turn towards our friends and family. I'm still surprised that any of my family actually came. My eyes meet Josh's before landing on a few others. Ryan. Alec. Jason. I shake my head with a soft smile.

"Oh, hush. All of you. I was not saying I believe any of that now. Geez." I smile a little brighter. Teasingly. Though, I blush furiously. "Don't growl at me on my wedding day." I turn back to my loves when people laugh.

All except my family. All except a few of them seem to look at me with disdain. I ignore them and smile up at DJ and Matt. They're all that matters anyway. Them and Beckett. The family behind me who I have chosen. Not those trying to ruin everything.

I won't let them.

"You both have made me believe in myself. You've accepted all of me." I pause a moment, but keep a soft smile on my face. "Including Josh and Jaxon. They'll always be a part of me, and you've all accepted them both and our tradition of visiting Jaxon each year." I smile softly at Josh before I turn to look at Beckett. "I love that you sat there and told Jaxon about everything going on in our lives. You even asked him questions and nodded along as if he was answering you while Josh stood with his chin on my shoulder. Your dads stood at my sides, holding my hands. They added in their own snippets when they could. I don't know what they said when they knelt down and spoke to him before we left, but I know it was something heartfelt and true. I don't know what I did to deserve any of you, but I'm forever grateful for whatever it was. I'm truly so proud that you've chosen me to be your mom." I look at them all as I tear up again. "I know I may slip sometimes, but you love me more and more each day. I love you all. So much."

Luca smiles. "I think we should probably let them kiss their bride, huh? So, with that, and with the power the state of Massachusetts gave me to marry people, probably a stupid mistake, but meh. Too late now." Luca laughs. "I now pronounce you husbands and wife. Don't hurt my sister, but kiss her already!"

They both lean down. DJ kisses me first. Sweet to begin with, but he moans a little and deepens it. When he pulls away, people are applauding. I blush but don't have much time to react before Matt's lips are on mine. He growls low and possessively, making me giggle into the kiss. When he pulls away, I'm breathless.

Beckett kisses me on the cheek. "You're ours for sure now. Can't run away."

I giggle. "There's nowhere else I'd want to be." I kiss his cheek back. "I'm finally home."

DJ swoops me in his arms and carries me down the aisle, Matt at his side. I giggle and wrap my arms around his neck, fingering my rings. We decided when we got them that we would wear them right away. To us, the rings were a symbol of the love and commitment we already had for each other.

Mine is a pretty, oval-shaped, princess-cut, diamond. My band is white-gold. I also have two other plain white-gold bands on either side of the diamond. They each have five, small, blue diamonds. Matt and DJ had the rings soldered together. Theirs are titanium bands with a strip of blue ion in them to match the blue diamonds in mine.

I smile as Beckett takes Layne's hand and runs up the aisle behind us. Everyone is applauding, but I can't help noticing my family isn't. Except my dad. He even wiped a tear. I notice that his wife, my favorite aunt, and my uncle are too. My mom, however, is doing nothing but glaring. Most of my family are shaking their heads or looking completely indifferent and uninterested. I refuse to let them ruin my day though. I choose, instead, to focus on all of the happy faces and the loves of my life.

DJ carries me to the front of the building where we are to meet our photographer for pictures. I don't want to miss a single second of any of this. I want it all captured from every angle. Which is the reason I asked for both videography and photography.

For the next couple of hours, we pose for photos with just us, with our families, friends, and even individually. There are some fun photos thrown in, like with Matt and DJ throwing me in the air and catching me. And both of them fighting over me. Josh even snuck into a few of them and photobombed them, which made me laugh so hard, I nearly fell over.

Our reception, though I was truly so excited for it, seems to be dragging on. It's not that I'm not having fun. I am. It's that I can't seem to stop myself from somehow overhearing snippets of conversations between my family members. It's like no matter what I do, how far away from them I am, I somehow hear something. I hate that our friends and family will have most definitely heard them, too.

I added them to our guest list because I thought they had to be there. That it was something everyone does. I don't know why they agreed to come if they were just going to complain the entire time. They're not even being quiet about it. I've heard my dad, my uncle King, and my aunt tell them multiple times to shut up. To stop complaining. But they just keep going.

I rub my chest and sit down at our table with my eyes lowered as they continue. I can hear them clearly from here. If I can, then so can everyone else. I sniffle and wipe my eyes subtly, making it look like I am moving my hair out of my face.

DJ puts his arm around my waist and leans into me. "Ignore them," he whispers. "Everyone else is. This is our wedding. And everyone else here is happy as fuck to see it. You know how excited the girls were when we told everyone we proposed. They all flew down on Ryan's plane to help plan it whenever they could get away."

"They're embarrassing me," I whisper with a sniffle.

Matt leans into my other side and puts a hand on my thigh. "There have been a few people who have snapped at them, sweet girl. Trust me. No one here is paying them any mind. They're trying to get under your skin. Don't let them."

DJ chuckles and squeezes my hip. "Though with the way your cousin keeps throwing herself at Chase, Ryan, Josh, and Jason, I think she's going to get her ass kicked. And you know how hard it is to piss Breetana, Arianna and Jessa off."

"She deserves to get her ass kicked," I grumble.

"Time to say goodnight," Luca says, handing DJ a microphone.

"That's it," Mariah mumbles, appearing at Luca's side and swiping the microphone away before DJ can grab it.

I watch her in shock. "Mariah?"

She winks and turns. I glance at Matt, DJ, and even Luca, but none of them know what's happening. So, we all just watch in fascination as Mariah walks towards where Jessa is sitting with Arianna, Breetana, Jessa, Raleigh, Dallas, Nicole, and Dani. They are all wives or girlfriends of the Cranes or Lucinios. Well, all except Dallas. Dallas is Alec's little sister but is like family to them all. They have all become my family. Family I never really believed I'd have. Real and true.

They all look deep in conversation but all eyes rise to Mariah when she approaches. She turns towards everyone with a huge smile. "I hope everyone enjoyed coming to this fabulous wedding between three of my closest friends. Give me a hell yeah if you had an incredible time!"

A rousing chorus of 'hell yeahs' go up through the courtyard.

Mariah giggles. "Yes! I'm so excited to hear that because this has been one of the best nights I've had in a long time." Her eyes and bright smile fall to me and my men. "Thank you, Lyric, Matt, and DJ, for throwing this incredible celebration of your love and letting all of us attend. And thank you so much for the incredible array of food! Oh my God, I don't think I've eaten so much since, well, forever."

"You're welcome!" DJ yells to her. "Now, get married already, so you can return the fucking favor!"

"DJ!" I laugh and swat his arm.

Mariah blushes but laughs. "Three weeks!" She turns back to the room. "I want everyone to join me right now in wishing DJ, Matt, and Lyric all a fantastic honeymoon. They're going on a family vacation with Beckett, and are even taking Layne with, to Universal Studios in Hollywood, California, for two weeks. Then, they're going to Aulani Resort and Spa in Hawaii for a week. They'll be flying back for our wedding. Then back to Aulani. I am so, so freaking jealous! So, everyone, give them a cheer!"

She waits for everyone to cheer.

"Seriously? Hawaii? That whore is going to Hawaii?" My cousin, Eamonn, whines in what I'm sure he believes is a whisper.

I can't believe the asshole, Eamonn, is high. In a room where there is more than a handful of cops, and he's fucking high. How he got it, I don't fucking know. Didn't they go through airport security? I shake my head to banish the thoughts. He probably found himself a dealer here. I hear Ellie whine under her breath. She's pouting like a brat.

When everyone quiets again, Mariah's eyes narrow. "While this night has been incredible, I can't help but notice a few of you have been doing all you can to ruin this for Lyric. Snide comments about her looks and weight." Her eyes meet mine again. I blush and look down because I truly hoped she didn't hear anything. I know she did, but I hoped she didn't. "You're beautiful, by the way. No matter what any of the idiots in your family think."

"I'd say she's fucking beautiful. I dated her. Had a handsome boy with her, too," Josh hollers from the back of the room with a grin that makes me blush for a completely different reason.

I smile softly as I think about Jaxon. We used one of those programs to find out what he would have looked like. He had Josh's dark hair, but my slight waves. His striking blue eyes. My full lips and button nose. A charming little smile that would have gotten him out of trouble, and probably into it, on many occasions. He was the perfect mix of us.

Strange as it may sound, but finding that out actually helped us. Jaxon wasn't unknown anymore. He became a real person. Josh keeps a copy of his photo in his wallet. Rebekkah has another on her mantle at her home. Mine is in a frame that DJ had placed in the den on the top of the mantle. All our other photos are spread around it. He said that Jaxon belongs in the heart of them, just as he is in ours.

I fell even deeper in love with him that day. Beckett surprised us all when he decided to have a canvas made in honor of Jaxon. It hangs above his bed in his room. It says, 'My little brother is an Angel. He watches over me.'

I'm so humbled at how much they have embraced Jaxon in their lives. They have even become closer to Josh. My smile falters, and I lean into Matt when Ellie glares at me.

"Couldn't agree more! She's gorgeous!" Ryan yells from next to him. He and Josh both put our bags down. I raise an eyebrow because I wasn't aware we were leaving tonight. I thought we were leaving tomorrow. Matt and DJ smile next to me as they both hug me close.

"It's pretty obvious that you don't want to be here. That really all of you don't want to be," Mariah nearly growls as she focuses on my family. "There are only a few of you who have shown any interest at all in Lyric's special day. So, tell me. If you didn't want to come, then why the hell are you even here?"

"We thought it was Luca's wedding. We wanted to be here for him. To see him marry whichever beautiful woman captured his heart." My cousin, Ellie, snaps. I'm surprised she cares enough to even speak up. She's the snobbiest person I have ever met. And considering my sister, that's saying something. "And where the fuck is this Jaxon they keep talking about?"

"Don't…," Ryan growls. His growl is echoed by others in the room, females included. I notice the men have gathered in a protective semi-circle around the women. Ryan grips Josh's shoulder when he lurches forward with a snarl. "Don't you fucking dare."

"What?" Ellie snaps back, mockingly. "Ain't my fault she wasn't able to keep her kid. Probably too busy spreading her legs to look after it."

"She miscarried him, you stupid bitch!" Layne yells. Matt and DJ might have something to say to him about his outburst, but I doubt that will happen. It's deserved. Beckett moves in front of him, stopping him from launching at Ellie, just as Josh tried to. Layne has become just as protective of me as Beckett has.

"Let me go," Dallas shouts. "She needs to shut up! She's hurting Lyric!" I notice her eyes move to Josh. Her movements become even more erratic at the look in his eye. "She hurt Josh! She's vile!" I watch wide-eyed as she struggles to get out of Alec's grip. Tyler moves to help calm her down as she thrashes enough for Alec to lose his hold. But I don't miss that it's the look Josh shoots her that gets her to stop.

"Why would we care about that heffa?" my youngest cousin, Autumn, snarls. "We finally got rid of her. Fat, ugly whore that she is. And from the sounds of it, a failure as a woman. We came for Luca."

Mariah cracks up. For a moment, I think she's gone insane. "Well, considering I'm the beautiful woman who captured Luca's heart, I can assure you of one thing. You aren't invited to our wedding." She turns slightly to look at Luca. He nods in agreement. "Besides." Her vicious glare returns to Autumn. "Lyric's name was all over that fucking invitation. Lyric, Matt, and DJ. Not Luca."

Jessa snarls dangerously as she stands. Mariah hands her the microphone. "Don't you fucking dare mock her. You have no idea the pain she and Josh went through when she lost Jaxon. The agony she went through for months. She almost died." She glares fiercely at Autumn.

I sniffle and turn my face into DJ's neck. He hugs me tightly as Matt presses against my other side, making sure I feel him. He rubs his thumb over the back of my neck soothingly.

"And I don't know who the fuck you're calling a heffa. Or a fat, ugly, whore," Jessa growls. "I only see one heffa in this room. And it's you. And the ugly whore? Well, guess what? Look no further than the bitch sitting next to you." She points to Ellie. I turn back to the girls once I have composed myself. I stifle a laugh as Breetana stands next to Jessa.

Jessa hands her the mic next. "You all should be ashamed of yourselves," Breetana begins. "Lyric is the strongest woman we know. She's not a failure. You were invited here out of the kindness of a beautiful woman's heart. She wanted to show you how far she came. How she's thriving. Did you know that she started her own business? I bet you didn't because not a single one of you bothered to ask. Well, guess what? I bet you my entire bank account, and it's worth billions, that Lyric makes more than all of you combined in a single month. Yeah. She's thriving. And she's doing it without any of you." She hands the microphone off to Raleigh. I wipe a tear away at all of their kind words.

"This wasn't even a real fucking wedding. She's with two men at the same time!" My mom throws her hands up in disgust. "It's just a way to show you approve of her being a whore." She turns to my dad. "Why didn't you object when I nudged you? Surely, you don't approve of this farce of a wedding or relationship. It's not right!"

"Amen," Autumn and Ellie grumble in agreement. My mouth just drops. I don't even know what to say. I'm close to bursting into tears, but DJ and Matt just hug me tighter.

"You wanted me to ruin my little girl's wedding? Are you fucking insane? She just got married to two incredible men who see her for who she is and embrace it completely. I wasn't going to do a damn thing to ruin it. And as her mother, nor should you!" My dad growls at my mom.

He's been a lot happier since they divorced when we were kids. He remarried a few years after their divorce when he met someone else. His wife is next to him. She places her hand on his to calm him. I really like her. I always have. I know it must have been awkward when he first introduced me to her and her two kids. Her son is a few years older than me, and her daughter is four years younger. But she didn't hesitate to include me in every activity. It really helped me to connect with them. I'm still quiet around them, but it's gotten better in the years they have been together.

"I don't understand how she first got him." Ellie points at Josh then Matt and DJ. "Or how she managed to snare hot men like them. She must have fucking cocaine in her pussy." She crosses her arms with a whine. "I'm so much sexier than she is. I'm skinnier. I have a perky ass and boobs. Yet, none of the men here want to fuck me. I don't get it." She shakes her head. "What man won't take what is being offered?"

"Every man here is either in a committed relationship or married, you two-bit slut," Luca growls. "Why would they want you when they can have the partner that they love and have devoted themselves to? Shut the fuck up, you spoiled brat."

"Enough!" Raleigh yells. "No one, and I do mean no one gives a shit about you or your opinions. None of you. You're all trying to ruin the best night of Lyric's life. Well, guess what? We're not going to let you. Not a single one of you gets to say another word. In fact, you all can leave. Mariah literally just said you're not invited to hers and Luca's wedding. The only people in your little posse who I can see being allowed to stay for their wedding is Luca's father, his wife and Luca's and Lyric's aunt and uncles. At least his father has told everyone else to shut up more than once. The rest of you? You all can fuck the fuck off."

Dallas stands then and takes the mic Raleigh gives her. Nicole and Dani both stand next to her. They all position themselves as a united front, but what surprises me is when Nicole reaches for my hand. DJ and Matt both kiss my neck and nudge me up. I take Nicole's hand. She places me in the center of the girls as Dallas waits. I lower my head to keep everyone from seeing my tears.

Tears of joy.

Tears of relief.

Tears of only God knows what.

As Dallas begins to speak, Jessa and Mariah both put an arm around my waist. "I don't know who any of you people are. But I can honestly tell you that your behavior here tonight is so appalling to me. And I'm only fifteen! This is coming from the sister of the President of a very powerful, large, dangerous, and crude motorcycle crew. I've seen it all. Literally. But this?" She shakes her head. "This is disgusting. But it's okay. You all have shown your true colors here tonight. Lyric doesn't need any of you. She has all of us. We are her true family. So, good riddance." She hands the mic back to Mariah.

I giggle quietly when I see that their men are staring at their respective partners with awe, pride, and not a small amount of lust. If I didn't know better, I would think they were about to throw their women over their shoulders and march off to their rooms caveman style.

"Everyone, let's wish Lyric, Matt, and DJ an incredible night and exciting honeymoon!" Mariah kisses my cheek with a squeak. "You're going to have so much fun!"

Everyone's loud cheers drown out the grumbles of my family. Matt and DJ appear in front of me and each take a hand. They both lean down and give me a deep kiss. The cheers turn into hoots and hollers.

"My jet is gassed up. Limos waiting outside. The driver already grabbed your bags while the girls were giving your family a verbal fucking smackdown." Josh leans down and kisses my head after Matt and DJ leave me breathless. "Go! Get out of here!"

"I know Uncle King will be here, but make sure my dad, his wife, and my aunt and uncles stay, please. I don't want them to have to fly back to the UK then back here," I whisper to him quietly.

"You got it, sweetheart," he whispers back. He hugs me tight, kissing my head again.

I giggle as my husbands run towards the limo, dragging me with them. Beckett and Layne follow us, laughing. I hear clapping and shouts of love and support. Some tell us to have fun. Everyone drowns out the negativity from the family I've just decided isn't my family anymore.

I have a family right here. All of the people who supported us in there. Matt and DJ, the loves of my life slide into Josh's limo next to me. Beckett and Layne, who slide in and sit across from us. And last, but certainly not least, Jaxon, who I always feel in my heart.

My entire life, my world, is complete.

Perfect.

Epilogue

☆ Matt ☆

(Three Weeks Later)

Lyric squeals when I grab her around the waist and throw her over my shoulder. I haul her purple bikini clad ass back into our private suite as DJ laughs and follows. Beckett and Layne have taken a day off from our Hawaiian adventures to relax inside their own suite across from ours at the resort we're staying in.

It's been almost three weeks since we married our girl. We're heading back to Gainesville tomorrow for Mariah and Luca's wedding, then coming back here, to Hawaii, to finish our honeymoon. I feel like all we've been doing is running around on one adventure after another, and haven't had enough time by ourselves.

I'm sure DJ and Lyric would both disagree, considering our nights and mornings are spent locked in one position or another, but I don't care right now. I've been waiting for a lazy type of day for a long time. Now that I've gotten it, I have big, big plans.

"Matt!" Lyric laughs. She swats my ass. "Put me down! I can walk, you know."

I swat her ass in retaliation and bite it with a low growl that makes her both squeak and moan. "Where the fuck would the fun in that be?"

She giggles when I toss her on the bed in our room. DJ laughs when she bounces a little. He pounces on the bed and covers her with his body, smothering her in kisses. I remove my swim trunks and toss them before crawling into the bed. I tug DJ's off while he removes Lyric's bikini with his teeth, making her moan underneath him.

He kisses up her thighs and nips one of them while I watch. He teasingly licks her pussy before sliding up her body, covering her mouth with his, and sliding his cock into her without warning. She arches with a moan and squeals when he rolls them over without slipping out of her. She braces her hands on his abs as she sits up. She lets out a sexy little moan and shivers when he sinks even deeper into her pussy.

While I love watching, my plans don't include it. I want both of my loves. I do all the time, but something about today makes it far more intense. So, without wasting any time, I position myself behind Lyric, between DJ's thighs. I shift so the backs of DJ's thighs are braced on mine and slowly sink into him with a low moan.

DJ's eyes widen, and he groans when he thrusts down on my dick as he pulls back to thrust up into Lyric again. "Fuck…," he moans.

I grin when I see Lyric's eyes widen. "Oh… God…," she breathes when DJ fills her sweet little pussy even more when I thrust into him.

I grip DJ's hips with a low growl. He's tight around me, but the instant pulsing is really what gets me. "Christ, DJ…"

When he's used to my size, I start thrusting into him again and again. I let my head fall back, enjoying the feel of him. When I push into him, DJ moans and thrusts up into Lyric. Lyric writhes above him, meeting each of his thrusts with a bounce down on top of him of her own.

Matching my rhythm, DJ pulls out of Lyric when I pull out of him. We're slow at first, but our thrusts are deep. Hard. Lyric seems to shatter with each thrust she's given. She bounces harder on his dick as she spreads her legs wider, taking him deeper. Her moans and whimpers harmonized with his grunts and groans are the sexiest things I have ever heard.

But I'm not even close to being done with either of them. I quicken my pace. I grip DJ's hips harder and thrust faster. Deeper. Harder. My dick jerks into him again and again, faster and faster, until he clenches so tightly around me, I know he's dangerously close to careening into the dark abyss of passion. He grips Lyric's ass harder and slams her down onto his dick. I can feel his impending release just by how tight he's getting around me the longer I thrust my cock into him.

Lyric throws her head back. "DJ! Oh fuck! Yes!" She starts twisting her hips on him. I don't need to look to see her fingers are dug into his abs. Nor do I need to feel her pussy around my dick to know she is pulsing erratically around him.

"Fuck!" He slaps her ass and starts trembling. "Fuck, baby, you need to come. I'm not holding on much longer."

"Damn right you're not. Fuck, DJ. Your ass is so tight, you're going to squeeze my come out of me."

It's exactly what I want. I want Lyric to take his come while he takes mine. I want her to soak his dick when she gives him the release that he's desperately chasing. And then I plan to do it all over again until we're all so spent that we can't fucking move.

"DJ... DJ!" Lyric moans. "Please!"

DJ starts moving her back and forth over his dick as she bounces. The only thing I regret about my hurried need to take my husband's ass is not being able to see his dick fucking our wife's pussy. Or those perky tits of hers bouncing up and down while DJ slams into her.

"Ask me right, baby." He slaps her ass again, causing her to jerk over him. She must clamp down on him, too, because he groans and clenches around me, nearly sending me off my own desire cliff.

"Oh fuck," I grunt as I bury myself balls deep into him again and again.

"DJ! Please! Please, sir, let me come. Captain! Please! Please, let me come! Captain!"

"Good girl. Such a good little girl for me. Come for me. Now." DJ rumbles dominantly, sending electricity through me at his tone. His eyes meet mine. "Both of you."

Lyric shivers. His tone does exactly the same thing to her as it does me. "Yes! DJ! Ah!" She keeps bouncing over his dick slamming down on him again and again until she finally throws her head back and comes. "Yes!"

I watch her body jerk as I keep thrusting into DJ until, finally, I can't take anymore. I give him one last thrust that forces him to jerk into

Lyric and come. Hard. "Fuck! DJ!" My dick jerks and jolts inside him while I fill him.

He holds Lyric down on him and comes deep inside her, milking my come from me. "Lyric! Holy God, baby! Matt! Christ!" He holds Lyric with one hand and grips my arm with the other. His ass pulses around me as he comes inside her.

I relish in the feeling as we all come down. Lyric falls back against me. I wrap my arms around her and hug her while I slowly pull out of DJ. I love the way she melts into me. How her neck tilts automatically, giving me the access I need to kiss it.

"I don't know where that came from," Lyric says as she trembles against me.

I smile against her neck. My hands make their way up her body to her tits as I kiss the soft flesh of her neck and lick it. I squeeze her tits as DJ sits up slowly. He wraps his arms around both of us as he slips out of her and starts kissing the other side of her neck.

She whimpers at the loss of DJ's dick, and probably his come. I frown a little when she reaches between her legs like she's trying to keep his come from spilling out of her. "Are you sure you aren't upset about us having vasectomies? You know we'll get them reversed. If that's something you want."

She turns her head towards me and reaches up with her other hand to cup my face. I lean into it slightly as she shakes her head. "No...," She says softly. "You would think at my age that I would. But I don't. You know that at one point I wanted kids. And you know about my miscarriage with Josh that almost killed me. How depressed I was. How I simply can't go through that. Not again. I have everything I need. I have Beckett. And even Layne, considering how close they've become. I'm so happy, Matt." She kisses me, and I feel all of the reassurance I need sometimes pouring out of her.

"I love you, baby," I whisper against her lips. "So damn much."

"I love you, too," she whispers back.

DJ smiles and hugs her even closer while I clean up. "You got one more in there for me?" he asks her.

She nods and kisses him. "I love you," she whispers as she leans her forehead against his.

"I love you, too," he says right before kissing her again.

He pulls back slowly as I toss the wipe I used to clean my dick. I love that I don't even have to tell him what I want. DJ and Lyric both know me so well, I'm pretty sure they can read my mind at this point.

DJ lays back against the headboard, reclining slightly, and shifts Lyric, guiding her so her back is to him and she's straddling him. I move between his legs and help Lyric get into the position we want her to be. I don't know about either of them, but what we're about to do is my favorite way to take our girl. I get the feel of both Lyric and DJ at the same time while teasing them both.

After Lyric is situated, DJ guides his dick into her already soaked pussy. I grin as I watch. This. This is everything. All I want. Right here. Lyric's eyes flutter closed as she lets her head fall back onto DJ's shoulder. DJ groans against her neck as he wraps his arms around her, gripping her tits and teasing her nipples. She arches into his hands.

I lean down with a wicked grin and lick from DJ's balls, up his dick, to Lyric's pussy, and finally, stopping at her clit. I smile at both of their moans. DJ's cock twitches. Lyric visibly shivers and gets wetter. I groan as I watch her pussy pulse around his dick.

I shift to my knees and fist my cock while DJ fondles her pretty breasts and kisses her shoulder. He makes his way up her neck to her jaw. I slide my tip from her pussy to her clit teasingly while I soak it in her essence.

"Matt…," she whimpers. "Please… Don't tease me." She reaches for me with an adorable pout.

"But it's so fun to." I grin teasingly. "And your pussy pulses so prettily around DJ's dick."

DJ groans again when I rub my dick against his. "You're such a fucking asshole."

I laugh. "You love my asshole."

DJ and Lyric both laugh, but my cock is throbbing. As much as I'd love to keep going on with my little game, I can't. I need to be inside her. I need my dick rubbing against his. I need her pussy pulsing around us both. So, I lean in and position my tip at her entrance. They both inhale sharply in anticipation.

I brace myself against the headboard and kiss Lyric as I slowly slide into her. It's my turn to groan. I close my eyes and pull away slowly. I kiss across her jaw as I slide deeper and deeper. Her breathy whimpers in my ear make me impossibly harder. When I reach DJ's lips, the kiss quickly becomes heated and out of my control. DJ slips his tongue into my mouth with a commanding groan, and all control I had falls to him.

I bury myself in her to the hilt. With DJ's thick cock against mine, Lyric feels so tight. We're both beyond hard. Lyric's pussy is already clenching and pulsing. I know if either of us move, she's going to come, and I'm not ready for that.

Not yet.

So, I stay still while she moans and whimpers. I wait for DJ to make the first move and let him fuck my mouth with his tongue. His hands slide down her body and up my thighs. He grips my ass and pulls me closer. I sink deeper into Lyric, and in my sex-filled, lusty haze, I completely forget about DJ's tongue until he bites mine when he pulls away.

"Fuck," I moan when he flexes his dick against mine. "Oh fuck."

"Please," Lyric whispers. Her hands grip my ass trying to pull me even deeper into her. "You have to move. I need… you… to move… please…"

"God, I love when you beg," DJ growls against her neck.

I let one hand fall to her tits while I brace myself with the other. I roll her nipple between my thumb and forefinger as DJ and I both begin to move. "It's so fucking sexy when you beg for us." I lean down and take the other nipple in my mouth while we both thrust slowly but deeply.

"Oh…," Lyric moans. I feel her arching into us both. Her hands slide from my ass to the backs of her thighs. She pulls them back, spreading her legs wider, opening herself even more for us. DJ and I both moan as we sink even deeper. Our dicks flex against each other inside her, making her moan. "Mmm… So full… So good… So fucking full…"

DJ grips my ass and pulls me into them both as we thrust, completely in tune with one another. I lavish Lyric's tits with my tongue. DJ devours her mouth. We both damn near melt into her when her hands spear our hair and pull us both closer. DJ moans against her mouth. I groan against her nipples. We both thrust harder, thickening against each other and inside her, making her feel even tighter.

I nip her nipple before kissing my way up to her neck. "Fuck, Lyric. How do you feel better and better every time we're inside you, baby?"

"Oh… Matt… DJ…" Lyric's arm wraps around my shoulders. Her lips trail across my shoulder to my neck. She pauses and sucks hard, leaving her own mark to match the ones we've left on her. I groan low and thicken inside her even more at the thought of her staking her claim on me the way we do her.

I turn her face to me and kiss her while DJ kisses down to her neck. With each thrust he pulls me into, I feel myself getting closer and closer. Lyric is so tight around us. Her pussy is spasming uncontrollably as we both thrust hard and deeply. Fast, because that's how our girl likes it.

Her tits against my chest drive me closer and closer to my breaking point. DJ's dick sliding against mine makes me almost forget my name. I pull slightly away from her and kiss along her jaw to DJ's lips once more. The delirium they both put me in is something I'll never be able to get enough of. My heart is pounding in my chest. The sound of Lyric's wetness as we both pound into her sends me spiraling.

"Fuck…," DJ moans against my lips. His head falls back. "Fuck, you both feel so good."

"Oh my Christ…," Lyric moans. "Oh yes. Yes…! I'm… gonna…" She meets our thrusts. Her thighs tremble. Her pussy clamps down around us.

"Goddamn, pretty girl," DJ moans against her neck. "Come for us, baby."

"Now. Jesus, baby. Now. Come now," I plead.

DJ and I both slam into her one last time. We all shatter together.

Lyric grips my shoulders and digs her nails into them. "Ah! Matt! DJ! Oh my God, yes! Yes!" She comes hard around us both, soaking our dicks and thighs as she sucks us into her.

"Lyric! Matt! Mother fuck, yes!" DJ yells as his head falls back against the headboard. His dick jerks into her and against mine, but I feel like it's slamming into us both.

I collapse into her, pushing her further against DJ and growl against her neck as we both fill her tight little pussy. "Oh God, baby. Lyric… DJ!" I moan as I tremble. My dick spasms with every pulse of her pussy and jerk of DJ's dick.

It takes us all quite a bit longer to come down than it did the first time. The second time seemed so much more intense. More like we were making love to not only her, but to each other. While it wasn't slow by any means, the passion was there and was just as powerful.

After a few long moments, DJ and I both pull out of Lyric. I lean back as she slowly opens her eyes. She blushes and looks at me shyly before looking at DJ the same way. She slowly gets up and climbs off DJ, sitting on her knees next to us. We watch her curiously as she folds her hands submissively in her lap.

"Do you think you both could give me one more?" she asks. I know she's teasing, but she looks so fucking shy and adorable doing it that I can't help but laugh.

"I don't know, sexy girl," DJ teases back. "I'm so much older than you." He dramatically yawns.

She swats him. "Twenty years is nothing, old man." She giggles before she laughs and smothers him in kisses.

I teasingly tap her ass. "What are you thinking, pretty girl?"

She squeaks as DJ's hand falls to her ass. He rubs it as she looks at me with a blush. "Well... I rode DJ..." She blushes darkly and looks down. She lifts her lashes and glances at me.

I smile. "What do you want, honey? You know I'll never deny you."

She takes a deep breath. "I thought I could ride you... while you're on him."

I can't help the little flip my stomach does at the idea of DJ inside me while Lyric rides me. I lean in and kiss her before straddling DJ. I settle over him. His arms slide around my stomach as he kisses my shoulder.

I let my head fall back as he slides his thick cock into me. It's like I've been waiting for that feeling for days, even though I just had him like this last night. I clench over him a few times, making him moan low against my shoulder, before settling. Lyric's eyes are riveted to us both.

I smile again. She loves to watch us as much as we love watching her. I crook my finger at her. "Come here, beautiful."

She looks at us both submissively as she crawls to us. DJ bites my shoulder lightly. His dick twitches inside me. I know he wants to move as much as I want him to, but this time it's all for her. I'll do whatever she wants as long as she's happy.

Not that I have any issue with her riding me while DJ is fucking me from behind.

I help her position herself on me and grip her hips when she drops herself slowly on my dick. Her head falls slightly, her cheek resting on top of DJ's head as she kisses my temple. She lets out a breath as she takes me as deeply as she can.

DJ chuckles as Lyric's eyes flutter closed. She loves relishing in the feeling of us before either of us start moving. His hands move from me to her thighs. Mine wander up her body to her tits. I squeeze them both, making her moan and clench around me. DJ grips her ass. I lock my arms around her. When her beautiful, hazel eyes open, they're consumed with desire and fire.

And it's at that very moment that DJ and I both know we're in for it.

Lyric rises off me and slams her pussy down on my cock as she spreads her legs wider. I sink deeper into her, but it's DJ's dick jerking into me that has me moaning louder. The sudden motion makes DJ grunt and pull her closer to me. Lyric puts her hands on DJ's shoulders, bringing her tits within the dangerous territory of my mouth, and starts bouncing on me.

Fast.

Hard.

She takes me deep. DJ, not even moving underneath me, pushes deeper with each of her bounces. She kisses me passionately, pulling away when we both need to breathe. She presses her tits against my chest as she leans forward to kiss DJ just as passionately. I turn my head to watch and groan. Fuck if watching them kiss doesn't affect me just as much as when I kiss them both.

I watch as she trails her kisses lower and nips along his jaw. His neck. She stops when she reaches his shoulder and bites down with a low moan. She never stops bouncing. DJ groans as she sucks hard leaving her mark on him. I know he gets just as turned on as I do when she claims him like that. She might be our submissive, but we belong to her just as much as she does to us.

"Mmm... Fuck, yes...," she moans and spreads her legs as widely as she can, taking me even deeper than I would have thought possible. She moans into his neck as she clenches purposely around me and twists her hip. My head falls back on a guttural moan as my dick jerks inside her, causing me to jolt back harder onto DJ's dick. She pulls away from his neck with a low moan as she bounces harder and faster.

"Good Christ," DJ grunts.

Each of her bounces slams me back onto his dick. He's getting thicker and impossibly harder. I clench around him, pounding my dick into Lyric as I meet her thrusts. I nip and suck her neck as my dick thickens even more.

I refuse to come before she does.

"Fuck, little girl... So tight and wet for me... I don't know how much longer I can hold on," I groan against her neck. I pull her into me and kiss her deeply. I fuck her mouth with the same rhythm she bounces on my cock. She moans into the kiss. I feel her hand spear my hair and tug, knowing she does the same with DJ's when he moans.

When I feel her bounces start to become erratic, I know she's close, even if I couldn't feel her soaked pussy pulsing erratically around my dick. I grip her hips and thrust her over my dick as I grind over DJ's.

"Oh fuck... Matt... DJ... Please... I can't... I'm gonna....," she whimpers and moans as she bucks into me. Her pussy is clenching tighter and tighter around me. Her thighs tremble as she tries to hold on.

"Ask the right way, baby." I pull back and slap her ass, nipping her lip as she moans. I feel her pussy get even wetter when DJ tugs her hair gently, pulling her lips to his as he kisses her passionately. My eyes roll back when she slams down on my cock while clenching around me.

Fuck.

I love when she does that.

"Captain! Lieutenant! Please! I need to come for you! Please!" She whimpers and moans writhing against us.

"Christ, baby girl. Such a good little girl. Come for us. Come all over his cock. Show us who you belong to," DJ growls against her lips. He grips her hips and slams her down on my dick. The motion forces his dick to sink deeper into me. He keeps thrusting her over my cock relentlessly.

"Fucking Christ, DJ....," I groan.

"Oh fuck! Yes!" She throws her head back with a scream, arching as her pussy clamps down tight around my pulsing cock. She comes hard, drenching my dick and our thighs as her body spasms against mine. "Holy fuck! Captain! Lieutenant! Yes! Yes!"

"Come, Lieutenant," DJ commands low and dominantly in my ear. "Right fucking now," he rumbles, slapping my ass as he slams me down on his cock one last time. He holds himself deep inside me.

"Holy fuck, Lyric! DJ! Baby, fuck! Yes!" My eyes roll back as she rips my come from me. Her pussy clenches and pulses erratically. I clench tight around DJ's thick cock as I come hard, my dick jerking and pulsing inside her, filling her pussy with everything I have to give.

"Holy fuck, Lyric! Jesus Christ, Matt!" DJ lets out a shout of his own as he comes hard, his dick spasming and jerking inside me as I clench around him.

Lyric collapses against my chest, panting as her body experiences shockwaves from her intense release and mine. I hug her close, running my fingers through her hair as DJ rubs her back to help her come down while he fills my ass. I lean against DJ's chest as I fall limp from my orgasm, taking all he has to give. His arms wrap tighter around us both as we enjoy the afterglow. I kiss her neck and feel DJ do the same.

After several moments of holding each other, I gently pull out of her. I guide Lyric back just enough so that I can rise off DJ and grab some wipes for us to clean up. After we're finished, DJ shifts and settles in the bed, cuddling Lyric into him. I crawl into bed after throwing everyone's wipes away. I snuggle behind Lyric as she curls into DJ's chest.

As I hold them both close, I bury my nose in Lyric's hair and hug her closer. I can't help but think to myself that if someone had told me twenty years ago I would be here right now, I would probably have had them committed.

But right now, I feel like the luckiest man in the world. I have a kid who I love as if he was my own. Two sons, if I count Layne. I have a husband and wife that I love and adore with my entire being. Something I would never have believed possible all those years ago. I never thought I would have something so pure, so special, as what I have with Lyric and DJ, but I can't ever see myself living without them. They complete me. Just as I complete them. Our family is perfect.

We have made so many incredible friends over the course of our relationship, and I don't doubt that we'll continue to make more. Our future starts right here. And I can't wait to see what comes next for us.

This is one of my favorite moments that we get to spend together. Lyric tucked into one of our chests, with her fingertips pressed lightly against the heart of the one in front of her. I asked her about that once. She told me it's a reminder that we're together. She said when she presses her fingers against our chests, she can feel us. Our hearts beat in time to hers. She believes it's a symbol.

A symbol of our union.

Our love.

Our hearts beat as one.

Forever and Always.

The End

Next In The Beautiful Dream Series

The sweet and sinfully sexy Beautiful Dream Series continues with
Cherished By The Texan.

They say a cop is sixty to seventy-five percent more likely to get a divorce.
As a Captain with Gainesville, Florida's, Police Department, I can attest to
just how accurate that statistic is. I'm currently getting a divorce from wife
number three.

I'll fight her with everything I have, but my divorce has raged on for over a
year with no end in sight. Needless to say, I've sworn off love forever.

I'm done.

With the woman I consider one of my best friends by my side, I'm pretty
sure I'll be able to stay sane and focused on what matters.

Soon, though, lines we've drawn between us blur. Walls we've built are
bulldozed to the ground. And just as we're emerging from the dust, another
mystery girl drops into our lap and knocks us both off our feet. I know
immediately none of us are getting out of this with our hearts intact.

As my own, personal battle rages on, will either of them come out on the
other side with me? Or will the flames licking at our heels consume us?

Order **Cherished By The Texan** Today!

The Beautiful Dream Series

Available Now

Loving You
My Love, My Heart
Softening Lyric
Undercover Temptations
Captain Charming
Breaking Boundaries
Crashing Into You
Tactical Inferno
Ravishing Our Queen
Cherished By The Texan
Unveiling Our Passions

Box Sets Available

The Beautiful Dream Series: Box Set: Part 1
The Beautiful Dream Series: Box Set: Part 2

Other Books By Melony Ann

The Crane Family Series

Available Now

The Reluctant Mafia King
Sweet Lies
Billion Dollar Love Story
Be Mine
Protecting Her
Dangerously Forbidden Love
His Heart
Love In The Dark

Box Sets Available

The Crane Family Series

The Deimos Trilogy

Available Now

Connor's Legacy
Aryan's Alpha
Kade's Redemption

Box Sets Available

The Deimos Trilogy

The Forbidden Temptation Series

Available Now

The Detective's Forbidden Temptation
The Running Back's Forbidden Temptation

The Lucinio Family Series

Available Now

Rising From The Ashes
The Player's Rebel
Encrypting My Heart
Fighting My Fate

Multi Author Series
Piper Falls: Firehouse 49

Available Now

Ignite My Fire by Melony Ann
Regain My Fire by Kindra White
Playing With My Fire by D.L. Howe
Fight My Fire by Darley Collins
Against My Fire by Anneke Boshoff
Relight My Fire by Louise Murchie
Harness My Fire by Ayana Lisbet
Quench My Fire by Havana Wilder

Let's Be Friends

Follow me on

Bookbub

Facebook

Goodreads

Instagram

Tik Tok

Visit my website
www.melonyannauthor.com

Subscribe to my newsletter and get a FREE never-seen-before NOVELLA
just for subscribers!
https://www.melonyannauthor.com/exclusive-content

Join my Facebook Reader Group!
Melony Ann's Sizzling Book Nook

The official Beautiful Dream Series Playlist on YouTube
https://youtube.com/playlist?list=PLGEiD5wbQmDe1z4_FeeKbMLcBkOz
1M4L4

Dedication

Our hearts and souls.
Forever and Always.

Acknowledgements

Brad - I love you. Your continued guidance and support means the entire world to both of us. Even if it comes in the whispers of a breeze or a gentle nudge. Or a very blatant, "Are you kidding me? No. Do this." Yes. I definitely hear that.

Laura - I love you. This book would not exist without you. Literally. The twists and turns. The spicy sex. It's all because of you. Your help. Your guidance. I truly hope with all of the work that we put into this book that it's something you can be proud of. I love you with all of my heart. With everything I am.

Jay - I love you. Your laughter. Your hugs. Everything about you. Sometimes, when life throws curveballs, I find myself sitting here just blinking in confusion. Thank God you make sense of it all and help us to.

Anneke - You are seriously such an incredible woman. I'm so proud to see you grow as an author each and every day, but mostly? I'm proud that you're more of that family that I got to choose.

Jason - Thank you for always being my voice of reason.

Kayla - You're honestly this incredibly sturdiness in a storm of shit. Thanks for protecting me from it all.

To the Bookstagram Community.

To my family.

To all of those who believe in me and support me.

To all of those who don't.

Cover by: Carter Cover Designs

Edited by: Alyssa Skaggs

About Melony Ann

Melony Ann began writing short stories and poetry as a child. She continued honing her craft over the years until she took the plunge and began publishing her work, despite having severe anxiety.

Melony writes contemporary romance stories that are full of suspense and a lot of steam.

When she isn't writing, she is loving her family and working to make her life something she deserves.

Melony believes that if her writing can inspire just one person, then all of her hard work is worth it.

Her hope is that her writing allows each and every one of her readers to escape for a little while. To dive into a different world one book at a time.

www.ingramcontent.com/pod-product-compliance
Lightning Source LLC
Chambersburg PA
CBHW071906220626
47052CB00002B/234